"Would it be so wrong to take whatever happiness we can find together and worry about the future in the future?"

Ashley swallowed. "You mean like Scarlett O'Hara? Think about the bothersome things tomorrow?"

"Maybe by tomorrow they won't be so bothersome."

Why was it so hard to find the right words? She made her living with words, but at the moment it was as though someone had stolen her mental dictionary. She shrugged, shaking her head. "You're still a Boston lawyer, and I'm still a Broadway lyricist."

"We had more than a love affair," Zach said. "It was a wonderful friendship as well. Wouldn't it be worthwhile to renew all that, without demanding blueprints for the years ahead?"

Ashley knew—*knew*—she was about to slide her heart under a steamroller, but she closed her ears to the cries of warning sounding in her head. "Yes," she said. "I'd like that very much."

Dear Reader,

Sophisticated but sensitive, savvy yet unabashedly sentimental—that's today's woman, today's romance reader—you! And Silhouette Special Editions are written expressly to reward your quest for substantial, emotionally involving love stories.

So take a leisurely stroll under the cover's lavender arch into a garden of romantic delights. Pick and choose among titles if you must—we hope you'll soon equate all six Special Editions each month with consistently gratifying romantic reading.

Watch for sparkling new stories from your Silhouette favorites—Nora Roberts, Tracy Sinclair, Ginna Gray, Lindsay McKenna, Curtiss Ann Matlock, among others—along with some exciting newcomers to Silhouette, such as Karen Keast and Patricia Coughlin. Be on the lookout, too, for the new Silhouette Classics, a distinctive collection of bestselling Special Editions and Silhouette Intimate Moments now brought back to the stands—two each month—by popular demand.

On behalf of all the authors and editors of Special Editions,
Warmest wishes,

Leslie Kazanjian
Senior Editor

MARY CURTIS
Love Lyrics

Silhouette Special Edition

Published by Silhouette Books New York

America's Publisher of Contemporary Romance

SILHOUETTE BOOKS
300 East 42nd St., New York, N.Y. 10017

Copyright © 1987 by Mary Curtis

ISBN: 0-373-09424-8

First Silhouette Books printing December 1987

America's Publisher of Contemporary Romance

Printed in the U.S.A.

MARY CURTIS,

a former Californian who now resides in Massachusetts, divides her artistic energy between writing projects and work in community theatre. This author of a dozen romance novels and mother of three daughters also finds time to play heroine herself in musicals such as *Guys and Dolls*, *Kiss Me, Kate* and *The King and I*. When not performing, directing or writing, Mary is likely to be found traveling with her husband, gathering new story and setting ideas along the way. She is also known to romance fans as Mary Haskell.

REGAL THEATER

Jerry Jerome presents

LOVE LYRICS

lyrics and book by
ASHLEY GRAINGER

music by
MATTHEW ROBBINS

based on an idea by Ashley Grainger and Matthew Robbins

with

SAMMY KIRK **KELLY ADAMS** **LYLE BAKER**

set and lighting designer
BUZZ CRAWFORD

costume designer
CLAIRE HANSTON

stage management
JOE CASPER

general management
WEILER/MILLER ASSOCIATES

conductor
HANS SCHMIEDE

choreographer
SONJA HAAGER

director
CRAIG CLARKE

Chapter One

Ashley sat curled like a sulking cat at the end of the pale lavender cut-velvet sofa, a clipboard propped on her knee. She stared mournfully at the last two lines of the stanza she'd just finished:

When did heaven become the wrong side of town ...
When did the green of springtime turn so brown?

It must be good, she told herself; otherwise, why would she have such an urge to cry? Of course, to be honest, it had taken very little to make her feel like crying during the past couple of weeks. Sadness had invaded every part of her body like a long, attenuated sigh.

The pencil, barely held by fingers too listless for a firm grip, lay against the board as though it, too, had been exhausted by the effort to inscribe these words—words that bore no resemblance to what she'd settled down to write. They were the indelible imprint of her rotten mood. The way her emotions automatically arranged themselves into a rhythm, and the rhythm into rhyme, still surprised her, even though the pattern had been formed in early childhood. It was a habit she had honed into a skill, and the skill had brought her to heights that amazed and sometimes dizzied her.

Her eyes rose from the page to roam around the over-sized room decorated with furnishings that all but shrieked their newness and expense. Despite determined mental efforts to assert ownership, she still felt like a visitor in this elegant apartment and found herself glancing around guilt-ily when she curled up on the couch, half expecting some-one to jump out and tell her to get her feet off the furniture.

Her melancholy was interrupted by a sharp rap, and she called, "Come in, it's open!" She heard the slam of the door and the heavy tread of determined footsteps crossing the room. Her fingers made a feeble attempt to cover the scrawled evidence of her nonproductive day. Without rais-ing her head she said, "Hi, Matt."

"How the hell do you write in that position? I should think you'd get kinks in your brain." Matthew Robbins loomed over her, his tall form blocking the afternoon sun. Matt was her musical collaborator, the other half of the prize-winning team of Robbins and Grainger, whose first full-scale Broadway musical had run for two years and won the Tony award.

"Sounds like a good idea."

"Oh, no, don't tell me. Gloom still looms." Matt plucked the board from its precarious perch and quickly scanned the contents of the paper it held. "Terrific. I need lyrics for two jump tunes and a humor/patter song, and what do I get?" His voice held dismay as he read: "Why did our love song go out of tune? And spring become winter so soon?"

He cocked his head and stared at her accusingly. "The sixth sad ballad in a week. Ash, shall I call Jerry and tell him that, much to his surprise, both leads of this musical will

have to slit their wrists during the finale, or do you anticipate pulling out of this funk?''

"I don't know." Ashley, with considerable effort, sat up
straight. "I just can't seem to come up with any cheerful
lyrics."

"Uh-huh. I wish I didn't know the reason. That would
sure make me happier."

She looked up at the familiar face, which bore an unfamiliar expression of worry. "If you know the reason, perhaps you'd be so kind as to share it with me."

"Come on, babe. You know as well as I do it's a rare but
virulent disease called Zachary Jordan." Ashley cringed as
the name rippled through her, causing extreme turbulence.
"After the case you had of him, I'd think you'd have built
up an immunity." Matt tossed the clipboard onto a nearby
chair and sat down on the edge of the couch.

Ashley ran her hand over her eyes, amazed at how tired
they felt. "Where did you learn to add two and two and
come up with five?"

"Same place you learned heart control. The Show Biz
School of Irrational Behavior. Wouldn't you know it! In a
country where lawyers proliferate like wire coat hangers, our
biggest potential investor has to choose Zachary Jordan."
His scowl deepened. "I know Joe Sanders lives in Boston,
and it figures he'd have a Boston lawyer. But why *that*
one?"

She laced her fingers together tightly. "He's one of the
best in New England, and Joe Sanders can afford the best."
The best of the best, she thought. Not only in law, but in
every category she could think of. Why, after all this time,
did he still seem so incomparable?

"Yeah. The thing that boggles my mind is that Jordan
didn't talk him out of the idea of investing in a Broadway
musical. He probably considers it about as safe as shooting
craps in Las Vegas." His hand made a sweep of dismissal.
"Anyway, that's out of our hands. Jerry has the backers'

audition all set for Wednesday night. I understand there's enough money already on the line, so if Joe Sanders comes in, that may be all we need."

Jerry Jerome was a flamboyant showman and the most successful producer now on Broadway. It seemed miraculous to Ashley that he had approached them about handling their new show. Success was still too new to her to have any feeling of familiarity.

"Now, if we can get your mind off Zachary Jordan long enough to write a few sprightly lyrics, we should be in good shape."

"Matthew, once and for all, my mood has nothing to do with Zachary. I just have a case of writer's block."

"How come the only other case you've had occurred three years ago when said lawyer departed from your life? Just some weird celestial malformation that brings on writer's block and Zachary Jordan at the same time?" His hands flew up in a dramatic gesture.

Matt rarely departed from his usual state of joyous optimism, and he seemed to relish this brief excursion into alarmed concern. There was a theatrical quality to his discourse, as if he were scoring his words as he spoke them. Ashley could practically hear the wail of a clarinet.

"I shudder at the memory of that other slide into funereal pentameter; it lasted six months," he continued. "We don't *have* six months." His head bobbed up and down in emphatic conviction. "You must avoid him like the plague."

"Your line of logic would baffle Carl Sagan." She frowned at him. "Besides, you're all wrong. I could walk right past Zachary without missing a pulse beat." An inner howl of "liar!" was followed by an overall tingling sensation, as though each inch of her skin held private memories of delicious contact. With determined indignation at the traitorous reaction of both mind and body, she added, "That's over. Three years is enough recovery time for anyone, even me."

He patted her knee in patent disbelief. "You don't have to see him, you know. It's the producer's job to work with investors . . . and their lawyers. It's your job to write lyrics. Snappy lyrics, the kind that make people smile. At your present rate, you're going to turn this playful froth of a musical into a Greek tragedy."

"So? That might not be so bad. *Sweeney Todd* was no bucket of laughs, and it won all kinds of awards."

"Honey, the book and the lyrics should bear some resemblance in mood. This musical is a *comedy,* as in ha-ha."

"I know already—I wrote the dialogue."

"You wrote the very *funny* dialogue. We now need some very *funny* songs. The star is supposed to have one rather woeful ballad, and his lady friend, two. I timidly venture the opinion that two and one make a total of three." He tapped his finger on the paper. "We now have nine." He squinted emphatically: the impatient adult teaching basic addition to a recalcitrant child. "Would you agree that's ample?"

"Okay, agreed." She stretched her arm to retrieve her clipboard, hastily scanning the verse. "I guess there's no way to turn this into humorous patter."

"Well, it might tickle Dracula's funny bone."

"Ha-ha."

"Ashley." Matt jumped up, unable, as usual, to restrain his restless energy. "Why don't I take you out to dinner? Somewhere outrageously posh, where we might be recognized and fawned over. In fact, I'll call ahead and remind the maître d' who we are, so he'll make a fuss. Wouldn't that cheer you up?"

"You know that's not my thing."

"Phooey. You enjoy a little public recognition as much as any of us. You and I, against heavy odds, have cut our path to success through the Broadway jungle like voracious beavers. We have every right in the world to enjoy it."

Ashley wished she could summon a smidgen of humor in order to fully enjoy Matt's colorful rhetoric. He was in rare form today. She sighed. It was a good thing *somebody* was.

He pointed his finger at her in stern admonition. "And you were doing just that until that stuffy Bostonian made you think there was something vulgar about having your name in print."

"Matt, that's not true." There was a definite lack of conviction in her tone. She added, somewhat defiantly, "Zachary isn't stuffy at all."

"Humph." Before she could say anything further, he doubled back to the previous subject. "Now, concerning an extravagant dinner in a posh restaurant...how about it? After all, were we not touted as the hottest new writing team in town by *Time* magazine? Should that not entitle us to a bit of personal flaunting?"

Ashley shook her head, grinning helplessly at her dear friend. "You certainly know how to muck up a perfectly good deep-purple mood. How do you know you're not turning off a wonderful streak of creativity? When have I written six lyrics of any sort in one week? One of them might become a hit someday!"

"All of them will, babe, but in due time. We happen to have a deadline baring its ugly teeth. We should follow dinner by going to a rock joint. Loosen up, jiggle our spines. Might get you in the mood to turn out something that can be sung in this particular production. We still have one of the two rock numbers to do, you know."

"All right, all right. I get the message. We were probably nuts to make him a rock star. I don't even like most rock music."

"Hey, lyric-wise they're easy: just repeat the same line eight times, throw in a bridge and repeat it four more."

"In that case, we can skip the nightclubbing. But what about Amy? Didn't you tell me you had a date tonight?"

Matt's expression clouded. "Amy and I have had what was, in gentler times, termed a falling out. She is not answering my calls."

"Oh, Matt! Not again!" She scowled accusingly at him. "Did you take that girl out? The one who auditioned the other day?"

His eyebrows rose in an expression of wounded innocence. "What girl is that?"

"The one you said had the greatest set of gams you'd seen in years."

"Oh . . . *that* girl."

"Stop evading. Did you?"

Matthew's eyes slid away from hers. "All right, so I took her over to the pizza place. Poor kid hadn't had a square meal in ages. I was just being kind."

Delighted to have the focus turned away from her, Ashley moved to the attack. "You idiot. One of these days Amy will close the door on you completely, and you'll have lost one of the nicest women in this rotten town."

"How can you call New York a rotten town? This is the hub of the world! This is where it's all happening! This is the source of our riches! This is home!" He resumed his place on the edge of the sofa.

"Stop!" Her hands came up in a defensive posture. "You're giving me a headache. Besides, right now New York seems more like the pit of my funk than the hub of the world. I'm seriously considering buying a nice quiet place somewhere in the country."

"As in the country just outside of Boston?"

Ashley swung her legs out, avoiding Matt's lanky form, set her feet firmly on the floor and stood up. "Listen, once and for all, my state of mind has nothing to do with Zachary Jordan. I barely remember what he looks like." She squeezed her eyes shut, trying to obliterate the picture still vividly etched in her mind. That beautifully sculpted face with dark, dark eyes and thick black hair.

"Liar."

She slapped her hands against her sides in exasperation. "If you want to cheer me up, I shouldn't think you'd call me names. Maybe it would be a good idea to go out tonight. I bought a divine dress yesterday, at that little boutique down the street. It cost a fortune, and I want to start amortizing it."

"You bought another dress? Oh, boy, all the signs are in place. The only time you go shopping is when you're feeling depressed." He stood and crossed to stand beside her. "Ashley, are you still—"

"No!"

"Then why..."

"Hearing his name again brought back some painful memories, that's all."

"Babe, you were crazy about the guy. You had a very bad time when you split up. I offer you this advice free. Do not see him. Let dead affairs remain buried." He gave her a peck on the cheek and headed for the door. "I'll pick you up at eight-thirty. Meanwhile, think lovely thoughts. Call the Video shop and have them send over an old Laurel and Hardy movie. Eat bonbons. Stand on the balcony in your all-together and flash Seventy-first Street. Lighten up!"

Ashley, who had neglected to ask where they were going, was surprised when the taxi stopped in front of the 21 Club. "Matt, we come here every time there's an out-of-towner we have to woo! I thought you were taking me somewhere like the Côte d'Azur."

"Nah. This place caters more to our kind of people."

"You mean the kind that might know who we are?"

"Right. It's about time we got a little recognition. Stars get all the glory. People like you and me just sweat and slave in the background."

Ashley shook her head in resignation and followed him inside. She'd long since accepted Matt's craving for fame.

The regular maître d' was missing, and a stranger stood in his place. "Uh-oh, Matt," her voice was teasing, "you'll have to tell him who you are." But the maître d' came forward immediately, a smile of welcome on his face. "Good evening, Miss Grainger, Mr. Robbins! What an honor to have you with us!"

"You called ahead!" Ashley hissed in Matt's ear.

"I didn't either. He must have seen the *Time* article." His guilty expression belied the disclaimer.

"We have a lovely table for you, right this way." They were led to the center of the room.

Ashley shot daggers at her escort as she whispered, "This is the kind of table they usually give to tourists from Dubuque, Iowa, who are too intimidated to complain."

"Or celebrities who want to be seen."

"Matthew, please get us something more private. I do not share your fishbowl mentality."

"Okay, okay."

After a few discreet words to the maître d', they were seated at a more secluded table. The waiter was at their side before they were completely settled. "May I take a drink order?"

Ashley nodded. "A white wine spritzer, please."

"Dry martini, straight up, with a twist."

The waiter backed away for a few steps before turning to cross the room. Ashley frowned at her self-satisfied companion. "What did you do, come over early and bribe all the help? That man is in danger of smiling himself to death."

"Now, Ashley, don't be so cynical. The waiters at 21 are always pleasant. Besides, you're beautiful and you're famous, and you look positively smashing tonight. In fact we're both beautiful and famous and look positively smashing tonight. Why shouldn't we elicit cheerfulness from the waiter?"

"I may throw up. Matt, please. Let me work my way out of my mood on my own. Don't subject me to jollity over-kill."

"All right, my sweet. But do try to turn the sides of your mouth up instead of down." Matt's gaze made a lazy circuit of the room. He always liked to know if anyone important was around. His eyes moved slowly, right to left, stopped and darted back to a spot just over Ashley's left shoulder. "Oh, no."

"What's the matter? Spot someone more famous, beautiful and smashing than we?"

"Worse. The bearer of the plague is here."

"What? What on earth are you talking about?"

"Gird your loins, he's coming."

"Matt . . . ?" But before she could even turn around to look, she heard a disturbingly familiar voice.

"Well, hello."

She had almost forgotten the sonorous timbre of that voice, the way it bushwhacked trails through her nerve endings, straight toward her fluttering heart. "Zachary." Her eyes rose to his face. He didn't look five minutes older or one millimeter less attractive. She had hoped for signs of rampant aging or premature sag. It was ludicrous for a Boston lawyer to be that handsome.

"This is quite a coincidence." He smiled, his teeth brilliant against his bronzed skin. Where had he been to get such a tan? Out on a sailboat? Like the one they'd moored in that secluded cove off the Caribbean islands while they... Ashley forced her attention to what he was saying. "I guess that's a pretty hackneyed line, isn't it?"

Matthew stood to shake hands with him. "Any line sounds terrific delivered in that upper-crust Bostonian accent. How are you, Zachary? We heard you were around and about, but who'd have guessed we'd meet at the 21? Isn't the Four Seasons more your style?"

Ashley's eyes moved from one face to the other as the two men stood poised like fencers parrying for a thrust. The tightening of Zachary's jaw brought back memories far different from the scene on the sailboat. She hastily interrupted. "Uh...will you sit down and have a drink? I'm sure the waiter would bring over an extra chair."

"Actually, I'm with my client, Mr. Sanders."

Matt whistled softly. "He's the one with the bulging pockets and the angel wings. Tell him the show'll be a smash."

"I was hoping you'd tell him yourself. He'd like you to join us for dinner."

Ashley's heart leaped up and lodged in the base of her throat. "I, uh, we..."

Matt shot her a warning look. "Sure. We'd be delighted."

"Good. I'll have the waiter bring your drinks over and put two more settings on the table. Give me just a couple of minutes, okay?"

"Sure—dandy."

The moment Zachary left and Matt sat down, Ashley leaned forward, her eyes narrowed, her tone threatening. "You nerd! What was all that advice you were giving me? 'Don't see him, Ashley; let the producer take care of it, Ashley; avoid him like the plague, Ashley; just write happy lyrics, Ashley.'"

Matt tugged at his collar. "Yeah, but this is practically a command performance. I mean, this man is Mr. Goldfinger-and-Toes. He's the kind of angel every show needs. We're all in this together, Ash. If the money doesn't roll in, the rock doesn't roll onstage."

"Clever. Very damned clever. Why don't you just write your own clever lyrics for your clever music, since you're so clever?"

"Now don't be a sorehead. What was I supposed to do, spit in his eye?"

"That's what you looked like you were about to do until he mentioned the golden name."

"Listen, babe, money talks. In fact it sings...a very sweet tune."

"You are so unbelievably mercenary!"

"I have two ex-wives. Do you know what two ex-wives cost?"

"Why don't you try staying married? It would be cheaper."

"Ashley, we must cut short this erudite discourse. Mr. Jordan awaits. Not to mention Mr. Big Bucks."

"You'd best try," she muttered, as she got up, "to recall that his name is *Sanders*."

As they approached the table, both men stood to greet them, but Ashley's focus homed in on just one. Zachary's six-foot-three-inch frame dominated the corner in which he stood. He wore an elegant gray suit, which must have been hand-tailored to fit the broad shoulders and muscular chest developed from years of competitive swimming throughout his school days. She had kidded him about his conservative clothes, but in truth, she liked the way he dressed. Zachary exuded class. As Matt had once put it: old money and old family tree, complete with wooden attitudes about a woman's role.

"Ashley Grainger, Matt Robbins, meet Joe Sanders."

"Well now, this is a real treat!" Joe Sanders looked to be about sixty, with neatly trimmed gray hair and blue eyes that snapped from face to face, as though on command. Ashley got the instant impression that he was no dummy, and throwing around stars' names was not going to impress him.

"How do you do, Mr. Sanders." She put out her hand and smiled, catching the glance of approval from Matt. "We've been looking forward to meeting you. I hope you'll be pleased with our show."

"I hope so, too, Miss Grainger, and so does my banker." His gaze whipped to Matt. "I like your music, young man.

You have a real talent. And you were smart enough to hook up with the perfect lyricist.''

"Thank you, Mr. Sanders. And I agree." Matt grinned. "About both my music and my lyricist."

"Sit down, sit down."

Zachary held the chair for Ashley, the one right next to him. As she slid into the seat her arm grazed his, and the momentary contact was like an electric shock. Not fair, she mentally railed, not fair! After all these years! Her mind was in turmoil, churning up emotions all too reminiscent of those that had dominated her when they were together. When they were together. When God was in his heaven, and they were there, too.

"...and I agreed. Right, Zachary?"

Zachary started, and Ashley could see that he had no more idea what Joe had just said than she did. He looked flustered as he replied, "I'm sorry, I missed the question."

Joe laughed. "If you'd quit ogling the beautiful woman next to you, you'd be more aware of what's being said. But you'd also be a damned fool, and I wouldn't want you for my lawyer. I said that Jerry Jerome considers it money in the bank to have the Grainger and Robbins names on a musical."

"His very words." Zachary nodded. "Of course Jerry *is* the producer and therefore less than objective."

Ashley sat a bit straighter. "Are you saying you disagree?"

"I'm saying that, as a legal and investment consultant, the money is in the bank when the money is in the bank."

Matt raised his glass. "Hey, Ash...write that down. Sounds like it would make a great song!"

The glare of Zachary's dark eyes brought an unwelcome memory to Ashley. That awful night in her apartment with these two men, nose to nose, fists clenched. She could still hear Zachary's shouted words. "If there's nothing per-

sonal between you, as you claim, then why do you act like
a jealous husband?''

And Matt's angry answer. ''Who the hell would be this
upset over a wife? Ashley is the other half of my liveli-
hood. You're trying to steal away the best lyricist in the
business! Your problem, Jordan, is that you're such a
bullheaded, old-fashioned stuffed shirt you can't believe a
man and a woman can be just friends, and you sure as hell
can't envision adjusting your male ego to a wife whose career is at least as important as yours!''

And that, Ashley thought, was about as succinct a sum-
mary of their problem as could have been made.

''These old-family lawyers,'' Joe Sanders tilted his head
toward Zachary, ''are so damned conservative. I inherited
enough money to take care of me, my wife, my children and
any progeny of theirs...with plenty of leeway for a few risks.
Show business fascinates me; and after all, what's the use of
being rich if it isn't any fun?''

''What indeed?'' Matt had obviously taken an instant
liking to the man. He took a deep swallow of his martini and
sighed with pleasure. ''Ah...here's to the dry martini. May
it never be submerged in the new wave of fainthearted
drinking!'' He leaned forward, his twinkling gray eyes centered on the man with the bulging pockets. ''This is going to
be a good show, I guarantee it.''

''Can you guarantee a profit?''

Matt laughed. ''In a word...no.''

Joe obviously liked his candor. ''So what happens if I
don't invest? Does the show still go on?''

''Most definitely. Jerry has a lot of backing already. He'll
get the rest. In fact he's so sure of it that the schedule is all
set for Boston.'' His eyebrows went up as a new idea struck
him. ''Listen, Mr. Sanders...''

''Please...Joe.''

''Joe...we're about to go into rehearsal. In fact, we start
the day after the backers' audition. You should come down

and watch. The first few days resemble battle drills, but I bet you'd get a kick out of it. Gives you a chance to see the show biz crazies at their wackiest.''

Ashley blanched. "Matt, isn't an investor supposed to be shown a more positive view of a show? If Mr. Sanders..."

"Joe."

"If Joe sits through the mayhem on Thursday, he'll pack his bag and flee!"

Joe laughed. "Don't underestimate my tolerance for madness. I live in such an orderly environment that I have a perverse craving for it. What do you think, Zach? Can you stay over for a few days?"

Ashley could feel the heat of Zachary's eyes on her cheek and commanded her own eyes to stay focused on Joe Sanders.

"Zach?"

"Oh, sorry, I was trying to picture what was on my calendar. I'll have to call my secretary to find out. But even if I have to return, you could stay. Just don't sign any checks without me beside you!" His smile looked strained.

Matt, who had clearly noted the building tension across the table, signaled the waiter for another martini. "See there, Ash? Like I told you this morning, you've got to finish those lyrics. It will be a decided detriment to rehearsals if the songs have to be sung with la-la-las.''

Joe turned his attention to Ashley. "What? You mean you're behind on the lyrics? Jerry told me it was usually the other way around, with you pushing Matt to catch up with you!"

She gave a helpless shrug. "Well, all of us bog down occasionally. No cause for alarm, I'll get them done."

Matt's voice cut through, lacking its usual lilt of humor. "Actually, she's down to the last three songs, but they're all upbeat, and Ashley is stuck on sad ballads. I haven't seen this happen to her in, oh...three years or so. Everything's been great, Ash. You must be coughing up some bad memories or something.'' He nodded his thanks at the waiter as he placed the second drink before him.

Joe Sanders looked puzzled by Matt's comment, but Zachary's expression was evidence that the message had hit its target.

Zachary turned to Ashley, pinning her with his incredible eyes, so dark they looked black until there was enough light to reveal their unusual shade of navy blue. ''I was surprised to hear you were working on a rock musical, Ashley. It doesn't seem your forte.''

She fought to hold her gaze steady, a visual lie of calm. ''It isn't actually a rock musical, even though it is about a rock star. We're using a libretto and songs that are reminiscent of musicals of the forties and fifties in most of the show, the part that tells the story; the actual rock just comes in twice, when the star is shown in performances. Sort of a mixing of musical metaphors.'' She was experiencing an unnerving déjà vu. She and Zach had once talked about everything, consumed with the joy of sharing ideas and challenges, successes and disappointments. They'd discussed her story lines, her lyrics, her love of the theater; his legal cases, his expanding base of investment clients, his fascination with problem solving. So much they'd shared. Too much they couldn't.

''Do you think it will be accepted by a big enough audience?''

Matt's voice, edgy with annoyance, gave the answer. ''If we didn't, we wouldn't write it that way.''

Ashley sighed. Obviously, Zachary Jordan brought on not only her unusual cases of writer's block but an equally rare show of bad temper in Matthew. She aimed a smile at Joe. ''You know, they have a fascinating wine cellar here. If you'd like, I'm sure we could go down for a tour.''

''Thanks, but I've seen it. I'm interested in this discussion. Is that why Jerry feels this show is going to set some new trends on Broadway?''

Ashley could imagine their ebullient producer, his hands waving about, creating images of giant pies in the sky. "Jerry is extraordinarily successful at mounting hit shows because he has a knack for spotting elements none of the rest of us see—" She took a deep breath, wondering if her words sounded as contrived to them as they did to her. Spurred by a need to fill the silence with sound, she plunged on "—or inventing them, as the need arises. We're mixing styles in a way that hasn't been tried, both musically and through contrasting production techniques. You know... full-stage choruses under pink gels, followed by a punk rocker with green hair under a stark white spot. If it works, and we think it will, I suppose it might be called a trendsetter." She shrugged. "But Matt and I just write them, then chew our fingernails while the producer and director and choreographer turn them into something at least slightly different from what we had envisioned."

Joe looked fascinated. "Doesn't that tick you off?"

She shook her head. "No. That, as they say in the trade, is show biz, and the sum is better than the parts."

Zachary's voice was low. "Two hits in five years. How can you fight the numbers?"

She raised her eyes to his. "It would be greedy, wouldn't it, when all your dreams have come true, to want even more?" The moment the words were out of her mouth, she wanted to recall them; they seemed to verbally lay out her scarred heart for his inspection, as though she were wailing, "Look at what you did, aren't you ashamed?" But the expression in his eyes made her wonder if he still bore scars, too.

Joe tilted his head inquiringly. "*Two* hits?"

Ashley smiled. "You're probably only familiar with the last one. Our first was a small, low-budget, off-off-Broadway musical, but it *was* a hit, and it opened a lot of doors to us—like catching the interest of investors like you."

"Same old story, huh? Need success to draw the money and need the money to make the success."

"You've got it." Matt nodded.

Zachary, whose proximity was already causing her acute anxiety, leaned closer. "You look wonderful, Ashley; the years have done you service."

Joe remarked, "That's right, you and Ashley are old friends, aren't you?" He smiled at her. "Zachary is one of those lucky people who can claim to have known you when you were still struggling."

Matt opened his mouth—caught Ashley's glare—and closed it again.

The waiter, who had been inconspicuously hovering in the background waiting for the right moment to approach, came to the table. "Would anyone like another drink, or may I take your order?"

Joe nodded. "I know what I want, but I don't think these two have had a chance to look at the menu."

Ashley, relieved by the interruption, hastened to say, "Why don't you and Zachary order, while Matt and I take a quick peek?"

The ordering was taken care of with speedy dispatch, but the serving, eating and conversing ritual seemed, to Ashley, to drag by at a turtle's pace. She listened halfheartedly to Matt's voice, as he recounted to Joe how their collaboration had started.

"So I was sitting at the piano, and this was a *big* party, lots of noise and . . . well, we'd all had a few. Then someone challenged me to make up some songs on the spot. They'd ask for a jump tune or a ballad, and I'd whip one out. I was still a young punk, trying to get from off-off Broadway to off-Broadway, and I loved strutting my stuff. Then this gorgeous girl—" he tilted his head toward Ashley "—sits down beside me and starts fitting lyrics to the tunes. Now I want to tell you, even half in the bag I knew clever improvising when I heard it. So I got her name and number and called her the next day. The guy I was working with at the time wasn't cutting it. Well, the rest is history."

Joe's face was alight with interest. "How long ago was that?"

"Let's see. A little over eight years."

"You *both* must have been pretty young."

"Yep. I was twenty-nine and Ashley was a kid of twenty-four."

"Young genius. That's very exciting."

Matt was in his glory, responding to questions about himself. Ashley was totally drained. When the second cup of coffee was finally consumed, and it was late enough to excuse herself without seeming rude, she said, "I'd better say good-night and get home. As Matt pointed out, I've still got work to do and little time left to do it. I need my sleep."

Matt started to stand, but Zachary held up his hand to stop him. "Matthew, why don't you stay and finish telling Joe about your musical background? I can see Ashley home."

Ashley knocked a spoon off her plate onto the floor. A waiter stepped in to retrieve it, and she gave him a shaky smile, clasping her hands in her lap so they wouldn't further betray her turmoil. How could she go with Zachary? She couldn't picture being alone in a dark cab with him, attempting to make polite, "remember when" conversation, while fighting the onslaught of memories, the trembling of long-dormant emotions. If she combined the hundreds of love lyrics she had written, they wouldn't begin to express the magnitude of what she had felt for this man. And all of her "woeful ballads" put together could never chronicle the agonizing hurt she'd suffered when she lost him.

"I wouldn't want to take you out of your way, Zachary. Besides, Matt should turn in, too. He still has a bad habit of staying up too late."

"Have a heart!" Joe's face beamed at her, pleasant and friendly. "I'm fascinated with Matt's stories, and if I can't keep both of you, at least indulge me a little and let me persuade Matt to stay. You don't know what a kick it is for a staid old businessman like me to be sitting in the 21 Club gossiping about show business! And don't worry about Zach, he can go out of his way. After all, his meter is running on my account, so he can just add it to the bill. Besides, I doubt it's any sacrifice for him."

Ashley's mouth was dry. She wanted a drink of water but was afraid that if she reached for it, she'd knock that over, too. "You could all stay. I can get a cab. After all, I'm accustomed to operating on my own; I don't really need to be escorted."

"Nonsense, my pleasure."

Zachary stood, his hand on the back of Ashley's chair. It wasn't touching her, but she could feel the penetration of its warmth. She had a sensation of a trap snapping closed around her, offering no chance at escape. She rose on trembling legs, praying they'd hold her. "Well, all right, then I'll say good-night. Don't stay up *too* late, Matt. We have a conference with the musical director tomorrow at ten."

"I'll be there." Matt's face was an open statement of his dismay at seeing her about to leave with Zachary, mixed with his reluctance to leave the gold-laying goose before the egg was safely delivered.

Ashley led the way out of the restaurant. The other tables, the customers and the waiters seemed eclipsed by a foggy haze, while all her awareness tuned to the unseen man behind her. She knew there were eyes following them, there always had been. Zachary drew as many admiring glances from women as she did from men. It had been remarked, so many times, that they were a stunning couple. It had also been remarked that their love shone about them like a spotlight. Damn. She couldn't stand this. It hurt too much.

Chapter Two

The chill air of January hit her as she stepped outside, almost stumbling over one of the little figures of a jockey as she hastened to the curb.

"Taxi?" The doorman tipped his hat.

"Please." Zachary's voice still held that special tone of command.

They were silent until the door to the cab had been closed and it had pulled away into the snarl of after-theater traffic. She felt Zach's eyes on her cheek but continued to stare at the back of the cabbie's neck as though enthralled with the long, stringy hair that covered it.

"I hope you don't mind that I asked to see you home."

She had to look at him now. She couldn't carry on a conversation with her eyes averted. After all, they had parted on a friendly basis. Two reasonable adults, coming to the reasonable conclusion that their life-styles were just too different to be reconciled. He had no way of knowing of the carnage of her emotional system that followed the breakup, and she had no intention of telling him.

"No. Of course not. It's nice to see you again, Zachary. I've wondered, on occasion, how you were and what you were doing." Dear God, such tripe! Wondered! She thought of the endless nights spent staring into black loneliness while she tried to imagine where he was, who he was with, what he was thinking. . . .

"I've been fine. Good health runs in the family. It seems to persist in spite of anything." There was enough emphasis on the last word to imply that his health had persisted through a great deal of strain. "And the law practice continues to thrive."

"And your family? I still receive Christmas cards from Emily." Emily, his sister, had become, in the eighteen months that Ashley and Zach had dated, a good friend. "She writes a brief note now and then, so I know your brother got married and your parents sold their house and moved into a condominium."

"Yes. Jared is very happy. His wife, Diane, is a gem, and they're expecting a baby in about four months."

"Dear heaven, how time disappears! He seemed such a kid when I last saw him."

"Understandable. He was only twenty-one." There was an uncomfortable pause. This was just as deadly as she'd thought it would be. "Mother and Dad seem content in their new place. By the way, I told them I'd be seeing you, and they send you their best."

Ashley could feel the treacherous heat of tears gathering. Zach's parents had been cool to their affair for quite a while, obviously concerned about the vast difficulties a marriage would present, but had finally warmed to her as they grew to know her. She had often wondered if they'd been at all saddened by the breakup—or just relieved.

"Please tell them hello."

"I will. And Curt and Doris. How are they?"

Her parents, on the other hand, had engulfed Zachary in total acceptance from the start, clearly delighted to see their only daughter finally dating someone outside the questionable theater set. Their demeanor had been somewhat frosty when she'd told them the engagement was broken, as though she'd deliberately denied them a proper son-in-law. And a rich one, she thought, without bitterness. How could she blame them for wanting the security for their daughter that they'd never had themselves?

"They're very well. Dad's retired, so they have plenty of time to relax." One of the thrills of her success lay in her ability to augment her father's meager pension with regular "gifts" of money.

"And your brother?"

Ashley gulped, squinting into the street to see where they were. How long would this torment last? Small talk between two people who had once fallen eagerly into each other's arms the moment they had the slightest amount of privacy! She glanced down at his hand, lying on the seat between them. Such a beautiful hand, long-fingered and strong, with the leathery weathering that came from hours on the ocean hoisting sails and on a court swinging a racket. He was a fine athlete. He was a marvelous lover. She pulled her eyes away from the hand, fastening their attention, once again, on the back of the taxi driver's head.

"Johnny is still Johnny. Crazy and funny and, miraculously, still alive."

"I take it he's still a Hollywood stuntman?"

"Yes. Much to my parent's dismay. He keeps talking about quitting and becoming an agent. He'd be so good at it, too. But I'm afraid he has too much love of danger in him."

"I like Johnny."

"Everyone likes Johnny. Although I think your parents had their doubts that time they met him and he described his job. Of course, they may have been nervous about the genes in my family. A Broadway lyricist and a Hollywood stunt-man must look suspect to people of such respectable background.

"Ashley, my parents never voiced any uneasiness about you, except the demands of your career and the fact that it tied you so firmly to New York City."

"How nice, that you and your parents agree so well." There was a dreadful silence. Ashley wanted to bite her tongue but realized it was too late, by about three years.

There was no missing the angry edge to his retort. "I wasn't the one who broke the engagement. I trust you remember that."

Something inside her coiled and tightened, reminding her of the dreadful hurt, physical as well as emotional, that followed that breakup. She heard the memory of that pain in the angry tone of her own voice. "Officially, yes. But it was at least as much your decision. You couldn't imagine a lifetime of mixing with us odd theater types."

"You're not being fair, or honest. You were no more willing to compromise your life-style than I mine."

She gave an apologetic shake of her head. "You're right. I'm sorry. The pressure becomes intense at this point in writing a show, and my disposition shows it." She was desperate to plant the conversation safely back in the soil of banality.

He reached over and ran one finger across her cheek in a gesture so tender she had to steel herself against collapsing in his arms. "You're so lovely, Ashley. I have missed you so very much."

Bitter words snapped from her. "Not *too* much, obviously. You never contacted me in all that time!"

His hand grasped her chin and turned her face to him as he bent disturbingly close. Their eyes met and clung in the flickering lights of the passing cars. "You sound as though you were the only victim. There is no way, Ashley, *none*, that you could have suffered any more than I."

"Oh, Zachary, if only you'd called!"

"I could say the same to you. And I'm sure we'd both have the exact same answer. We had talked the subject to death. There was nothing to add to all that had been said."

She nodded, her anger subsiding as quickly as it had erupted. "I know. And nothing has changed."

"No. Nothing has changed. Including the fact that you are the only woman I've ever truly loved."

As the cab pulled to the curb and stopped, she laid her head back against the seat, closing her eyes for one brief instant. She felt like a plug had been pulled and her vital juices drained. She wondered where she would summon the energy to stand up and walk into the lobby. The doorman opened the door, said, "Good evening, Miss Grainger," and stood back discreetly.

She opened her eyes and looked at him for a long moment, then dropped her gaze. "Good night, Zachary."

"Good night, Ashley."

Ashley swung her legs out, took the hand of the doorman, who stepped forward to assist her, and, without looking back, went through the bronze door to her town house.

Ashley lay in bed, staring sightlessly into the blackness of her room, listening to the cadence of her heart as it banged its protest against her chest. No more, no more, no more, no more, in 4/4 time.

"Quiet, you traitorous thing." Her words were muttered aloud, an incongruous intrusion on the stillness. Did other people honestly put themselves to sleep counting sheep? She'd sent dozens of them flying over a mental fence and succeeded only in heightened frustration at their absolute refusal to leap gracefully in synchronized patterns. "Ashley, you idiot, you can't even suffer insomnia without setting it to music." She pushed her hands against the headboard as she pointed her toes, attempting to stretch out her tangled nerves. She felt awful.

She reached for the light switch, propping a couple of pillows behind her as she sat up. Damn. How she hated this sleeplessness. Everything seemed more ominous in the middle of the night. A glance at the clock heightened her anxiety. Two-forty. She'd be a wreck all day, too tired to think straight, let alone write articulate lyrics.

Zachary. The name had pounded a persistent duet with her heartbeat since she'd gone to bed at midnight. His words kept ringing in her head, "You're the only woman I've ever truly loved." Oh, Zachary. She pulled the blanket up under her chin, feeling a need for cover. Was it possible that he meant what he said? That he had lived three vacuum-packed emotional years, just as she had? And if it were true, where did that leave them? Back at square one. A love song without lyrics.

She massaged the back of her neck, wondering why tension always centered there, corkscrewing the cords into tight purveyors of pain. If she didn't find some release soon, the tension would work its way up and form into a splitting headache. Without giving herself time to reconsider, she picked up the receiver of the bedside phone and punched one of the preset buttons.

It was answered on the second ring. "Hello?"

"I'm surprised you're home."

"Sis? Listen, I get enough action at work. I can hardly wait to get back to my quiet house."

"Is that my madcap brother speaking? Could it be that you're aging, right along with the rest of humanity?"

"Rumor has it."

"I hope you weren't asleep."

"No. I was watching an old Charlie Chaplin film." There was a pause. "Now. Unless my calculations are wrong, it is somewhere in the vicinity of 3:00 a.m. back east. Since it has never been your custom to call in the middle of the night to make sure I'm at home and not sleeping, may I ask what's up?"

"I saw Zachary tonight."

"Ah. Just as you'd feared. And it didn't go well."

"Actually, the meeting was very friendly and civilized. And my stomach feels like it's been put through a Waring blender."

"Ashley, what did you expect? You've never gotten over him."

"What makes you say that? I haven't mentioned him in ages, at least not until I heard he might be coming; and I've dated several other men in the last couple of years. I've just been too busy to get serious."

"Don't try to con your brother. I can read your mind . . . more to the point, your heart. You were a sitting duck for a full-scale relapse."

"Oh, Johnny, what am I going to do?" The plaintive wail seemed to come from her toes.

"Is he married?"

"No."

"Then call him up, tell him you made a mistake and propose."

"Johnny! Can't you be serious?"

"I've never been more serious in my life. Zachary is, on all accounts, the most thoroughly decent man I ever knew, and he loved you so damned much it was embarrassing to watch. If you'd had any sense, you'd have latched onto him and worked out the problems later."

"That's a very simplistic thing to say. Especially from you, of all people. If it's so easy, how come you let Leslie get away?"

"Because I'm a wild bastard and I lay my life on the line every day and I'm not going to subject a wife to that."

"Then why don't you stop that nonsense and settle down?"

"I could ask you the same thing." His retort stopped the conversation cold for several seconds.

"That's the problem, isn't it, Johnny? I can't stop. Is there something wrong with us?"

"Yeah. I'm still a wild kid and you've got a fire in your belly. You must've been hexed by a crazed boy scout when you were in your crib." They laughed uneasily. It was an old family joke that didn't always seem funny. "Hey. How did I get into this analysis? We'll examine my id on another occasion and on my dime. Back to Zachary. How does he look?"

"Just the same. Exactly the same. Except..."

"Except what?"

"His eyes don't twinkle like they used to."

Johnny's answer came back coated with sarcasm. "I wonder why?"

"Johnny..." Ashley sounded, even to herself, like a lost child. "He said he'd never loved any woman the way he loved me."

"God. He said that at the first meeting? Was he vertical or horizontal?"

"Johnny! What kind of a woman do you think I am?"

"A dumb one, if you let him go to his own bed after a statement like that! Ashley, for crying out loud! You're a top-flight lyricist, an expert on all the descriptions of love. Don't you know you've got the real thing in the palm of your hand and all you have to do is close your fingers? Don't you know how rare the real thing is?"

"It's been three years! That's a very long time. People change."

"Evidently he hasn't, and you know damn well you haven't. And, Ashley, we're both old enough to know that three years is approximately two blinks of an eyelid. If you blink much more, you'll die a spinster."

"I wish you and I didn't live three thousand miles apart. I need to be hugged."

"Yes, you do. But you don't need a brother hug. Call Zach."

"I can't. It's three o'clock in the morning."

"Call him anyway. He's probably not asleep either."

"I'll think about it. I love you, Johnny."

"Love you, too, sis. Be good to yourself. Snare him!"

"Goodbye."

"Talk to you soon."

Ashley waited an instant, then took the phone book and looked up the number for the Hotel Pierre. She started to press the first number, then stopped. What would she say? That she loved him and needed him and wanted him? She'd said all of that three years ago, just before she said goodbye. She put the receiver back in the cradle and leaned against the pillows, her eyes closed. A fire in the belly. It brought back a wave of memories....

She'd been introduced to the expression when she overheard a conversation between her mother and father. They were talking about Johnny, which wasn't unusual. Johnny seemed to defy definition and frustrate all attempts at taming. He was the "wild kid," the one who had to try everything. He was full of passion and love and unquenchable curiosity, none of which was directed at books, and he drove their parents nuts. Ashley had heard so many worried confabs about Johnny that she started to pass the open door to the kitchen without pausing. Then the subject changed to their older brother, Jimmy. She could still hear the pride in her father's voice: "He has a real fire in his belly, that boy. Such dedication. Never been any doubt, has there, about what he wants to do...."

And her mother's pleased reply: "Oh, my, no. He'll be a wonderful doctor. He has such ambition, such dedication. It's so unusual in a youngster these days."

It was later—weeks? months?—before she heard the expression applied to her. This time her mother was talking to her Aunt Lorraine on the phone: "Yes, it was a cute play, wasn't it! Ashley wrote the whole thing, you know, music and all. We were so pleased when the teachers decided to use it as the class production. Quite an achievement for a four-teen-year-old.'' Then a pause, followed by her mother's worried reply. ''Well, yes, she does. She spends far too much of her time writing plays and songs. She doesn't seem interested in clothes or the new fads, and hasn't even mentioned any boys yet. She does have such a fire in her belly about show business. Oh, well—'' she uttered an indulgent laugh ''—we'll just hope she works it out of her system before she meets the right man, so she'll be ready to settle down and raise a family....''

It was the introduction of a theme Ashley had heard over and over, a theme that hadn't really changed all that much, despite the hoopla about women's liberation. When a boy had the ''fire in his belly,'' it meant ambition and drive, both positive attributes. When it blazed in a woman, she was compulsive and aggressive, both negative.

She sat upright, staring straight ahead, lost in thought. *Was* it abnormal, this driving force inside her? Should she be able to pat herself on the back with pride over her success in such a competitive field, then walk away from it and find even more fulfillment in providing a tranquil home for a husband and producing and raising children? She, like a lot of other young women she knew, had assumed that question was out of date, like girdles and the vapors, but it wasn't, really. It was all right, apparently, for a female to go partway up that proverbial ladder—but to the top? Only if she could survive in a very lonely territory.

There was no doubt about her mother's opinion. Ashley could still hear the incredulity in her voice: ''You've broken up with Zachary? Ashley, he's the kind of man every girl dreams of! Why, you'd never have had another worry in your life. He'd provide every comfort you could possibly want, and you could get out of that grimy city....''

In so many ways, her mother was right. Zachary *was* the kind of man that women create in their fantasies but rarely actually meet. And he had become not only the center of her reality, but the core of her existence; and he had left a hole that nothing—not fame, nor awards, nor the intoxicating sound of applause—could fill. What Johnny said was true: she'd been crazy to let him go. Surely she could confine her career so it demanded less of her, allowed time to concentrate her attention on a marriage, a home, children. On the man who still owned her heart....

She shook her head. She couldn't. For better or worse, the fire in her belly still raged. Her eyes swung back to the phone. Zachary, despite all his efforts to understand—and he *had* made an effort—had still, in the end, equated her need for a career in the theater to a failure of love. Ashley rubbed her aching eyes. Was it a failure? Was it peculiar for a woman to thrive on her work the way she did, particularly when it meant losing a man she loved so much that his absence caused a chronic ache in her heart?

She was so tired, she couldn't think about it anymore. If only Zachary hadn't come back into her life; if only this yearning for him had ended as it should have; if only... she reached over with an impatient flick of her fingers and switched out the light, knowing, all too well, that sleep was still a long way off.

Zachary stared in frustration at the beeping phone in his hand. Who in hell could she be talking to at this hour? Probably Matthew. Ashley had laughed about the state of near-mania that overtook them as the first rehearsal date drew closer and closer. As he sat there, his hand still resting on the telephone, Zachary began to remember a great many things: the canceled dates and the all-night sessions because one or two of the songs were bombing and had to be replaced, Ashley's fury over the conductor's refusal to bring down the sound of the orchestra for one of the singers whose voice couldn't carry over it. Zach couldn't understand the paranoia that engulfed all of them at the least hint of crisis. It was all so... *dramatic*. He took his hand away.

What had he been thinking of anyway, to try to call her at this hour? He rubbed his hand over his forehead. At least that one was easy to answer. From the moment he'd seen her enter the 21 Club, his mind had been possessed with the desire, no, more than desire, the *need* to hold her, to feel her closeness, her special warmth. There'd been no way to foresee the effect it would have on him to sit next to her again, to have her perfume teasing his nostrils, to see the familiar way her lovely hazel-green eyes widened when she was listening and narrowed, ever so slightly, when she was thinking. She still wore her reddish-brown hair long, only now it was feathered around her face, accenting even further her considerable beauty. It had been downright painful, seeing her slim hand resting on the table, her fingers so close to his. So difficult to keep his hand from creeping over to cover hers. He felt as though someone had taken a giant eraser to the past three years.

He jumped up impatiently. Fantasy. Pure fantasy. He'd already made an ass of himself by telling her how he still felt about her, and she hadn't even replied. That should tell him all he needed to know.

He went to the small refrigerator in the corner of the room and took out a beer. He thought he was through with sleepless nights, yet here he was again, pacing the room and watching the minutes trail by like tiny creatures with lead shoes. Hell and damnation, how could a grown man of supposed intelligence let himself get so out of control? That settled it. He would fly back to Boston in the morning. There was no way he would subject himself to this torture again. Joe Sanders could do the hobnobbing with the "exciting" theater people. He was going back home, where life was sane and relatively safe.

And boring.

The thought bobbed to the surface and was quickly banished.

Chapter Three

By the time Ashley and Matthew had finished the morning meeting, her head was throbbing. The music director was anxious to line up the best available musicians in Boston as quickly as possible for their out-of-town tryout and wanted to know the instrumentation needed for all the music. This gave her an immediate problem. There were those three important songs to be done, and she still couldn't come up with a single funny idea, let alone in rhyme.

But the bit of information that had given her the headache was that Zachary had returned to Boston.

They walked outside into the blinding sunlight, shivering as the cold air hit them with the cruel dichotomy of winter. "I'm starved. Where shall we go for lunch?" Matt turned up the collar of his jacket. He never remembered to wear a topcoat.

Ashley winced at the impact of the light. "I just want to go home. I feel like I've got a headful of crazed drummers."

"Yeah, no doubt. It's called 'Jordan aftershock.'"

"Matt..."

"Okay, sorry. In fact, I'd like to apologize for my crummy manners last night. It makes me so mad to see how wobbly kneed you still get when that guy is around that my usual charm deserts me." He shrugged, a gesture of helplessness. "It brings back terrible memories of what a basket case you were after...well, after."

"I know." She put her hand on his arm, grateful for his dogged loyalty and unquestioning friendship. "But it really isn't Zach's fault, you know. He was a perfect gentleman through the whole thing. It was obviously pretty hard on him, too."

"I'm sure, and why not? He lost the classiest broad in these here parts. He was too much of a gentleman. He should've tossed you over his shoulder and carried you off into the sunset."

"That only happens in Hollywood Westerns. Besides, if he'd done that, you'd have needed a new collaborator."

"I doubt it. You'd've stolen his horse and ridden back into town just in time to go to work on the next production."

"Yes. And there, my friend, lies the rub."

"Well, the evening had one productive element."

"Impossible."

"Now don't nay-say so quickly. Let's both go to your place. I want to play you a tune."

Ashley started to protest, then, with a shrug, stepped into the cab that Matt had hailed.

When they reached her building, the doorman met her with a smile. "Miss Grainger, I hope you don't mind, I put something in your living room...a delivery."

"Oh? I wasn't expecting anything."

His smile broadened. "Well, it's the sort of thing that isn't usually expected."

"You're not going to tell me, are you. What is this, a conspiracy?"

"No. Just a nice surprise."

Her curiosity piqued, she hurried through the door and into the elevator, with Matt close on her heels.

When they passed through her foyer, Ashley gasped. "Oh, how beautiful!"

Matt stepped into the large, rectangular living room, looking around and shaking his head. "What is this, Ashley? Have you lost faith in your penmanship and gone into the nursery business?"

There were vases everywhere, containing forced bulbs of hyacinth, daffodils, iris, crocus, tulips. "But who...?" She walked around the room, her spirits lifting as the visual taste of springtime infiltrated her senses. "It must be Joe Sanders."

"Should be a card somewhere. Although an extravaganza of this magnitude might be accompanied by a homing pigeon with a note in its beak. Have you looked on your balcony?"

"Oh, there...see? On the piano." She crossed to the gleaming Steinway grand that dominated the decor and picked up an envelope balanced against a pot of freesia. Ripping it open, she pulled out the card and read aloud, "Ashley...I wish you endless springs—" Her voice stuck in her throat, and she read the rest of the message silently: *...and how I wish I could have shared them with you. Zachary.* She sank into the pale pink chair next to the piano, clutching the note in trembling fingers.

"Not Sanders, I gather."

"No."

"I didn't think Boston Yankees were prone to this sort of extravagance."

"They aren't. Usually."

"Not to intrude, but why the spring bulb show, why not roses?"

"I told him my favorite time of year was springtime; that even in New York City, just seeing the first crocuses pop up was enough to renew my spirits. I'd often dreamed of having a house in the countryside, with so many bulbs planted that every spring there'd be flowers as far as the eye could see. We..." She stopped. She couldn't share the rest of the daydreams with anyone else. The two of them cuddled in front of a roaring fire, planning the home they would someday share, making long lists of bulbs they would plant as far as the eye could see....

Matt sat on the arm of the chair, his hand on her shoulder. "I'm sorry, babe. It still hurts, doesn't it?"

"Yes."

"It's too bad it went bad. Zachary is a damned nice man."

She stared up at him in surprise. "I thought you disliked him!"

"No. I disliked what the relationship was doing to you." He stood up, running his fingers through his hair. Matt wasn't very comfortable with emotional situations, so he gravitated to the position of his utmost comfort, the piano bench. "Why don't I limber up the fingers while you place the call?"

"How did you know I was going to call him?"

"We've worked together a long time, babe. And you wear your feelings on your face."

She nodded, knowing he was right. "I'll be back in a minute."

"Take your time. I'll call the deli and have them send up some sandwiches."

"Okay. Make mine pastrami on dark rye." She almost ran to the bedroom, her stomach doing a series of half-gainers. If his work habits hadn't changed, he'd have gone straight from the plane to his office. But suppose he was out for lunch? Suppose he was with a client? Suppose... She picked up the phone and placed the call before all the 'supposes' could dissuade her.

"Jordan, Purnell and Ware. Good afternoon."

"Good—" Ashley cleared her throat. "Good afternoon. Is Mr. Jordan in?"

"May I tell him who's calling?"

"Ashley Grainger."

"Just a moment, please."

How was it possible for the second hand on her bedside clock to move so short a distance in what surely had to be five minutes?

"Ashley?"

As soon as she heard his voice, her entire body became one giant container of misgivings. What should she say? Her mouth opened, closed, opened again, and, miraculously, something came out.

"Thank you." It was the best she could do.

"You're welcome. I hope they brighten up your home."

"They brighten up my life."

There was a moment of silence. What was he thinking? Why was the slightest pause so excruciating?

"I'm glad. Things got a little tense last night, and I hated to leave it like that. I wanted to call you, but I didn't know what to say, so I took a hint from the commercials and said it with flowers."

"I love the flowers." She swallowed. How much truth could both of them stand? "But I wish you had stayed."

"Ashley, one look at you completely undid me, so I took the coward's way out and ran. My stalwart ancestors would be appalled."

She smiled, glad to hear the first touch of the wonderful humor that was so much a part of him. "You were just following my example. You said something I'd wanted to hear for three years, and it struck me dumb."

"What a pair."

"Yes."

There were, she was amazed to notice, tears running down her cheeks. What a pair, indeed. A perfectly matched set, in so many ways. No wonder she still felt halved.

"Ashley, I know you're about to enter a hectic period, but I'd like—" her heart stopped, waiting for the rest of the sentence "—I'd like to talk to you." There was a little throat clearing on his end of the line, too. "Obviously we can't be around each other without, well, remembering."

Her head bobbed up and down. "Obviously."

"It seems only sensible to attempt to make it easier on ourselves."

"Yes." They'd need a magician to accomplish that.

"I'd like to have dinner with you...."

"I'd like that, too." The most flagrant of understatements.

"When?"

Her mind unreeled a scroll of the insane schedule of the coming week. "I'll make time. Whenever you say."

"Why don't I come down in about a week? That would at least get you through the first rehearsals."

"I'm sure that's wise." Wise, yes. But a week was such a very long time!

"How about a week from Friday night?"

So far away. "All right. What time?"

"Seven-thirty? Let's go to the Veau d'Or."

"Oh, yes." They'd both loved that small, cramped, noisy restaurant with its happy atmosphere and delicious food.

"This may well break a record."

"What do you mean?"

"It may be the longest nine days in recorded history."

She breathed a sigh of relief. She wasn't the only one having trouble with unruly emotions! "Without doubt."

"I'll see you."

How wonderful. "I'll look forward to it."

When Zachary replaced the phone in its cradle, he leaned back in his leather chair and stared out the picture window at a jet airplane, miniaturized by distance, making its descent over the blue harbor into Logan airport. He wished he were there now, waiting to board the shuttle to New York. His gaze shifted to the brightly canopied buildings of the Quincy Marketplace, alive with noonday shoppers and restaurant goers, rushing or strolling across the cobblestone and brick walks. As he sat there, he realized that the morning's frown had been replaced by a wide grin.

He'd hesitated so over sending the flowers, skeptical about opening a door that had been firmly closed three whole years ago. Just being in Ashley's presence a few short hours had wrought a miracle of sorts, an instant time crunch that eliminated those intervening years, resurrecting in full degree the rampant yearning that had once been his constant companion. He was probably nuts to hazard even one dinner with her. Obviously his resistance to her was nil. If he listened to his sensible side, he'd call her back, break the date and flatly refuse to handle this particular venture for Joe Sanders. There were good lawyers in New York who knew a lot more than he about the theater.

The momentary lapse into good sense was quickly lost in the still-resonating memory of Ashley's soft voice.

Whistling softly under his breath, he pressed a button on the intercom and said, "Janet. Would you bring in the Thompson folder, please?"

"Be right there."

"Thanks." With the silly grin still glued in place, he returned his attention to the papers on his desk.

Ashley all but danced back into the living room, humming a tune from their last musical. All of the recollections of unsolvable problems that had so diligently marched through her mind the night before had faded away.

Matt looked up and watched her approach with raised eyebrows. "Uh-oh."

"What does that mean?"

"Has the premature spring heralded by all these blossoms infused your eyeballs with sunshine, or is that gleam powered by *flowerescent* bulbs?"

"Oh, Lord, that's corny." Her eyes had a newly acquired twinkle as she said, "You told me to 'lighten up,' and I'm just following orders."

He grimaced. "Stop! I surrender!" He ran his fingers over the keys in an extended glissando. "When is he coming?"

"A week from Friday."

"Then you'd better work your little fanny off between now and then." He stopped, and a worried frown creased his forehead. "Ashley, be careful."

"I will, I promise. He just thinks that because we're going to be seeing each other, we should try to remove some of the tension."

"Humph. Fat chance." His mercurial mood swung again, and the frown disappeared. "At least, now that you've got a smile on your face, maybe you'll respond to this marvelous idea."

"Let's hear it."

"Remember when I somewhat callously mocked Zachary's line about 'the money's in the bank when the money's in the bank?'"

"Yes, and you *were* callous."

"Agreed. But creativity hath o'ercome callousity, and so—" he held up his hand eloquently "—bear the 'money' line in mind whilst I play this catchy tune." His fingers began to move on the keys. "Remember the scene where our about-to-be-star, Christo, is mulling over the wisdom of signing the contract that offers nothing more substantial than vague promises?"

"Yes."

"And he shows it to his mentor, Uncle Hermie?"

"Still with you." The dialogue was suspended while she listened to the tune. Her eyes widened in delight. "Of course, it's brilliant!"

"Yes, it is. So glad you can hear it."

Ashley sat down in the pink chair, her "working" chair, and took the clipboard and pencil Matt handed her from the piano. She listened while he played the tune over and over, then she started to write like mad. "Okay. Hermie has a lead-in verse that talks about the pitfalls in the contract and how they've both worked so hard to get where they are and how Christo shouldn't sign anything without lots of dollar signs...."

"Yeah...yeah..." Matt leaned forward, his eyes on Ashley, his hands still playing the melody line.

From there on, the song almost wrote itself. Ashley sang the lyrics as they appeared on the paper, and Matt adjusted notes to fit. The chorus and the repeat were done within twenty minutes. The bridge all but sprang out of the blossom-scented air, and they were soon winding up the last chorus.

So don't count your chickens until they're hatched
And don't call your socks a pair until they're matched,
Never sign a check if the check is blank, and
Don't count your money...
Don't count your money...
Don't count your money till the money's in the bank!

"Yeah!" They jumped up at the conclusion and hugged each other, dancing around the flower-bedecked room.

Matt held her at arm's length, his face gleaming. "Ataway, babe! One down, two to go!"

"I have a feeling it will be a piece of cake."

"I have a feeling I know why!"

* * *

By week's end, Ashley had finished one more lyric, revised another she wasn't entirely happy with and was hard
at work on the last song. She was producing like an automatic word machine. And the results, she knew, were good.

The read-through had taken place on Thursday at the first
get-together of the whole cast. Once the schedule was posted
and the sketches for the scenery and costumes had been
displayed to the cast and the press, the hall was cleared of
everyone but the company, with the exception of Joe Sanders, who sat through the whole procedure with an ecstatic
grin on his face. Everyone was seated on the stage while the
script was read by the cast and the songs, at least all those
that were complete, were played by Matt and sung by Ashley. The reaction all around had been extremely positive.

Now, a week later, the rehearsals had settled into their
working format, with the director, Craig Clarke, blocking
the scenes with the leads in one building, the chorus and the
music director down the street in a vacant studio and the
choreographer and dancers in a third location. Ashley and
Matt attended most of the late-afternoon rehearsals held
with Craig and the principals and worked on the score in the
mornings. It was a familiar routine, with each moment
crammed full of stimulating activity; but to Ashley, the
hours seemed endless. She found herself doing something
she'd never done before in her life—crossing the days off the
calendar as they passed.

Zachary called her on Friday morning to confirm their
date. "Are we still all set?"

All set? If he didn't come, her next reviews would be on
the obituary page. "Yes." She hugged the phone closer to
her ear, wishing she could crawl through the curled cord and
be zapped right into his arms.

"Ashley, I have a couple of appointments this afternoon
that I couldn't cancel because both of them involve out-of-
state clients. Could we meet at the restaurant?"

"Of course. Zach, is this going to be too difficult? We could postpone it, if you need to." If he said "yes," she'd die.

"I wouldn't dream of standing you up. Besides, what's inconvenient about flying to New York for dinner? All of us jet-setters do it."

Despite the bantering tone, the words made her shiver. "Too many years and too many tears and it isn't funny at all." The line sprang to mind from a song she'd written shortly after they quit seeing each other, the last time she'd been stuck in sad ballads. She forced a note of levity into her tone. "I'm glad to know the sacrifice isn't too great."

"The sacrifice has already been offered to the gods. My peace of mind for the past eight days. I was right, it *was* the longest such period in recorded history."

"Zachary..."

"I know. We must keep it light. See you at seven-thirty."

"Yes."

She replaced the receiver, alarmed at the way her hand shook. Had he been as nervous as she about how to handle that first moment when he came to pick her up? Or did he really have out-of-state clients? In either case, it eased some of her apprehension. Far better to start off in a public place.

She stood quickly and went into her dressing room to get ready to leave, wondering where tonight's meeting would lead. It was a blessing that the lyrics were practically finished; if this evening aroused too much of the pain of separation, her sense of humor could well be incapacitated indefinitely.

By that evening, it took a long soaking in a bubble bath to wash away the tension of the day and prepare her for the tension of the night. After examining every garment in her closets, she selected an outfit, laid it out, looked at it and put it back. This routine was repeated approximately ten times before she settled on a softly pleated dress of white, light-weight wool that clung to her slim body in a very becoming manner. After a great deal of cogitation, she put on an amethyst necklace with matching earrings that had been a gift from Zachary. Never had so much indecision gone into the simple act of dressing for a date. Even the choice of a coat was a major event. A glamorous fur or a classic wool or the new high-fashion cape that Matt said made her look like Batman's assistant? She settled on a white wool coat. The lack of other colors starred the amethysts, which she knew would be a statement in itself.

The intercom buzzed, and when she picked it up, the doorman said, "Your taxi is here, Miss Grainger."

"Thank you. Be right down."

With a last, agonizing look in the mirror, she steeled herself against rushing in to change the whole outfit and rushed, instead, out the door.

Zachary arrived at the restaurant shortly after seven, wishing he'd swung by after all to pick up Ashley. It was murder to sit alone, staring at the door, bombarded by the memories this place revived. They'd had such fun here, sitting at one of the small, jammed-together tables, half-yelling at each other over the hubbub, enclosed in the peculiarly secure privacy of a crowd.

He'd never known anyone with whom he could share his thoughts so completely. Nothing, not the deepest hurts or insecurities or the most flagrant bragging over a personal victory, had ever seemed out-of-bounds. As a fourth generation Bostonian, his upbringing, though done in a close-knit, caring family amid scores of relatives and lifetime friends, included a solid tradition of keeping problems to oneself and never "blowing one's own horn." So the "all-levels" communication he'd shared with Ashley had been like letting a significant part of himself out of jail. Looking back, it was appalling, the speed with which the parole had been revoked when he quit seeing Ashley.

He twisted his glass around, rattling the ice against the sides. For a light drinker, he'd certainly dispensed with the Scotch in a hurry. There was no ignoring his jittery nerves. Strange, he was rarely uneasy. There were few situations in which he felt insecure, but waiting here for the only woman who had ever completely dominated his world was shattering his aplomb.

"Mr. Jordan!"

He looked up, surprised at the greeting. "Why, Charlie, hello! How nice of you to remember me! So, you're still working here."

"Oh, yes, probably will be until I'm ready to retire. It's been a long time, Mr. Jordan. I hope it wasn't a problem with our food or our service."

"No, of course not. Both were always superior. It was just that, at a certain point, I had no reason to come to New York."

"Oh. Well, it's good to see you again. Can I get you another drink?"

"No, thanks. I'll wait until my dinner companion arrives."

Charlie glanced over his head. "Well, unless I'm mistaken, she just did."

Zachary's eyes flicked to the door. Ashley had just stepped inside. Her cheeks were flushed from the cold outside air, and she was smiling at the maître d'. She looked absolutely beautiful. He stood up, and as their eyes met across the room, everything else disappeared from view.

He heard Charlie say, "I'll be right back to get your drink orders."

"Thanks, Charlie."

Ashley handed her coat to one of the waiters and followed the maître d' through the maze of tables, her eyes never leaving the face of the man who stood waiting for her. His black hair looked slightly rumpled, as though he'd run his fingers through it. She'd seen him do that so often. It was the only nervous habit he had. Zachary wore self-confidence like a second skin; it must have been passed on with the thoroughbred genes that had also endowed him with the aristocratic structure of his handsome face and his beautifully built body. He had much for which to thank his ancestors.

When she reached his side, he pulled out a chair and she sat down. Only then did they say, in unison, "Hello."

They both broke out in laughter.

Zachary nodded toward Charlie, who was fast approaching their table. "Do you remember our old friend from bygone days?"

Ashley looked up and smiled. "Why, Charlie, how nice to see you again!"

"It's good to have you back with us, Miss Grainger. We've missed seeing you here. Now, *you* can't say it's because you've had no reason to be in New York. I know better, from reading the theater page in *The New York Times*."

She raised her shoulders, not knowing how to answer. "I seem to have been moving in different directions, Charlie. But it's nice to be back."

"I'd say you'd been moving straight up, Miss Grainger. Congratulations on your successes."

"Thank you very much."

"Now, what can I get you to drink?"

They placed their orders, both watching in some trepidation as he walked away, leaving them alone, mentally fishing about for words to fill the void.

Zachary found them first. "You look beautiful, Ashley."

"Thank you, so do you."

He smiled, remembering all the times she'd insisted he was prettier than she was. "You wore the amethysts; that was thoughtful of you."

"Not thoughtful. Brave."

They stared at each other, muted for the moment by their awareness that the footing on this path of renewed contact was very tricky. Zachary took a deep breath and tried a different tack. "Are you pleased with the way the show is coming?"

"Very pleased. Especially since I've almost finished the lyrics, and the music is very nearly complete."

"So, you worked your way out of 'woeful ballads'?"

She laughed. "Finally. You provided an inspiration."

His brows rose. "I did?"

"Yes. Remember at dinner that night when you said that the money is in the bank when the money is in the bank?"

He winced. "Not a very cogent remark, I'm afraid."

"Oh, I beg to differ. That remark has now been immortalized in song."

"You're kidding!"

"No. It will be a big number, a humorous patter song, sung to our hero by his uncle. Now, since the man playing Uncle Hermie is not only an able singer, but also a remarkable dancer, it will be quite a production number."

"Well, well. I must say that never, in my most fanciful imaginings, did I picture myself as a song writer."

"Life sometimes takes peculiar turns."

"Doesn't it."

Ashley glanced around the restaurant, a wistful smile on her face. "We spent a lot of hours here."

"Yes. I was recalling some of them before you came in. This was where we came that first night, after we ducked out of the party."

Her eyes moved to his and were instantly trapped by their riveting gaze. She'd never known anyone with eyes like Zachary's. The dark blue seemed a surface to layers of tantalizing shades: gleamings of aqua and moss green and sunflickers of gold; deep-sea caverns, beguiling, bedazzling. They did not make false promises. The treasures were there, real and rich. Intellect, humor, sensitivity, an enormous capacity for love. She blinked, forcing a disconnection. She had almost drowned there once before and feared she was no better able to withstand the force of this particular current.

"How well I remember! You know, I don't think I ever asked you how you happened to be at a party in Greenwich Village."

She had been too entranced to think of such a detail. He had stood out in that crowd like a Rodin bronze in a display of amateur clay figures. It was about three weeks after the opening of her and Matt's first major Broadway musical. The reviews had been so good they might have written them themselves, and for weeks Ashley veered between ecstasy and apprehension, sure it was all a dream from which she would be rudely awakened. When she first sighted Zachary, the dreamlike illusion increased. He looked more a product of fantasy than reality.

"One of my classmates from Harvard law school lived there. He had decided that life as a hidebound lawyer wasn't his 'thing,' and was trying to write poetry."

"Is he still there?"

"Yes, and still writing."

"How's he doing?"

"Terribly. He's a very bad poet." They laughed together. "However, I'm glad he decided to try. He was the one who took me to see your musical and invited me to come to the party the following evening to meet you."

She knew it might be a chancy question, but she had to ask it. "Are you sorry?"

"Not at all. In spite of everything, Ashley, I wouldn't have missed our time together. Otherwise, I might never have known how it felt to be entirely happy." His eyes clouded. "Or, for that matter, entirely sad."

"You'd have been better off without the latter."

"Not necessarily. It gives me insight into what some of my clients are going through when they're faced with a death or a divorce. I suppose, in the long run, even the most hurtful of experiences builds something of value in us." He paused while Charlie put their drinks in front of them. "But I would be glad to be spared that kind of pain again."

"So would I." She took a sip of her wine, then looked at him squarely and asked, "So what are we doing to ourselves, Zachary? If you're experiencing any of the feelings I am right now, we're putting our own thumbs in the screw."

"Or our own feet on the cloud."

Ashley felt caught in a whirlpool—in imminent danger of going under. "How could we? We split up because you couldn't accept the demands of my career, and I knew I'd be deceiving myself as well as you if I said I could be happy without it. The demands haven't changed, Zachary, and my love of the theater hasn't changed."

"We're both older and probably wiser; maybe we could enjoy each other's company without expecting so much from the relationship."

She closed her eyes, trying to shut out the intrusion of hope; a hope so blinding that it blocked the flashing signals of danger that blinked on and off in her head. "Oh, Zachary, if only..."

"Ashley, I was terribly apprehensive about seeing you again, and I had no thought in mind about trying to revive anything. Three years is a long time. I thought I'd put our affair behind me and was sure you'd have done so. In fact, I assumed there would be someone else in your life."

She shook her head. "No."

"Nor in mine. I tried, a couple of times, but it didn't work."

"Same here."

"I'm so glad."

She couldn't move her gaze from his, and she was about to go under for the second time.

"Would it be so wrong of us to take whatever happiness we can find together and worry about the future in the future?"

Ashley swallowed, trying to dislodge the obstacle to her speech. "You mean like Scarlett O'Hara? Think about the bothersome things tomorrow?"

"Maybe by tomorrow they won't be so bothersome."

Why was it so hard for her to find the right words to say? She made her living with words. But at the moment, it was as though someone had stolen her mental dictionary. She shrugged, shaking her head at the same time, body language expressing the myriad doubts she felt. "You're still a Boston lawyer, and I'm still a Broadway lyricist. That twain couldn't meet before."

His hand reached across the table to cover hers, and the simple contact obliterated any remnants of Ashley's common sense.

"Maybe we tried too hard. You and I are both used to planning everything far in advance. Perhaps that's a mistake, in this case. We had something unique. It was not only a love affair, it was a wonderful friendship, as well. Would it be so terrible to renew that, without demanding blueprints for the years ahead? I think it's worthwhile to try it."

She knew, *knew*, she was about to slide her heart under a steamroller. Her lips made a frantic effort to form the word "no" and failed. She was so miserable without him, that surely seeing him, even on a platonic basis, would be better. She closed her ears to all the cries of warning that were sounding in her head. "Yes. I'd like that very much."

His eyes deepened in color, eye-beacons beckoning, compelling. She took a deep breath just before going under for the third time.

Chapter Four

When they stepped outside to hail a taxi, the sidewalk was covered by a blanket of white, and snow was falling in steady, huge, wispy flakes.

"Oh, Zach, look!" Ashley tucked her hand through his arm. "It's snowing, just like it was the first night we met! It must be a lucky omen!" She ducked her head as they stepped from the shelter of the canopy and crossed to the cab that had pulled up at the curb.

Once inside, Zachary gave the driver the address, then turned to her with a smile. "Lucky omen. That's right, I'd forgotten how superstitious you are."

"All show business people are superstitious. It's bad luck not to be."

Zachary laughed. "That makes perfect sense, I'm sure." He brushed away the snowflakes that nestled on her hair. "I'd almost forgotten how your eyes dance when you're happy."

"I don't think they've done much dancing for quite a while."

"Oh? I should think you'd be on top of the world with all the success you've achieved."

"Do you really think that's all I want?"

"I think it's what you want most."

What she wanted most, at this moment, was to be held tight in his arms, to feel his lips on hers. She wanted to lie in bed with him, to reacquaint herself with the exquisite feeling of her skin touching his. She dropped her eyes, hoping to cut off the powerful pull of his magnetism. "This is a dangerous subject, Zach."

"You're right, I apologize. It'll take a lot of discipline."

"What will?" She raised her eyes to look at him and was instantly ensnared by the dark intensity of his gaze.

"Curbing this relationship." His hand reached out to touch her cheek, then slid down to her neck, his finger stroking the tender spot behind her earlobe. Ashley shivered as tingling currents began to vibrate just beneath her skin.

"Zachary..." Her voice had gone husky. "We made all those resolutions..."

"Very wise of us, too." His finger slipped into her ear and circled its contours. "Very wise, indeed."

She knew just where she'd like those fingers to go next. "We should think of something to talk about, something safe."

"Good idea." The devilish finger moved to outline the rim of her lips. "How about the weather? Looks like snow." His hand moved over her hair, then cupped the back of her head.

"Zachary..." The pressure of his long, slender fingers awoke cravings that had lain dormant for three years. The tingling currents, still rippling beneath her skin, moved down her body, tickling the hardening tips of her breasts, dipping to tantalize the center of her womanhood.

"Or maybe we could talk about old times. Do you remember the weekend we spent at my cabin in Vermont? We had snow there, too. Lots of snow, perfect ski conditions. But, as I recall, we never did put on our skis. Or much of anything else."

"This isn't fair..." Her hand, against all orders, rose to explore the sculptured elegance of his face.

"We had that roaring fire and took turns crawling out of the sleeping bag to throw on a log." His other hand moved to rest on her knee. How could such a simple touch send jolting tremors through her whole body?

His face was very near hers, those dark, velvet eyes inveigling, caressing. She should pull away, put a stop to this. She tried to force her mind from the indescribable pleasure of the scene he was recounting. Maybe she should try counting sheep now, the ornery little devils might divert her attention. His hand moved, ever so slightly, on her knee, and she had to stifle a gasp. "I don't think this falls within the guidelines of friendship."

His white teeth gleamed in the night lights. "Oh? It seems very friendly to me." The smile faded. "Oh, Ashley, it's been so long." His strong arms pulled her to him as his mouth captured hers.

Ashley leaned into the kiss with the grateful relief of a lost wanderer finally home. His lips moved hungrily on hers and were met with greedy ardor. She could feel all those wise resolutions melting under the heat of the kiss as she wrapped her arms around his neck. She couldn't believe this was real. Was it, perhaps, one of the nighttime dreams or daytime fantasies that had so often invaded the past few years? Her fingers inched up into the thick, wavy hair, and she savored the feel, soft and clean and so familiar. Oh, this was real, all right, real and so very right. She was finally back in his arms where she belonged.

He raised his head, just a little, his lips brushing her temple. "Damn."

She pulled back, her eyes wide with surprise. "What?"

"We're on the street where you live."

She giggled. "Oh, how sweet, you're talking to me in love lyrics! When we get out, will you sing that song to me?"

His chuckle was low, sexy. "I can promise you one thing: if I did, you'd wish I hadn't. One thing I do not do well is sing."

"It must be the only thing. I can't recall any others. No, none at all."

"Are you flirting with me?"

"Oh, yes, most definitely." The cab stopped in front of her building. Ashley glanced down at his arms still encircling her. "Unless you let go, I can't get out."

"That's the whole idea." His eyes had the texture of midnight sky, black and mysterious and very inviting.

"You folks getting out here or what?" The cabbie's impatient voice broke the mood.

"Yes, we are." Zach reached into his pocket and fished out his money clip.

Ashley took the momentary distraction to counsel herself sternly against inviting him in. "Are you sure you'll be able to get another taxi?"

"Doesn't matter. I can walk."

"You might get mugged."

He shot her an offended look. "Me? One karate chop and the guy is mincemeat."

The cabbie handed Zach his change and accepted his tip. "Thanks. Y'know, I wouldn't take no chances if I was you. Some'a the guys on the street're animals."

Zach reached across Ashley to open the door. "Thanks for the kind advice, but I'm not worried." He gave a short chopping motion with his hand. "Believe me, mincemeat!"

"Okay. S'yer funeral. G'nite." They slid out and shut the door, laughing as he pulled away.

Ashley looked up at him reproachfully. "That poor man, I do believe he thought you were serious."

One of his black eyebrows rose. "What makes you think I'm not?" He gave the same chop motion, his forehead creased into scowling ferocity. "Mincemeat!" The doorman waited at the entrance, trying to be unobtrusive. Zach motioned toward him with his head. "It's your move. Aren't you going to ask me in?"

Ashley glanced over at the door, then up at the handsome face. "I don't think that's such a good idea." Actually, she thought it was a wonderful idea but was making a last-ditch effort to nudge some discipline into her character.

"You mean you're going to leave me out here, alone and defenseless? Don't you know some of the guys on the street are animals?"

"What happened to the old 'chop-chop' mincemeat number?"

"It gets very messy, and this is a new suit."

The giggles were again threatening eruption. Ashley shook her head in surrender. "I'd almost forgotten your weird sense of humor. Yes, do come in. You may have a nightcap and then call a taxi to take you safely to your hotel."

"What a woman. You're all heart." As they walked inside, Ashley gave a friendly greeting to the patient doorman. When they entered the elevator, Zach amended his statement. "No, I take that back. There is definitely far more to you than just heart."

Ashley pushed the button for the third floor. "Are you flirting with me?"

"Most flagrantly." He leaned down to place a kiss on the side of her neck.

She could almost feel the flesh singeing under the touch of his lips. She counseled herself against letting him inside her apartment. She should kiss him good-night before unlocking the door, assure him she'd call a taxi for him and send him right back down in the elevator. He pulled aside the collar of her coat so he could kiss the sensitive spot just below her ear. The elevator stopped. Ashley looked up into those beguiling eyes and handed him her key. "We shouldn't be doing this; I think we both know that!"

He turned the key in the lock, opened the door and stood back for her to enter. "But you're wrong, Ashley. Don't you know it's terrible luck not to offer hospitality to an old friend and even worse luck for the old friend to refuse it?"

"I never heard of that."

"You'd better bone up on your superstitions. It's far more dangerous than black cats or ladders."

She narrowed her eyes at him. "How did a partner of a prestigious law firm, a man with a high-class social background, ever become such a con artist?"

"Now see, that question just proves how naive you are. Most of the so-called social elite have at least one robber baron in their ancestry, and everyone knows how shady lawyers are, so on both counts I come by it naturally." He slid her coat off her shoulders, his fingers leaving hot trails down her arms. While she hung her coat in the closet, he tossed his overcoat on the chair in the entrance hall, glancing around in the process. "My, my, these are much fancier digs than what you used to have."

She moved into the living room, acutely aware of his nearness as he followed. "Yes, I know. I still feel more a visitor than a resident. How do you like it?"

"Well, as my Aunt Phoebe would say, it's really rather swell. But I have to admit a slight preference for the old place. It seemed so much more..."

"Cluttered?"

"Intimate was the word I had in mind. But yes, clutter was part of its charm." Zachary moved around the room, looking at the highly polished wood floor, partly covered by a spectacular Navajo Indian rug, the deep-cushioned, pale rose sofa with two chairs in complementary patterns, the wide expanse of sliding glass doors leading out to a small balcony. He stopped by the piano and ran his hand over the smooth surface. "And here is the center of it all. Much more elegant than that little beat-up upright."

"Oh yes, I'll never forget it. It had such a lovely finish— early black-pitted."

"It may not have been beautiful, but it did real well by you. I still remember you sitting there, in that crowded corner, plunking out a melody while you set words to it. I always thought how awesome that was, the way the words just flowed out of you in exactly the right sequence. I really admired that ability; it's quite a talent."

She turned and looked at him, surprised. "I didn't know that—that you admired it. I thought you just resented it."

He crossed the room to her and took hold of her shoulders. "Oh, Ashley, what an ass I must have seemed, always jealous of your incredible craft because it was such an insurmountable rival. Of course, I admired it, and I also resented it. I wanted to be the source of your riches. I wanted to give you a beautiful home and your first taste of luxury. I wanted to hand you the world on a silver platter. But that wasn't the world you wanted. The one you wanted could only be gained by your own talent, and it made me feel so...empty-handed. That's what comes of being hopelessly old-fashioned."

The heat from his hands sent streams of warm comfort down her arms. Just having him here, touching her, made her feel completed. "I only wanted one thing from you, Zach. I only wanted your love."

"You had that. In fact, you still have it. Unfortunately, it isn't that simple. You can love and still have to walk away."

"Did you have to walk away?" She stopped and leaned her forehead against his chest. "I'm sorry. We're getting into old territory we swore we wouldn't enter." He kissed the top of her head, which imbued her with a heightened sense of well-being. It had always made her feel protected, secure, and it did now.

His voice was muffled in her hair. "This seems to be a night for breaking resolutions." He tipped up her chin. "I'd like to break at least one more."

He was so near. His face mere inches away, those firm, tantalizing lips so close. Her whole body signaled its yearning, and as his arms enclosed her, she leaned into the embrace, desperate to close any gaps, to connect completely and irrevocably with him. As soon as his mouth met hers, the last torn remnant of her defensiveness slid away to join the rag pile of sensible vows. Her lips opened, and his tongue slid past them to join a circling, probing, winding reunion with hers. The kiss deepened as they longed for the ultimate closeness.

"Ashley." Her name from his lips thrummed through her throat, surged through her pulsing veins to her heart. She rejoiced in the taste of him, wanted to consume and be consumed, to devour and be devoured. She moaned her need for haste, as his fingers moved to the zipper on the back of her dress. Without interrupting the kiss, he slid the suddenly constricting garment off her shoulders, down and down till it dropped to the floor. Frantic to be naked, to be flesh to flesh with him, her shaking fingers moved to his belt, awkwardly undid the buckle, the zipper, pushed at the intrusive pants until they, too, fell.

Zachary stepped back and quickly shed his clothes while Ashley impatiently kicked off her shoes and took off her slip and panty hose. Within moments, their clothes lay in two heaps on the floor, and they faced each other, he clad only in shorts that betrayed his arousal and she in lace bra and bikini panties.

His eyes caressed her, inch by inch. "I have held the picture of you in my mind. But it doesn't compare to the reality." He reached over to undo the clip and parted the bra to display her full, smooth breasts. "God, Ashley, you're so perfect." He leaned over to kiss the top of each curve, then on to gently nip the taut nipples.

Ashley gasped as shock waves of incredible pleasure careered through her body. How had she lived without this, this exquisite torture? Her greedy hands pushed at his shorts, but their descent was stalled by a significant barrier. As she worked them free, she heard a low growl of reaction from her too-long missing lover. His body was still as magnificent as ever: wide-shouldered and muscular, sinewy, taut and lean. The ruggedly smooth skin with its perpetually lingering tan. She was intoxicated with craving.

He looked down at her, his eyes smoky with desire. "Where's the bedroom?"

She gave a weak wave of her hand. "That way."

He grinned, that lopsided smile that gave him such a devilish air. "Shall I carry you, like the triumphant warrior come to collect his due?"

"Oh, yes." Her voice was a mere whisper, stilled by the hoarseness of passion. "I'd like to be your prize. I want to be ravished."

With a rumbling chuckle, he swept her into his arms with an ease that reminded her of his immense strength, garnered on playing fields and rolling oceans. Everywhere they touched felt tingling hot; the rest of her ached for the warmth. He carried her into her bedroom, over the deep-piled rug to the king-size bed, where he lowered her to the soft quilt cover. His hands moved over her silken body, over each curve, leaving delicious shivers in their wake. He hooked his fingers over the edge of her bikini and eased it off, bending to kiss the triangle that lay revealed.

Ashley was one seething cauldron of smoldering desire. As Zach stretched out beside her, she turned toward him. "Zachary, I want you so."

"My love."

A muffled cry escaped her as his lips took her nipple, his tongue sliding and circling, sending spasms of ecstasy streaking through her. His tongue teased, moving back and forth, back and forth, while his talented fingers explored the contours of her form, making their way slowly, maddeningly, to the nub of her need. She felt the danger of explosion when they reached their goal, gently probing, arousing her to a pandemonium of passion.

She wound her arms around his neck, sighing in pleasure as her palms explored the familiar feel of smooth skin covering hard muscle. Her fingers danced over the short, curled hair on his chest, moved to touch each ridge and ripple of taut muscle.

When his relentless fingers strayed down to nip the electrified flesh of her thighs then return to the torment of her throbbing core, she reeled under the volcanic burst of her senses.

"Zachary, Zachary, I need you so."

With a low groan, he slid on top of her, his mouth grinding hers with the ferocity of ignited passion. Her mouth opened, wanting total intrusion, offering total submission as her hands slipped downward to enclose the hot shaft of his need. A deep growl accompanied the spasm of his body.

"Please, darling, please. Now!" There was pleading desperation in her tone.

He breathed her name deep into her mouth as he entered her, joining love to love, need to need. She felt at once complete, whole. The undulation of their combined bodies, gyrating in rhythm with their quickening pulses, beating harder, faster, until, with a synchronized cry of release, they bucked and arched in the agonizing splendor of climax.

They lay, totally spent, their breathing slow and satisfied. Although a master of words, Ashley couldn't possibly have described how she felt at that moment. Such sheer, unadulterated contentment defied simple syllables. Zach shifted his weight slightly, and she whispered, "Umm, that feels good."

"Everything feels good. There isn't a spot on my body, inside or out, that is not sated with pleasure. Oh, my sweet, this feels like heaven. If aery visions in gossamer and wings should flutter by, I won't be the least surprised."

"You're right, that's just where we are. And they say you have to die to go to heaven. Should we pass the word that it's not true?"

"Uh-uh. If word of this ecstasy got out, crowds would gather, lines would form. It could lead to a riot. No, we'll keep it to ourselves, hoarded and safe."

"Can you stay right here with me for the night? I couldn't bear it if you went away. I'm sure I'd plummet straight back to earth, and that's a very long fall. I shouldn't think you'd want to be responsible for the injuries."

"I hadn't thought of that. But now that you bring it up, of course that's true. I could never stand to have such a calamity on my conscience, so I'm ready to make the supreme sacrifice of staying right here in your arms."

"What a guy."

"I've always had philanthropic tendencies; they're bred into my genes."

"They're not the only wonderful things carried in your jeans."

He hoisted himself to his elbows and gave her a sardonic scowl of mock disapproval. "Tch, tch. What would your mother say?"

Ashley laughed. "By this time she'd be far beyond speech." Her forehead wrinkled in thought. "No, I take that back. As long as it's you here, indisposing me, she'd probably say, 'Atta girl, Ashley, way to go!'"

"Your mother is a woman of profoundly good judgment." He settled back down, his head on the pillow beside hers.

"True. She was terribly put out with me when I told her I'd broken our engagement."

"She wasn't the only one." A touch of sadness played through the jesting tone.

"Zach..."

"What, my love?"

"Did your parents mind at all? I mean, were they the least bit disappointed, or do you think they were just relieved?"

His head came up again, his dark blue eyes warm with his love. "Ashley, of course they were disappointed. They'd come to care very deeply for you, and had already mentally added you to the family."

"Had they really?"

"Does that surprise you?"

She sighed. "I have to admit it does. I'm afraid I never got past being a little intimidated by them."

"Why?"

"Well, they seem to belong to another world from the one I grew up in. I mean, they're so...refined, so..."

"Stuffy?"

She laughed. "No. That's really *not* it at all. In fact, they weren't the least bit stuffy, they were always kind and welcoming. But you saw the difference, Zach, between your home and mine. I grew up thinking maids just existed in fancy movies, and only royalty dressed for dinner."

Zach chuckled as he moved over to lie beside her. "It might surprise you to know they were a bit intimidated by you, too."

"You're kidding."

"Not at all. They'd never known anyone who had a hit show running on Broadway. And after they came to New York to see it and realized how much of it was your creation, they were thoroughly impressed."

"That's nice to know."

He kissed her cheek. "How could anyone, given half an opportunity, fail to love you?"

She turned her head on the pillow, meeting his gaze. "I wish..."

"What?"

"That it *was* as simple as that. That love really did cure all problems."

"Maybe it does, if given half a chance." He rolled onto his back and put his arm under her head as she snuggled close with her head on his chest. "Umm, I'm getting drowsy. It *is* rather late."

"It sure is. I'm sleepy, too. And I can't imagine anything lovelier than falling asleep in your arms."

His arms tightened around her, and his hand stroked her hair. "You know, I have a great surprise for you in the morning. I've learned to cook a smashing breakfast. If you have the right ingredients, I'll prepare a sumptuous repast, and we can tarry over our coffee for hours."

Ashley drew in her breath and held it for seconds, while her drowsy mind snapped to attention. She exhaled slowly, ruing the need to say what she had to say. "I can't honey. I have an eight-thirty meeting with our director. We have to go over some of the scenes that aren't blocking exactly right."

His silence was only momentary. "Okay. So you must be dazzled by my culinary arts at a later date. I'll meet you for lunch. Perhaps at the "

"Zach." Ashley was developing a knot in her stomach. "You know how much I'd love that, but..."

"Another meeting?"

"A working lunch, with Gregory, our scenery designer."

The silence was slightly longer. "All right, moving right along. Dinner. Somewhere with soft music and candlelight..."

"Damn." She turned her head away, feeling the threat of tears behind her lids.

"No dinnertime? Don't you people eat?"

"Not formally. Not during rehearsal weeks. It's too much of a madhouse, honey. You have no idea the number of problems that arise before opening night. And especially when there's an out-of-town run. Every day brings something else that has to be changed or polished or finished."

"I thought that became the job of the producer and director."

"Zach, it's my show. Mine and Matt's. There's no part of it that we're not involved in—not one. If it succeeds, it's ultimately our success. If it bombs, it's our turkey. We *have* to oversee everything."

Zach slid his arm from beneath her head. "I'm getting a cramp." There was no missing the change of tone, though it was nothing more than a fiber of withdrawal. "Well, that takes care of Saturday. I don't suppose Sunday is set aside for resting?"

"Matt and I have to finish some songs . . ."

"I thought they were finished."

"All the lyrics and melodies are done, but final arrangements are still going on. It takes a lot of time." She was developing a cramp, too. In her heart.

"Funny. Your schedule seemed wild before, but I don't recall its being this bad."

She turned on her side to look at his fine profile. His features had, without question, stiffened. "The play I was involved with when we met was in its third week on Broadway. Most of the kinks had been ironed out. If you think back, we had a lot of time together for quite a while, until Matt and I started on our next project. And then, of course, the play opened in England . . ."

"And a few other countries."

"Yes. Zach, I have to be honest. The weeks before an opening night are just plain insane. We attend most of the rehearsals, at least the principal rehearsals, and spend the rest of the time rewriting and smoothing and dealing with glitches."

"How did you get away tonight?"

"I just took a night off."

"But it's pretty clear that can't happen very often."

"No." Her cramp was spreading; it now included her stomach.

"Well—" he swung his legs over the side of the bed and sat up "—in that case I'd better go back to my hotel so I can catch the early plane. I have a lot of things that should be tended to, and there's obviously no reason to postpone them to hang around here."

She reached out to touch his back. "Why can't you sleep here?"

He turned his head and looked at her, his eyes guarded. "Because, I wouldn't sleep." He got up and headed into the bathroom.

Ashley lay there, fighting tears, and listened to the sound of water running in the shower, then the bang of the stall door after the water was turned off. All the joy inside had evaporated and was replaced by a creeping dread. When Zach came out of the bathroom, a towel wrapped around his waist, he gave her a weak smile and walked toward the living room. The silence was awful. He seemed to be gone forever. Her mind seemed to be in some form of catatonia, no doubt a protective device to thwart the intrusion of speculation. The possibilities that faced her, at this moment, seemed nothing but catastrophic.

Zach came back into the bedroom, fully dressed, and sat on the edge of the bed. He looked perfectly groomed, incredibly handsome and remote. Something in his eyes, when they met hers, had retreated, leaving her unbearably alone. "Ashley, I must apologize. This was a mistake." Her breath caught in her esophagus, threatening strangulation. "And it's entirely my fault. You tried to keep us on a safe course, but I wanted you so badly that I refused to listen to my own good counsel." He bent over to place a gentle kiss on her forehead. "You're a remarkable woman, in every way." He glanced away, staring at some inner thought for a few seconds before returning to her. "I love you."

She couldn't hold back the tears. They began to slide silently down her cheeks. "That sounds like there's a 'but' at the end."

"It does, doesn't it. I wish…" He stopped and shook his head. "Hell, what's the use? Wishing *won't* make it so." He patted her arm, like a man consoling a sick friend, and stood up. He looked every inch the suave, sophisticated man of purpose. He looked like he'd stepped out of her world into another. One that had No Trespassing signs posted.

"Zachary," her voice came out squeaky and tiny, like a little girl's. "Don't go."

For an instant his stance changed and he appeared undecided. For only an instant. "Get some sleep, Ashley. You've got a lot of work ahead of you." He came back to the edge of the bed, leaned over, his hands on both sides of her head, and bent to kiss her gently on the lips. "Thank you for the view of heaven. Tonight was incredible." He stood and backed away. "I'll be in touch." With that, he was gone.

She listened to the front door open and close and strained her ears for the sound of the elevator before she released the full flow of her tears.

Chapter Five

Ashley reached her 8:30 a.m. meeting on time but looked and felt as though she'd left the better part of herself at home. Heartbreak, it was clear, was no easier the second time around. She felt battered, bruised and filled with despair. She couldn't blame it all on Zachary, much as she'd like to. Her guard had eroded just as quickly as his under the onslaught of desire. Unfortunately, as a result of the hours they'd spent together, the precious time in his arms, all of the inner doubts and ambiguities concerning life in the theater versus a life with Zachary had been reawakened. There was nothing to compare with the sheer joy she'd rediscovered last night. Though she thought she'd put a definite "period" after her decision of three years past, it had squirmed loose from its shape as an adamant circle of finality to curl itself into a wavering question mark.

The minute she entered the drafty rehearsal hall, it was obvious that at least one crisis was under way. Matt, who rarely made an appearance anywhere before 10:00 a.m., was hunched over the flat top of the piano, running his hand through his hair while Sonja, the choreographer, stood next to him and gesticulated wildly, her mouth going at a rapid rate. Ashley squinted, trying to adjust her eyes to the semi-darkness after the glare of the morning sun, as she scanned the room to locate Craig, the director. She spotted Craig on the far side of the hall and headed his way. As soon as he saw her, he signaled her to stay put and came to meet her.

"Hi, Ashley." Craig gave her the regulation hug and kiss, then gestured toward a door that led to a small sitting room. "Let's disappear before Sonja sees you, or you're sure to end up arbitrating between her and Matt."

"What's going on?"

"Beats me. Matt mumbled something about screwy tempos when he came in. I try to avoid contact with Sonja whenever possible. She never even says hello. She opens every conversation with 'Craig, you're allowing your body to settle. It needs stretching and pulling!' If she got me under her control for a week, I'd be dead."

Ashley made a good stab at a laugh. She had precious little humor in her this morning. "She's the only one I know who can get Matt out of bed this early."

"Isn't that the truth. Let's sit in here." He led the way into the other room and closed the door behind him. "We might stay undiscovered long enough to get some work done." He pulled a rumpled sheaf of folded papers out of his hip pocket. "I have a few notes here about the staging of the songs."

Ashley sighed. Craig was an exceptional director, esteemed and liked by everyone who knew him. She loved working with him because his attitude toward the play's author was one of complete respect. He consulted with her about every scene of the play, and unlike many directors, he believed authors should, to the greatest degree possible, be completely satisfied with the on-stage translation of their work. The problem, this morning, was that Ashley was finding it difficult to give a significant damn about any of it.

Nevertheless, giving herself a stern inner shake, she sat beside Craig on the small, hard sofa and focused her attention on his notations.

It was minutes away from midnight by the time she returned to her apartment, so exhausted she was surprised she was still vertical. When she reached her bedroom she stopped in the doorway, overwhelmed by waves of memory. Her eyes moved to the bed, neatly made up by Lulu, the housekeeper who came by daily to clean and run errands. She walked slowly across the room, pulled back the spread and ran her hand over the pillow that had supported Zachary's head so few hours before. She was filled with such a wave of loneliness that it seemed certain to drown her. What would it feel like to be Zachary's wife, to anticipate his return to her night after night, to be freed from the emptiness of sleeping alone, always missing him, always wishing he were beside her?

"Damn!" She threw her purse onto a chair and stomped into the dressing room to prepare for bed. "You *knew* this would happen, you dippy idiot! Why did you agree to see him?" No logical excuses came to mind, but one illogical fact slithered through the self-condemnation. If given the chance, she'd probably do it again.

Just as she reached over to turn out the bedside lamp, the phone rang. Her hand leapt to the receiver. "Hello?"

"Ashley."

Her heart wiggled free of its restraints and rose to lodge in the bottom of her throat.

"Zachary?"

"Yes. I was hoping you'd be home by now. How did the day go?"

"All right, I guess." Terrible, awful, horrible.

"I'm afraid we flunked our first stab at 'platonic.'"

"We got an F minus."

"Ashley, I'm sorry. I don't want you to be hurt anymore. In fact, I don't want *me* to be hurt anymore. I overestimated my willpower and underestimated your...attraction."

"It wasn't just your fault, Zach. Not by a long shot."

"Well—" He gave a sort of half-chuckle. "I did feel there was a significant element of mutual accord."

She actually smiled. "If we're speaking in legalese, I'm afraid I must plead 'no contest.'" Hope, a bright-eyed little creature, peeked over her black cloud of sadness. "I was afraid I wouldn't hear from you."

"Despite my too-frequent shows of petulance, I am beset, now and again, by periods of rational thought. I acted like a jerk. I'd like to throw myself on the mercy of the court and request a second chance."

Ashley wound the cord around her finger, surprised to feel her mouth arch into a smile. "May the court inquire: a second chance at what?"

This time it was a full-fledged laugh. "Umm. There is room for confusion, at that. I'd like to make another attempt at being a trustworthy friend. Of the hands-off variety."

She lay back against the headboard of the bed. "Oh, Zachary, do you honestly think we could keep our relationship confined to friendship?"

"We could be very *good* friends."

Little bubbles of mirth had formed in her stomach. What a pushover she was! Just hearing his voice, no matter what it was saying, fed happiness into her system like a free-running IV. "I'm beginning to fear we're both gluttons for punishment."

"Don't feel too sheepish about it. Masochism is rampant. We're not alone."

A couple of the joy bubbles popped up, forming into silly hiccups of laughter. "Do you have any sort of program for this endeavor?"

"That depends on you. Joe and I are coming to New York on Tuesday morning. There are bargains to strike and papers to sign, among which will be a significant check. Might we be allowed to dog your trail? Joe wants to see how a play comes together, and I want to go Ashley-watching."

She had a moment of panic. How could she possibly function, knowing his eyes were following her every move? How would she force her feet to head in any direction besides straight to him? "Sure. That can be arranged. Bring plenty of Excedrin."

"Will do. I will also wear my armor plating. I might suggest you get outfitted with a chastity belt."

A whole series of giggles bubbled out of her throat. "You fool. Neither of those things will do it. Try a bag over your head and don't, for any reason, touch me. That just might keep us out of trouble."

"That's one of the things I always loved about you. You're such an optimist. I'll see you on Tuesday."

"Zachary..."

"Yes?"

She bit her lip. "Good night."

"Good night."

She and Matt spent the morning reconstructing the sequence of tempos in the "Money in the Bank" number, which had been Sonja's primary concern. As usual, Matt came to Ashley's place to work. Lulu made a large pot of coffee and some cinnamon rolls.

Matt sat at the piano, stopping every few bars to take a sip of coffee and another bite of roll. "Jeez. Why don't we write our next musical without any dance numbers? It would make life a heck of a lot easier."

"The audiences love dances."

"Nuts to the audience. We'll reeducate them. Bring back stylized posturing and Greek choruses. Maybe we could start a rumor that watching dancers leap around on a stage causes loss of equilibrium."

"Better think of something else. There're probably lots of people who don't know the meaning of equilibrium. Matt, will you stop eating that roll while you play the piano? You're going to get the keys all sticky."

"Nag, nag, nag. You're beginning to sound like my last wife. Okay, listen to this." His fingers flew over the keys.

"Good. That's real good. I hope that's not the section you expect me to write another verse for."

"Sorry, kiddo, this is it. Don't sweat it; it's just a little simple syncopation."

"How in heaven's name can anyone dance to that beat and sing at the same time? You *know* what's going to happen. After the second try, we'll be asked to take it out again."

"Yep. Or change the rhythm to a mambo. Such is the sad dilemma of the composer."

"Well, you certainly are sanguine. What happened, did one of your ex's remarry?"

"No such luck." He came to the end of the section and ran his finger down the keys in a grand glissando. "Amy finally started taking my calls."

Ashley stopped studying the melody line in front of her and looked over at Matt. "Hey, that's great! You mean she actually forgave you, once again?"

"What's to forgive? A little human kindness? She came to her senses. Simple as that."

She shook her head. "Dear Amy. Much as I like her, I do at times suspect the poor thing suffers a degree of brain damage. If I were more of a humanitarian, I'd take her aside and warn her to run for her life."

"Leave Amy alone. She knows a good thing when she sees it. Where would she ever find another like me?" He shot her a warning look. "Don't answer that." His fingers picked up the melody of one of the show's love songs. "So, what about you, oh great purveyor of advice to the lovelorn? I have noted a slight shiftiness to your moods. After skimming around two feet off the ground for a week, you slid yourself in under the door yesterday morning. Now, once again, you resemble a round-eyed smile sticker." He paused just long enough to take another sticky bite. "How's Zach?"

"Now what makes you leap instantly to the conclusion that my mood has to have something to do with him?"

"Come on, babe, 'fess up. I bet you ignored my advice to be careful."

"Speaking of experts on love."

"Listen, I know all the pitfalls; I've taken every one. So answer the question. How's Zach? Is he due to show up today? Is that why you're twitching?"

"Matt! I am *not* twitching!"

"Either that or you're developing an unfortunate malady."

Ashley plopped into the rose chair. "All right, smartypants. So I ignored your advice and I took a whale of a pratfall. But he called last night, and we agreed to try again to be just friends."

Matt clapped his hands together and threw back his head in laughter. "That's rich! That'll happen about the same time cats learn to bark! Who came up with that cockamamy idea?"

"Oh, don't be so eternally skeptical! We *are* friends. We happen to like each other very much."

"Among a few other things."

"All right, so all we have to do is avoid those other things."

"Ashley, Ashley. For a brilliant broad you're awfully thick sometimes. Even I don't kid myself that much. What's he coming for, a test run?"

She huffed herself up to a dignified posture. "You'll be pleased to know he's accompanying Joe Sanders. Mr. Moneybags is ready to share the wealth."

Matt played a resounding "ta-dah" chord. "Whoopee! The money *is* in the bank. So Zach's coming along to read the fine print?"

"Yes. And..."

"Uh-oh."

"They want to stay with me for the day to see some of the preparation that goes into a play."

"Yeah, I just bet old Zach's dying to case the rehearsals." Both eyebrows rose to form twin arches of skepticism. "Friends, huh? Good luck, babe. It's a good thing the lyrics are done."

Ashley wrinkled her nose at him. "We can do it, just wait and see!"

How she wished she felt even a tad of confidence in her own words!

Ashley and Matt were in the middle of looking at costume sketches when she was summoned to the phone. All the way through the long corridor to the building's tiny office, she fed herself tidbits of gloom. "He's not coming, I just know he's not coming. Something's come up and he couldn't get away." By the time she picked up the receiver there were tears in her eyes. "Hello."

"That's a sad-sounding hello. Are things going badly today?"

"Hi, Zachary." She attempted to lighten her tone, with, she suspected, precious little success. "No, everything's fine." If he was still in Boston, she'd die!

There was a pause. He must have heard the anxiety in her voice. "All right, if you say so. I hope you're not having second thoughts about our sitting in on rehearsals today."

"Oh, no!" She caught her breath, not quite daring to hope. "You *are* coming to New York?"

"We're not coming, we're here. We've been to the law-yer's office and all the papers are signed. I have to warn you, Joe's eyes have acquired a proprietary gleam."

Ashley's eyes had acquired blazing glints of happiness. "That's wonderful. We'll try to make him feel right at home with us." So much so he'd want to come back again and again. With Zachary by his side.

"Tell me, do you eat lunch at all?"

"Yes." She fought a brisk skirmish with her conscience, trying to convince it she *could* accept a luncheon invitation from him. But the brief flight of speculation died. She sim-ply couldn't leave, there was too much to be done. With a sigh, she told him, "We usually have sandwiches sent in."

"I see. How many people constitute we?"

"What do you mean?"

"I'm talking numbers. How many sandwiches?"

"Hmm, let me think." She went through a mental head count. "About fifteen. Rehearsal doesn't start until two, so as yet we don't have the masses."

"Okay. Don't send out, Joe and I will bring lunch. About one o'clock be okay?"

"Fine." Marvelous, incredible, magnificent!

Ashley floated back to rejoin the costume conference. The moment Matt saw her, his eyes took on a knowing gleam, and he gave an almost indiscernible shake of his head that was just enough to convey his concern. It was all too clear that her collaborator thought she was doing a heavy gig on thin ice. Well, what did he know? His track record would certainly never be used as a guide to a smooth ride through loveland! Besides, there was no reason for him to be so doubtful. After all, their relationship was proof that male-female friendships worked! She ignored the inner voice that pointed out the vast differences between her feelings for Matt and those for Zachary. She believed what she needed to believe. If she faced too many realities, she'd *have* to stay away from Zach, and she didn't think that was possible. She glanced up at the big round clock on the wall. Twelve-fifteen. She wondered if she could survive the next forty-five minutes.

When Joe and Zach arrived, they were loaded down with cartons and bags, and they were accompanied by Jerry Jerome. The producer's face was aglow with triumph. Ashley couldn't blame him. Getting enough money to float a Broadway musical was no mean feat; the cost was in the millions. She got up from her seat next to Matt on the piano bench and rushed forward to meet Zachary.

"What in heaven's name have you two brought?" She tried to keep her eyes fastened on Joe's big grin, instead of allowing herself to fall head first into the deep pools of dark blue that so compelled her.

Jerry motioned toward the side exit with his head. "We'd better take all this to the back room." As he walked through the theater, he yelled, "Lunch! Follow me!" When they reached the other room, Jerry set down two big bags and helped unload the white boxes from Joe's arms. "They insisted on going to the Stage Door Café for sandwiches, so you know they're not low-cal."

"But good," Joe interjected.

"But good," Jerry agreed. "And Joe was bound and determined to bring champagne. I told him we'd lose everyone for the afternoon, but I was overruled." His wide smile and shining face indicated that he hadn't fought too hard to thwart any of Joe Sander's spurts of generosity.

Ashley, who had gone to Zach's assistance, was irritated by the shakiness of her hands as she lifted a couple of the containers from their precarious perch and put them on the long table against the wall. "I said fifteen, not fifty! This looks like enough food to feed the entire cast!"

He grinned. "Well, maybe they'll arrive hungry."

"You can count on it. Singers are always hungry, and dancers are always ravenous. They work so hard and always have to watch their figures. It's a tough combination."

His eyes slid over her covetously. "You don't have to watch yours. It's perfect."

Ashley actually felt the warmth of a blush. "Thank you, kind sir." The glib words failed to screen the electric currents of awareness crackling between them. As Ashley lifted a carton off the pile in his arms, she allowed her gaze to be ensnared by his and promptly dropped the box, "Damn!" She bent to retrieve it, feeling awkward and foolish. She was behaving like a lovesick schoolgirl. This friendship thing was going to be one tough assignment!

"Hey, watch the pastrami. That's good stuff."

With sheer determination, she kept her eyes away from the sapphire entrappers. "Um. I love pastrami." But pastrami was not going to satisfy her voracious appetite. There was hunger and there was *hunger*.

"We also brought corned beef and smoked turkey. And you're right, there's enough for the cast of a play or a busload of commuters. Joe is feeling lavish today. I'll have to stick close or he'll give away the store."

Jerry came over to give her an exuberant hug. "Hi there, lyric lady. I hear you've got this show completely written. We're neck and neck. I just got it completely paid for!"

Ashley laughed and returned his hug. "Congratulations, Jerry. I hope the finances stay put more firmly than what I've written will. There are bound to be lots of changes between now and our Broadway opening."

"Yeah, guess that's true." He flashed a smile. "But I don't worry about that—you and Matt can handle it."

Everyone quickly gathered in the back room, lured by the scent of food. Joe even provided champagne glasses. When they all held a glass of the bubbly, he proposed a toast. "Here's to a full-out, no-holds-barred, rip-roaring success!" With many echoes of agreement, the champagne was quickly consumed.

Jerry introduced Zachary and Joe to all the happy recipients of their largesse while Craig and Matt pulled up a circle of chairs. Ashley somehow managed to chew and swallow an entire pastrami sandwich, even though Zachary's proximity caused a significant constriction of the esophagus. Surrounded as they were, they had no chance for a private conversation, which was just as well. She couldn't think of one single platonic thing to say.

There were, as anticipated, lots of leftovers, all of which swiftly disappeared as the cast assembled. Rehearsal, which usually started promptly on time, was a little late, but nobody seemed to mind. Having the backing safely subscribed was well worth a celebration.

When the last of the food had about disappeared, Craig stood and called out, "Okay, cast, listen up! We're running late, so you'll have to concentrate extra hard. We have to finish getting this show on its feet today."

Joe leaned toward Ashley. "On its feet? What does that mean?"

"Doing the blocking." At his blank stare, she explained, "Setting the stage directions. When and where to move, that sort of thing."

"Very interesting." Zachary winked at Ashley, and she smiled in return. Joe was lapping this up like a kid with an ice-cream cone.

He was so clearly hungry for any and all bits of show biz lore, that she expanded on her explanation. "Some directors spend the first couple of days with everyone seated around a table for a read-through, but Craig says actors don't belong on their butts, so he starts right out on the staging. They'll be expected to have the movements, as well as the lines, memorized by the next time these scenes are run."

Craig was still giving instructions: "Be sure you get your directions written in the scripts. If you're not sure about them, ask. We can't take time to go back over this, and those scripts are out of your hands next time through. We start with act 2, scene 3, where we left off yesterday. On-stage, everyone!'' The usual rush to obey orders was more a ramble today. The champagne and heavy sandwiches had taken their toll.

Jerry pulled his chair closer to theirs, and Matt followed suit. ''Joe, maybe we can take a few minutes to answer your questions before we go into the theater. If we talk during Craig's rehearsal, we'll get yelled at.''

Joe nodded in compliance. ''Hey, I'm the last one to want to hold up progress. I've now got plenty of reasons to want this play to succeed. Each and every one of which is preceded by a dollar sign.'' He laughed happily. If he was at all worried about his investment, it didn't show. ''How does it begin, Ashley? Do you and Matt decide it's time to start writing and go searching for a topic, or do you wait till you're hit by an idea?''

Ashley almost lost Joe's question as Zachary hitched his chair closer to hers. The moment he got near her, every part of her became acutely tuned to his presence. She dragged her attention back to the matter at hand. ''It could start with either. So far the idea has come before we've reached the point of really *wanting* to go back to work.''

Matt snorted. ''You ain't kiddin'. After our last show, we were both ready to take a year off.'' He frowned. ''You know, I can't even remember where this idea first started, but it sure played hell with our plans.''

Ashley glanced at Zachary. His expression was unreadable. It had played hell with more than plans. She looked down at her fingers, clasped tightly together, as memories flicked through her mind. The attraction between her and Zachary had been instantaneous and incredibly potent. From the beginning, they'd spent every available moment together. It hadn't been difficult at first, because, with the show well into its run, the demands on her time were limited. She had flown to Boston often during the week so they could have dinner and, as time went on, breakfast, together; she'd met him at any number of trysting spots for weekends; or Zachary had come to New York on Friday nights and they'd played house in her crowded little apartment. All of that had altered when she and Matt got back to work. She could understand more clearly now, with the distance of time, the shock the change must have been to Zach. She'd quickly gone from almost total availability to practically none.

Her eyes rose to meet his. "It sort of takes over. Once an idea gets planted, it grows like crab grass, and there's nothing we can do but go with it." He hadn't understood the compulsion before, and the look in his eyes said he didn't now. He couldn't see why their work couldn't be contained, controlled in an orderly, reasonable time frame, like anyone else's. The burning need to stay with it, get it written down while it was flowing, eluded him.

Joe turned to Jerry. "How soon do you get involved with a production?"

"In this case, I was involved before there was one. I'd seen their last show and approached them about doing the next. So as soon as the play was pretty well sketched out and a few of the numbers written, I was on the trail, kicking up interest and contacting the production team we wanted. When it's an original, like this show, it has to be copyrighted, which is pretty simple. If it's an adaptation of a book, we have to go after the rights, which can really be time-consuming."

Matt nodded. "Most of the biggest hit musicals are adaptations of either a play or a book. We're hoping this will be an exception." He grinned at Joe. "I imagine you are, too."

"It's only money."

"Maybe to you, fella, but there are those of us whose investment goes beyond that—like our careers, for instance.

Besides, I've never been able to think of money in terms of 'only.'"

Ashley laughed. "Matt thinks of money in terms of 'gimme.' But then, as he keeps reminding me, he has two ex-wives to support."

Joe's eyebrows rose. "Two?"

"Yeah. 'Fraid so. Keeps me stuck to the piano."

Lyle Baker ambled in. The veteran actor was wiping his forehead with the small towel he kept looped over his belt, a practice that had earned him the nickname Halfback. "Boy, check this out. People sitting and relaxing. I knew I should've gone into the production end of this business."

Jerry stood up and pulled another chair over for Lyle, shaking his head at him as he did. "Bull. No one could pay you enough to stay off the stage." He gave him an affectionate jab to the arm. "Some people need regular transfusions of blood; with Lyle, it's applause. Sit down, Grandpa, and rest your weary bones." He grinned at the rest of them. "Lyle's trying to keep this a secret, but it's too delicious to keep to myself. He's just become a grandfather." There were unanimous exclamations of disbelief.

Matt looked skeptical, "Somebody's lying about something. We just helped you celebrate your thirty-ninth birthday."

Lyle shrugged. "So I'm caught." He gave Jerry an unconvincing scowl. The two men were old friends. Jerry had produced a number of shows that had featured Lyle Baker. "So maybe I'm a few years older. I should think little details like that could be kept among friends."

Matt nodded vigorously. "Absolutely. It's nobody else's business. Not a soul will know except those of us right here and Rona Barrett's entire video audience."

"Thanks, pal." Lyle sat down, still mopping his face. He could well get away with his claim of only thirty-nine years. His dancer's body was as fit as a body could be.

Jerry resumed his seat as he gestured toward Joe and Zach. "Lyle, you came in after the festivities this afternoon. I don't believe you've met Joe Sanders—" the two men shook hands and exchanged greetings "—and Zachary Jordan, Joe's lawyer."

Lyle's eyes widened in pleased recognition. "Hey, so you're the dude who came up with the idea for my big number. Thanks, friend."

Zachary laughed. "I'm afraid I'm getting entirely too much credit. All I did was make a hackneyed comment about investments."

"Investments? Is that your specialty?"

"One of them, yes."

"Hey, any chance of cornering you for a consult? I've gone and got myself into a partnership deal that's looking more and more crooked. Got no idea who to see about it. I've made a wide berth around lawyers for the last ten years, ever since one of 'em helped my ex-wife wipe out my life's savings."

Ashley glanced nervously at Zach, afraid he'd feel cornered into something he didn't want to do. But he actually looked pleased. "Sure, glad to help if I can."

Lyle glanced up at the wall clock. "Hell, time to get back to the grind." He leaned over and slapped Zachary's knee. "Hot damn, that's great. You helped provide me with a showstopper, and now you may help save my arse." He tipped his head toward Zach as he stood. "Good vibes. I get nothing but good vibes from this man." He stopped behind Ashley on his way out and bent to kiss the top of her head. "Hey, pretty lady, you're looking mighty tired these days. Why not take a couple of days for R and R? We can't let anything happen to you. Who'd mediate all the fights—not to mention writing the shows that keep us working?" He patted her on the shoulder. "Without people like Ashley and Matt, what would I do for a living? Softshoe to 'Tea for

Two'?" He bobbed his head at all of them. "See ya. And you, Mr. Z. Jordan—I'll catch you after my next scene."

"Fine." Zach watched him disappear through the door. "Seems like a nice man."

"Lyle?" Jerry nodded. "He's a gem. He's never satisfied with his own performance, always working like a son of a gun to do it better, all the time bitching at himself for not getting it right. But I've never heard him say one word to or about someone else that wasn't either complimentary or constructive. Guys like him are what make this business so great." He tapped Ashley on the arm. "And, of course, gals like you. And I think he's right, by the by. You should ease off a little. You get sucked into everything because you're such a good arbitrator, and that stuff takes its toll. Just remember, arbitrator and playwright are both full time-and-a-half jobs. You have to learn to say no."

Ashley gave a little salute. "Yes sir."

Just then the side door banged open and the conversation was stopped in its tracks by a grand entrance.

"Oh, no," Ashley muttered.

"Who's that?" Zach asked.

"Sonja Haager. She's our choreographer."

Sonja glided to them, her face a mask of despair, her voice sailing imperiously throughout the room. "We cannot go on! It is impossible! The dancers they are having trouble with too fast a tempo while they must also sing!" Sonja's accent was a combination of Rumanian heritage and Greek tragedy.

"I *told* Matt it wouldn't work," Ashley mumbled.

Zach leaned close to whisper in her ear. "Is the sky falling, or does she tend to dramatics?"

Ashley turned toward him and realized, too late, that his lips were mere inches away. The effect of his closeness was downright frightening. Everything else faded from view, even the agitated choreographer. All the invisible shields Ashley had so painstakingly erected against emotional disruption crumpled like so much tissue paper, leaving her completely vulnerable. Never in her life had she experienced a reaction even close to this magnitude with anyone else. How foolish to apply silly words like "platonic" to this relationship! She loved him. Still. With a passion that not only had failed to diminish during their separation, but seemed to have grown to uncontrollable proportions.

"Ashley?" His eyes narrowed in concern, deepening the fine lines at their edges. A very appealing expression. Ashley shook her head. This was a mistake, all of it. She hadn't exactly *dug* her own hole, but she'd certainly leapt in with mindless abandon.

"Oh, sorry. I'm afraid my mind was wandering." Sonja's high-pitched wail was re-entering her sphere of consciousness.

The dancer's whole body was one long dramatic statement. The near-skeletal thinness, the straight line of the back and the neck, the high carriage of the imperious head. She stood over Matt, arms flailing. "How could you do this to me? Are you expecting from me miracles?"

Matt started to open his mouth to answer, then turned instead to Ashley, a look of trapped panic on his face. "Ashley?"

Jerry looked over at her, his expression one of amused warning. "Ashley..."

She hunched her shoulders. "Who else is going to deal with it?"

Jerry grimaced. "You've got me there."

Ashley stood, turning to Zach. "Be back in a few minutes." She went to Sonja, laying a consoling hand on her arm, and led her off to another room, with Matt trailing after.

Jerry shook his head. "That girl's going to run herself ragged. Well, Joe, are you ready to go in and watch the fun?"

"Sure am." They all stood up.

"Zach," Jerry laid a restraining hand on Zachary's arm. "Could I speak to you privately for a minute?"

Zach looked at Joe and Joe nodded. "Fine with me. Like the man says, we can't talk in there, anyway."

"Okay." The two men sat back down as Joe headed for the side door.

"Listen, Zach—" Jerry shifted his chair a little nearer "—I don't want you to feel like you have to run for cover every time one of us comes near you, but I have this little problem...."

By the time Ashley returned, Zachary was sitting alone in the big room, a bemused expression on his face. He looked up and watched her as she walked toward him. "Well, pretty lady, who won the fight?"

"Sonja. Sonja always wins. She has an unbeatable tool on her side."

"Oh? What's that?"

"Intimidation. She intimidates all of us."

He cocked his head disapprovingly. "Now Ashley. That's basic Psychology 101. If someone intimidates you, it's because you're allowing yourself to be intimidated."

"I know. But you try reasoning with a choreographer. As Craig says, unlike you or me, they're wondrous but formidable creatures who accomplish incredible things without the detriment of logic."

"Sounds like a spoiled child who's been indulged too long." There was an uncomfortable silence. "Sorry. I know not whereof I speak, so I shouldn't. I have something else I'd like to talk to you about, anyway."

"Oh?" She sat down beside him.

He leaned toward her, his elbows on his knees, an intense look on his face. "Honey, how about flying up to Stowe this weekend to meet me? The snow is supposed to be superior. You could continue your ski lessons, and we could have a couple of days all to ourselves."

Her expression became stricken. "Zach, I couldn't possibly—"

He cut her off. "Come on, Ashley. Think about it before you automatically say no. Jerry told me again, after you left, that you really should take a rest—that he was sure everything could go along without you for a few days. You could fly out Friday evening and come back on Sunday in plenty of time for a good night's sleep. The whole show couldn't collapse in that amount of time!"

She jumped up, terribly agitated. "Zachary, this isn't fair! You're putting pressure on me to do something I've already told you is impossible. These weeks of rehearsal . . ."

"I know, are hectic. So tell me, how come you seem to be the only one who feels you're indispensable every second of the time? Craig came in while we were talking about it, and he agreed you should get away."

"Dammit!" She whirled on him. "That takes a lot of nerve, to go around discussing me behind my back! I can't go, and that's that!"

He got up slowly and stood silently for a moment, staring down at the worn floor. "This reminds me, unfortunately, of another period of time. When I not only slid way down from first place on your priority list but was, for all intents and purposes, dropped from your agenda."

"Zach . . ."

"You used to be quick to tell me I was unreasonable. Well, so be it. Heaven forbid someone else should have to placate some irrational, eccentric hothead while you wasted your time with me!" With that, he strode across the room, picked up his coat and left.

By the time Zachary reached his town house in Boston, it was once again past midnight. He headed straight for his bedroom. God, he was tired. He'd have to get off this crazy schedule soon, or he'd be a zombie.

He didn't know how he'd ever get to sleep; his mind kept turning their argument over and over, cringing at the memory of his tactless words, resurrecting her angry replies.

Without allowing time for reconsideration, he strode across the room, picked up the phone and punched out her New York number. What a routine he was forming: screw things up when he was with her, then call in the middle of the night to apologize!

"Hello."

Zachary almost hung up the phone, but social amenities were too deeply embedded. "Hello. Is Ashley there?" He'd never get used to the idea of calling the woman he loved in the wee hours of the morning and having the phone answered by a man. Especially when the man was related only by strains of music!

"Is this Zach?"

"Yes."

"Well, listen, Zach, she's here but she's asleep. She felt crummy so I told her to hit the sack."

Zachary tried to clamp his mouth shut, but before he made it, the question popped out. "If she's in bed, then what the hell are you doing there?"

"Hey, whoa. For God's sake, Jordan, lighten up. What the hell do you think I'm doing here? I'm finishing the arrangement we were working on while it's still in my head. I have all my clothes on, and I haven't set foot near the bedroom. Satisfied?"

Zach ran his fingers through his hair. "Look, Matt…I'm sorry. I don't know what the devil's gotten into me. I call to apologize to Ashley for being such a jerk today and end up apologizing to you for the same thing tonight."

"I hate to tell you, pal, but it's morning."

"Yeah, so it is."

"Listen, Zach, don't sweat it. You're in love. It does terrible things to the brain waves. Ashley's in love. She's also irrational. I wish you two would find a solution. Have you considered acupuncture?''

Zachary chuckled in spite of himself. "That's an idea. It's about the only thing we haven't tried."

Matt's voice took on a more serious tone. "I wish I could help. I really do."

"Thanks, Matt. I guess we'll just have to keep working on it. Say, would you do me a favor and not say anything..."

"Rest easy. I'll just tell her you called and said you were sorry she's feeling bad."

"Thanks."

"Anytime. Good night."

Zach put down the phone, feeling pretty crummy himself. They were both back on the treadmill, running in separate circles that seemed destined never to touch.

Chapter Six

As Zachary exited at the top of the Mt. Mansfield ski lift, he paused a moment to savor the beauty of the Vermont peaks. Stowe was covered with deep, newly fallen snow. A white-frocked wonderland. He sucked in a lungful of the clear, sharp air. With a wave at the young woman standing nearby, he shouted, "See you at the bottom!" She smiled and kicked off, heading down the steep slope with Zach a short distance behind.

He watched her slim body gracefully parallel down the trail, aware that his own movements displayed the same ease, the same sureness. He and his sister had been racing down mountains for so many years that it held the satisfying comfort of familiarity—and right now Zach needed both comfort and familiarity.

The bite of the cold air on his cheeks increased the exhilaration of his swift flight. How he loved it, the front of his skis skimming through the powder while the backs kicked up pure white wisps of flakes. He grinned as he slipped past his sister, pleased that this part of the pattern, too, was still in place. He always beat her, probably by dint of weight. He wanted no surprises, no alterations of habit; his psyche was jarred enough already. This weekend of skiing was designed to clear his head of stale New York air and jumbled emotions.

As he schussed down the trail, he remembered that wonderful winter when he'd brought Ashley to Vermont. She didn't consider herself much of an athlete, but she'd taken to skiing with an ease that amazed and delighted her. Zachary smiled, recalling her excitement when she had made her first full run down the beginner's slope and her pride when she conquered an intermediate trail. Ingrained as she was with cadence and rhythm, both enormous helps in the movements of the sport, she was a natural. They'd always had such a wonderful time together everywhere they went. Zachary relished his role as teacher, and Ashley proved an apt and eager student who quickly took to the disciplines of not only skiing, but sailing and snorkeling as well. She even learned how to sustain a fair volley on the tennis court. Each sport seemed brand-new and exciting to Zach as he introduced Ashley to them. She was like an eager child, interested in everything, willing to try.

Zach cut across under the ski tow to reach the steepest section of the trail. Life was so damned complex at times, so full of contradictions. In legal circles he was renowned for his clarity of thought, his ability to zero in on the core of a problem and find a solution. He could probably count the number of times he'd lost control of his dignity or his temper without getting to double digits. So how could a mind like his, orderly and disciplined, turn to mush merely through exposure to one woman?

He was chagrined by the series of events in New York. The dinner at the Veau d'Or had been his idea; he'd initiated the lovemaking; it was he who'd fostered the ridiculous notion that they could be just friends. All his own doing, each step of the way, and he'd marred every encounter by displaying the unforgivably bad manners of an adolescent having a snit. Matt must be right—being in love did crazy things to the brain.

He was approaching the final run, so he turned his skis straight downhill and crouched low. The speed was a tonic. The faint chance of danger a bracer. But even flying down the slope at a dizzying pace didn't stop the relentless churning of his mind. He was still so much in love with Ashley that the mere thought of her demolished all orderliness in his mental process.

When he reached the bottom, he flipped his skis sideways and dug in to stop. Emily was close behind him. She traversed to his side, a smile of pleasure on her face. "Hey, big brother, this is what I call perfect snow conditions!" Her skin was aglow, her cheeks red from the nipping wind.

"It sure is." He glanced at his watch. "It's lunchtime. Are you hungry?"

"Yes. I'm famished."

When they sat across the table from each other over steaming bowls of chili and grilled cheese sandwiches, Zachary moaned, "I'm afraid my days of winning are numbered, you're coming in closer and closer on my heels. Soon you'll beat me and do irreparable harm to my masculine ego."

"Oh, poor baby. You're losing your edge from lack of practice. What're you doing, spending all your time in court or behind that imposing desk of yours?"

Zachary stared down at his spoon, making lazy circles in the chili. "Well, not entirely."

"Mom said you had business in New York. That you planned to see Ashley."

"Uh-huh."

"Did you?"

"Yes."

"How is she?"

"Very well. More beautiful than ever. More famous than ever. Looks like she has another hit coming up." He kept staring downward, avoiding his sister's knowing eyes.

"How was it? Seeing her, I mean."

He shrugged. "Wonderful." He glanced up and met her questioning gaze. "Awful."

"Discombobulating?"

He laughed. It was their favorite expression for all unsettling events. "Yeah, every syllable's worth."

She put her elbows on the table and leaned forward. "I miss Ashley. She was always so much fun and so full of life. And it was exciting to hear about the different stars and all."

"Yeah, exciting. Her life is that, all right."

"Is her career still as important to her?"

"Probably more so. Certainly more important than anything else." That had been proven, once again, at their last meeting.

"Any chance of your getting together?"

"You mean for marriage?"

"Yes."

"I don't see how. It would be a little awkward to maintain two full-time households, one in Boston and one in New York."

"Oh, I don't know. It's not like you can't afford the plane fare."

He made a disgusted noise. "Come on, Emily. That's no way to live. I want a wife to come home to at night. I want to have children." He shrugged. "I guess, all in all, what I want is a conventional marriage."

"In that case, why not marry Joan?"

"How the devil did Joan get into this?"

"Well, she'd certainly be willing to be the kind of wife you say you want. And she's pretty and nice and from a 'proper' background. And she'd marry you in a minute. In fact, it wouldn't surprise me if she's got her wedding dress in the closet just hoping you'll pop the question."

Zach couldn't help laughing at that. "Oh, Em, how you exaggerate!"

"Not at all. In case you don't know it, brother dear, there are vast numbers of attractive, suitable women who'd jump at the chance to marry you. In fact, I'm sure I could make a bundle by raffling you off. If you'd go along with it, of course."

"Good Lord. What would you charge, five chances for a dollar?"

"Nah. I'd get more than that." She studied him sympathetically. "I have a feeling that you really still want Ashley."

He looked at her for a second, then nodded. "Yeah. You probably think I'm nuts."

"Not at all. She's the best of the bunch." Emily took a sip of cola, watching her brother over the rim of the glass. "Zach, your problem is that you've fallen in love with an extraordinary woman, and you want to turn her into an ordinary housewife." She paused. "Remember that old song Fred Astaire used to sing about an irresistible force meeting an immovable object?"

He plunked the spoon on the table in exasperation. "Em, what's the point?"

"Don't you remember the lyrics? 'Somethin's gotta give, somethin's gotta give'...."

"Does it have to be me?"

"In some ways, I think it does. Frankly, as far as I'm concerned, Ashley would be a fool to give up all that success to stay home to play the good wife and mother role."

Zach sat back in his chair, scowling at her. "There's plenty of theater in Boston. Why couldn't she be content with participating in that?"

"That's like suggesting that a major league baseball star make a permanent move to a farm team."

"Okay. I concede the point. So we're back to the same conclusion I've already reached. It's hopeless. Hurry and finish up, we've got some serious skiing to do."

Emily was not to be detoured. "What took you to New York in the first place? Is Mom right? Did one of your clients actually invest in Ashley's musical?"

Zach hesitated. He wanted to get off this subject, but he didn't want to hurt Emily's feelings by being curt. "Yes. Joe Sanders...you know, you met him about a month ago when you dropped into the office. Good-looking, in his sixties, with gray hair?"

"Oh, sure. Nice man."

"Uh-huh. That nice man has put a very large sum into that nice show."

"Why, Zachary! You mean you didn't advise him against it?"

"No, I didn't advise him either way. I simply pointed out the facts."

"Which are?"

"That only about five percent of the musicals produced ever repay the initial investment, and a significantly lower percent actually earn a profit."

"And that didn't dissuade him?"

"Not by a long shot. Joe's entranced by show biz. He's even got a couple of friends interested in putting money in a comedy that Jerry Jerome plans to produce. In fact, Joe's asking me to work with them on the legal angles, since I'm becoming such an expert." His words were well coated with sarcasm.

Emily laughed. "My goodness, do you mean to say my staid brother is getting sucked into the world of theater?"

"More than I want to, that's for sure. As if that weren't enough, Jerry Jerome's roped me into handling a lawsuit that's been hanging for a couple of years. Some joker who claims he was the actual author of *Criminals*. You know, the drama that won all those awards? Claims the idea was stolen.''

"Doesn't Jerry Jerome *have* a lawyer?"

"Of course. But he's not sure he's trustworthy. I asked him how he could be sure I am, and he said, 'I dunno how I know. I just know.'" They both laughed. "They're a different breed, no doubt about it."

She took the last spoonful of her chili. "Umm, good. Tell me, are you going to?"

"Going to what?"

"Look into the lawsuit for Jerry Jerome."

"As a matter of fact, I've already made some inquiries. He was right to be nervous about his lawyer. I'll bet that guy could play both sides of a tennis game."

Emily laughed aloud. "A little shifty, eh?"

"I still can't believe what I'm finding. He's with one of the best-known firms. He's savvy, he's expensive and he's as slippery as a buttered eel."

"Sounds like Mr. Jerome made a smart move when he got you involved."

Zach stood up, his expression closing off the way it did when he'd finished with a subject. "Maybe *he* did. But I haven't made a smart move yet. I have the feeling I'm trying to get free of the bog by walking across quicksand. All through? Come on, sis. Let's go ski."

With a knowing smile on her face, Emily followed him toward the exit.

Ashley scooted down in her seat and laid her head back. It bumped painfully on the narrow wooden rim. With a grunt of irritation, she rolled up her jacket and put it under her neck. She was so tired she simply couldn't sit upright any longer. Would this rehearsal never end?

The only good thing about the mad schedule was that it was leaving her no time to think. Thinking was about the most hazardous thing she could do right now; her brain, given even a half-inch of free space, crammed an unbelievable number of reminders of Zachary before her mind's eye.

She must have dozed off, because she came to suddenly, aware of loud voices raised in argument. With great reluctance, she opened her eyes and sat up.

Claire Hanston, the costume designer, was holding a couple of bolts of cloth in front of her while she yelled at the lighting designer, Buzz Crawford. "What do you mean, I can't use it!"

"Judas priest, Claire, have you any idea what my lights will do to that color?"

"Oh, you're impossible! You always, always, *always* light the scenery instead of the costumes. The show is supposed to be dominated by the *actors* Mr. Crawford."

Ashley flinched. She knew Claire was really heating up when she began to get formal. If only there could be one day without a blowup! She pushed herself out of the seat. "What's the matter?"

"I've chosen all my material for the gowns in the formal dance scene and this man tells me I can't use it! Just because he insists on focusing attention on the scenery."

"I am not focusing on the scenery. But it would be just slightly complicated to light one without touching the other." He turned to Ashley. "Tell her to calm down, will you? She'd really be furious if I let her make all those costumes and *then* showed her what happens when the spots hit!"

"Dammit, Buzz..."

Ashley held up her hand. "Wait a minute, Claire, please. Why not let him show you? It's better to know than to make a wrong guess. The scenery's all painted for that scene. There isn't much we can do about that without undue expense."

Clair, with a grunt of displeasure, followed Ashley and the grim-visaged lighting expert into his studio. "Okay

Claire," Buzz said, "Lay both bolts out on that table. I'll show you every gel we're using in that scene."

Ashley stood quietly, sympathizing with the flustered costume designer as the first spot fell on the fabrics. The bright color faded out to a sickly pastel.

Claire gasped. "Oh, my goodness!"

The next two gels were even worse; they washed the shades completely. "See what I mean, Claire? And at this point there's nothing I could do to salvage it. I wanted you to know before you went any further."

Claire rolled up the cloth, heaving a big sigh. "And they'd have been so lovely." With one last grimace of sorrow, she turned to Buzz and gave him a hug. "Thanks for rescuing me in time. It would have been a calamity. Expensive and time-consuming—and we can't afford either." With a wide, forgiving smile, she headed for the door, humming one of the jump tunes from the show.

Buzz grinned at Ashley. "I don't know if I'll ever get used to how fast her mood can swing."

"I know. At least she admits it when she's wrong, and she never holds a grudge."

"True. Well, guess I'd better get back to work. Have to double up on some of the lighting cues, 'cause some of what I've got for Broadway will never happen in Boston."

"Have you done a show in the Colonial?"

"Three. Not a bad theater, but limited."

She nodded, still feeling like a newcomer in this business; it was kind of depressing. But then, so were a lot of other things. In all regards, her mood was anything but joyful. Whenever she thought of Zachary, a dull, aching hurt spread through her. Their last confrontation, the day he and Joe had come to rehearsal, had left her terribly shaken up. Why had she reacted so angrily to a perfectly reasonable invitation? Was there more than a little truth in Zachary's allegations? She thought about Claire and Buzz. What would have happened if she hadn't been there, hadn't acted as arbitrator? The truth tactlessly bobbed to mind. They'd have settled it themselves. But, in any case, going to Stowe with him would—rather than helping—only have made the impossible situation between her and Zach more difficult. The more unforgettable experiences they shared, the harder the inevitable breakup would be. All things considered, there was ample cause for despair. The problems and emotions they'd walked away from three years ago were right back in place, stronger than before and just as insoluble.

She wondered if any addiction could be more powerful than her craving for Zachary. And sometimes the choice seemed so easy; all she had to do was say yes to have the sort of life most women dreamed of: a handsome, wonderful husband, a beautiful home, servants, travel, a full social life. Why would any woman in her right mind turn that down?

She had reached the side door to the theater. After a moment's hesitation, she went inside. She shut the door quietly behind her and stood there, silently, as the distinctive aura engulfed her. As she watched the leads on stage, singing *her* lyrics, working through *her* dialogue, a thrill of accomplishment ran through her. A yes to that bucolic life with Zachary would include a no to Broadway theater. She let the idea sink in, opened herself up to the full impact of that alternative. Unimaginable. She'd have to walk away from this, and she wasn't at all sure she'd survive *that* separation. And it wasn't the success and the fame and the money. Thrilling as they were, she could leave all of them without a backward glance. But writing shows wasn't just a job, a way to make a living. It was more than that. It was a way of life. Love of the theater ran through her like blood, sustaining, fueling, feeding her. She didn't blame Zach for being mystified by it; everyone who wasn't part of it was.

So there it was, the unsolvable conundrum. She had to have her career and she had to have Zach and she couldn't have both. The whole thing made her want to run—nowhere special, just hard and fast and away. She longed to take flight, to hide out. . . .

She closed her eyes and leaned back against the door, trying to stop her thoughts, to give her overworked mind a rest. Ironically, it was a product of her own trade that denied her escape, a song lyric that sang its refrain in her head, one more of life's truths set to music: "No matter where I run, I meet myself there. . . ." So here she was, once again, back in an impossible situation with no visible means of escape.

"Ashley?"

Her eyes snapped open. Craig stood before her, a quizzical expression on his face. "I thought maybe you'd fallen fast asleep standing up! Not that I'd blame you, but it is a precarious position for snoozing."

"Oh, boy." She ran her hand over her eyes. "I think I could sleep in any position right now."

"Couldn't we all! Everyone's been feeling down the last few days, but that's always the case in the third week of rehearsal. The songs seem a little stale, the jokes aren't funny anymore and the whole show begins to feel like a flop."

"Umm, that's right, I'd forgotten the third-week slump. I can't remember, Craig, does it get worse or better?"

He smiled and patted her arm. "Better. Have faith. The chorus and the dancers join the leads tomorrow and that's always a big boost for everyone. They all provide each other with a new audience. That reminds me. I'll have to be sure to put a check mark next to all the jokes the ensemble laughs at."

"Why?"

"Ashley, one thing you'll learn when you've been in this game as long as I have is that there are some irrefutable facts, one of which is that whatever the cast laughs at the audience won't. Never seen it to fail."

"Oh, God, now I'll really be a wreck tomorrow."

"Don't panic. Just hope they don't laugh at everything."

"That'll be the first time I ever hoped my material would lay an egg!"

"Everyone'll be back on high by tomorrow night. I promise."

She managed a weak smile. "I don't know how you do it. You keep your equilibrium through smooth runs and absolute disasters."

"Better than throwing tantrums. There's always plenty of those, in any case. Everyone involved wants the show to be a hit; we're all pulling together."

"It doesn't seem like it sometimes when the actors start biting off each other's heads."

"Some folks handle stress well and some not so well. And every last one of us hates to be wrong, so trying to pass the buck is, I fear, all too human."

Glancing over Craig's shoulder, Ashley whispered, "Uh-oh. Speaking of tantrums . . ."

He turned to the young man who had just left the stage and was now approaching him. "Hi there, Sammy." Sammy Kirk, who played Christo, was the main lead in the show. At twenty-five, he had an impressive number of stage and screen credits, a sizable roster of fans and a mammoth ego that required constant stroking. Craig's face tightened, just slightly, as he came forward.

"Craig. Ashley." Sammy's face, as usual, was a blueprint of discontent. "Craig, that damned broad is still upstaging me in that last scene. How the hell am I supposed to sing my song to her and project to the audience when she keeps drifting a couple of steps behind me?"

Ashley watched Craig's expression, searching for signs of annoyance, which she didn't find. Sammy was, increasingly, a pain in the butt. He was infuriated by the attention being paid his co-star, Kelly Adams, who was a relative unknown. Kelly's electrifying voice shook the rafters, and she was displaying an acting ability that was startling in a youngster of twenty with precious few theatrical credits. On top of that, it was more and more evident she had the elusive "star" quality that caught the eye the moment she set foot onstage. Sammy was being upstaged by talent, not footwork.

"Now Sam, she's just following directions. I want the audience to *see* her crying as she leaves you. Having her back off is very effective. You're only turned away from the audience for a few seconds, and your voice is carrying just fine. That scene is coming across beautifully; it's very poignant."

Sammy stared at his feet, visibly fighting for control. He was egotistical, but not stupid. Craig was the best director on Broadway, and most actors would kill for a chance to work with him. Even a hotshot like Sammy thought twice about cussing him out. Ashley figured the air inside his head must be bright blue by now.

"Yeah, well, tell her not to milk it so long. And keep that jerk, Lyle, off my back. I don't need his dumb suggestions." He looked straight at Craig while he said, "I get enough of those as it is."

There wasn't a hint of anger on Craig's face. In fact, he appeared to be having a tough time concealing a smile. "Yeah, Sam, we'll see if we can mellow out old Uncle Hermie. What could he teach you, anyway?"

Sammy's hauteur wavered for just an instant, as he searched Craig's face for sarcasm. Finding none, he nodded curtly. "Okay. I'm not in the next scene, so I'm going across the street for a Coke."

Craig's worried eyes followed the young man's swagger as he left, then came back to meet Ashley's. "Sure wish I was dead sure he meant a soft drink."

"Amen. I keep trying to remember why we signed him for the lead."

"Because he'll deliver a good performance and pull a sizable audience. God, why do some of these young punks have to take themselves so seriously? Lyle Baker has so much to teach him, but he figures he already knows it all. Too blown up with his own importance to recognize a master at work."

"Lyle is a master, isn't he? Every time I see him do a scene I'm impressed all over again. He's so good! This is the first time I've been lucky enough to see him in rehearsal."

"Quite a privilege, isn't it? The really great stars don't just rely on their talent to pull them through, they work harder than anyone else. That young gal, Kelly, I'd be willing to bet she joins the greats before she's through. I have to all but throw her out to make her quit practicing." He snapped his fingers. "I almost forgot! Speaking of greats, Jerry wanted me to tell you that your friend, Zachary, was a wizard. I'm not sure how it all came about, but evidently Jordan's on the way to having that old lawsuit thrown out of court. You know, the one that's been hanging over Jerry's head for some time."

"Zachary? I wonder how he got involved with that?"

"Dunno. But he's in it now. You know Jerry when he latches onto someone good. Tenacious as a barnacle. And from what he says, Zachary Jordan is one fine lawyer." Craig laughed. "More amazing still, I understand he's an *honest* lawyer."

She tried to look like someone responding to good news about a friend rather than fighting galloping trauma from the mention of a name. "Yes. He's both of those things. Good and honest." And enough to drive her out of her mind with longing.

"Evidently he'll be in town tomorrow to tie up loose legal ends. We'll probably see him sometime during the day."

Ashley's nerves leapt to attention. Tomorrow. Would he come, or would he deliberately stay away? "That's nice." She barely got the two words out, her mouth was so dry.

"Well, better get everyone back to work. See you later."
Craig walked toward the stage, shouting, "Okay, onstage
for scene 8!"

Ashley's legs gave out beneath her and she sank into the
aisle seat. Damn. This was going to drive her bonkers. Why
couldn't she fall in love with someone in the same screwy
business? Matt, for instance. That stopped her musings in
mid-thought. The idea of trying to live with Matt as well as
work with him was absurd enough to tweak her somnolent
humor. About two weeks of that, and they'd be writing for
Loony Tunes!

She stood up and walked toward the exit. She was too
pooped to be of any help to anyone tonight. At least she'd
made a firm decision about *something*: She was going home
to bed.

Unfortunately, alone.

Zachary stood just inside the back door of the theater, his
eyes searching for Ashley. He didn't see her, and the sense
of disappointment was acute. What the hell was he doing
here, anyway? He should grab the opportunity to disappear and get himself back to Boston where he belonged! The
conversation with Emily had been unnerving. It had
brought him right around circle to the same old conclusion. He and Ashley were poles apart, and no matter how
much they wanted each other, he didn't see how it could
work. One big problem was that the minute he got near her,
he forgot that fact. Just as he was about to take his own advice to leave, he felt a tap on his shoulder. He turned his
head and found Matt standing just behind him.

"Hi there, Zach. Come to watch the zanies?"

All traces of sarcasm had vanished from Matt's voice, and
Zachary was amazed at how pleased he was by the friendly
tone. He smiled at Matt and replied, "No zanier than a few
of the legal beagles I've been tangling with today. And
they're not supposed to be playacting."

"Oh, yeah, I heard about your taking on that weirdo, the one who sued Jerry. Thank God that wasn't our show—I'd've been a wreck. I'm never entirely sure my stuff is original, and I live in dread of someone saying, 'Hey! That's *my* song!' because they just might be right."

Zachary looked at him with keen interest. They'd been at sword's point with each other so much of their acquaintance that Zach had never had an opportunity to know Matt. In truth, he'd never wanted to know him, he'd just wanted him out of his life—or, more precisely, out of Ashley's. Jealousy, he acknowledged, was not only destructive, but limiting. "Do you really worry about that?"

"You better believe it. Hell, there isn't a really new tune left; they've all been used one place or another. You just have to keep hoping it didn't neatly pop into your head because you heard it on the radio."

Zach chuckled. "If that ever happens, I know a good lawyer."

Matt laughed and slapped him on the back. "Yeah, so I hear. I may be at your door one of these days. The only composer I *know* I've stolen from is Mozart. But what the hell, so has everyone else. More than one hit ballad has come from that source. Old Wolfgang wrote some good stuff."

"Too bad he didn't copyright it."

"Yeah. His royalties would be awesome. Might be tough for him to collect, however." He stretched and flexed his fingers. "Almost time to start. You've picked a good day to stop in. It's the first run-through with full company. Always gives the cast a big lift. You know, some new faces to play to, not to mention more hands for clapping."

Zach studied his profile as he talked. Matt was a good-looking man. And, of course, Ashley was a beautiful woman. It still seemed strange to him that they could have worked so closely together for eight years without one or the other wanting something more than friendship. He suffered a few pinpricks of the old jealousy before sternly ordering a halt. It was entirely possible the urge may have hit one or the other but was never mentioned. In their case, there was a far more important relationship to maintain. Fine time to get rational about Matthew Robbins, just when he was on the brink of accepting the impossibility of anything permanent between himself and Ashley! "Maybe I'll hang around and watch."

"Yeah, do. It's a kick. Have you seen Ashley yet?"

"No." No use letting Matt know he was on the verge of trying to avoid that when he came in.

"If I see her, I'll tell her you're here."

"Thanks."

"Sit down center, about the tenth row."

"Okay. Thanks again."

He settled into a seat in the designated row and tried to relax. Just as Craig and Ashley came through the side door, Jerry Jerome plunked down on the seat beside him.

"Hi there, Zachary old buddy. So you're here to see the mixing of the ingredients. This is the day we either sail home on a cloud or crawl home hiding under an inchworm."

Zach pulled his gaze away from Ashley and turned to Jerry. "Is this rehearsal as important as that?"

"Yes, sir, it sure as hell is. Of course, it'll all resemble a mixer in a madhouse to you, but after you've been through a few you can usually tell what's going to fly and what's going to dive. Get a grip on your popcorn, here we go."

Craig stood in front of the orchestra pit and yelled, "Full cast onstage!" When they had all crowded in, Craig continued. "I want as good a picture as I can get of the play as a whole today, so I'm not going to stop you to fix things unless it's absolutely necessary. You'll feel awkward at times, but you know where you belong, so get to your place and don't worry about anyone else. I'll be taking a lot of notes, so we'll go over all the mix-ups later. Okay, act 1, scene 1. Places!" When he'd finished, Craig picked up a clipboard and crossed over to sit beside Ashley and Matt.

Zach wanted to be there, too, right beside Ashley. But this was business for her and...what? for him. Certainly not pure pleasure. The air was thick with tension; he felt a little of it invade his system. He commented to Jerry, "It's funny, but this is getting to me, too. Like being at a Super Bowl game where you want your team to win."

Jerry nodded. "Know what you mean. And winning in this league means having a hit. It isn't just making money or losing it. People who invest in shows have some gambler blood in them and love the theater enough to toss the dice here. And they can usually afford a loss. The biggie is what this can do to careers. It can make stars or push 'em back down the ladder for awhile. Whole futures sometimes hang on the success or failure of one show. Not always, naturally, but for some. Watch Kelly, the young woman who plays Angela. If this goes, she's right on her way to the top. If it fails, she'll have to scramble for another chance to be seen."

"How about the other leads?"

"Well, Uncle Hermie's been right up there so long it'd take more than one turkey to do him any real damage. He's one hell of a performer and he works his tail off. The kid who plays Christo is already well-known. He'll probably be okay until his vocal chords do a little aging and his pretty face develops a few lines. It's my guess he'll never put out enough effort to grow into more mature roles. He's a juvenile hot dog, on and offstage."

"It all seems like another world to me."

"Hell, man, it is. A play in rehearsal is like a planet with only one town. The show is the only topic of conversation and the only thing anyone's interested in. Even though I'm the producer, I sometimes feel like I'm trespassing."

His words did nothing to lift Zach's spirits. He glanced at the back of Ashley's head. So close, yet so far away.

As the first scene got underway, Zach and Jerry settled back to listen and to watch. Zachary could see what Matt had been talking about. The delighted response started with the first solo, sung by Christo. The others, hovering backstage or sitting in the first couple of rows, broke out in enthusiastic applause, and that pattern continued through chorus numbers and dances as well as the other solos. The tension disappeared and was replaced by an excitement that was palpable.

Jerry leaned over at the end of act 1. "Yep," he said, "we've got a hit."

Zach wasn't at all proud of his reaction to that. Besides his feeling of pleasure for the participants, a negative registered in his mind. If it was a hit, Ashley would be even farther from reach, less willing to consider an alternative life-style. Damn. He'd like to rise above that sort of petty speculation, but it had staked a claim in his mind, and there it sat, gnawing little holes in his finer instincts.

Jerry stood up. "Let's go down and reassure Matt."

"Why would he need reassurance if it's good?"

"Matt will be absolutely convinced that all the songs are bombs and there isn't a decent melody line in the show. We'll have to practically tie him down to keep him from taking the next plane out of New York. To anywhere."

"You're kidding."

"Wait and see." The house lights went up and Ashley turned and saw them. Her eyes widened and she made a weak little flutter of her hand that managed to pass for a wave. Jerry smiled and waved back. "Come on, we've been sighted. Let's go join the fun."

With some trepidation, Zach followed. The word "fun" didn't apply to what he saw ahead. As he walked toward the woman he loved, he really did feel like a visitor to another planet. It was the only time in his life he wished he was an actor.

Chapter Seven

Ashley watched Zachary's tall form come toward her, trying to tell herself, all the while, that he was just an ordinary man, like any other. Two arms, two legs, one head. One pair of shoulders that just *seemed* wider and more muscular than others; one chest, admittedly broader than most and covered with fine, curling black hair. One pair of lips that could inflame her with their touch and ten fingers to drive her mad. She shook her head to stop the progression. Give her mind a little rope, and it swung her right out over a precipice and started to unravel itself.

All resolutions to maintain a safe distance, all vows to protect her emotions, all efforts to accept the fruitlessness of hope—in short, all her instincts for survival—were slain by his mere presence. He didn't have to lift a sword.

"Hello, Zachary." That wispy, wimpish little voice belonged to a star-struck child, not to a mature, successful woman of the world! She glanced quickly to the right and left to see if anyone was looking at her strangely. They weren't. But Zachary's eyes were burning holes to her heart.

"Ashley." Her name sounded different when he spoke it, a one-word caress. "Jerry thinks you have a hit."

"Oh, I hope so. Matt's a wreck."

"I understand that's not unusual."

She managed only half a smile. "Not at all. But his paranoia gets to me. Makes the whole show seem terribly iffy. Could you follow the story line okay?"

He smiled, the brilliant whiteness of his teeth catching the light that still flooded the stage. "No problem at all. I think the first act went—" there was the slightest of pauses "—quite well."

Matt, who had come up behind Ashley, blurted, "See there? See there? He can't even say it's okay without choking on it! It's a disaster, anyone can tell that! We should cancel the opening, cut our losses right now and get out! If we go to Boston the theater will be empty when the second act begins."

Jerry stepped forward and took him by the shoulders. "Hey, man, believe me, it's good. I told Zach before it started that it'd look like a mad scramble to him. It'd seem like that to anyone who hadn't seen the first day of putting a show together."

Zachary was staring at Matt with keen interest. "You were absolutely right, Jerry. I couldn't imagine you would be."

"What does that mean? Come on, I can take it. What do you mean?" Matt showed every symptom of the first stages of dementia.

Zachary jumped in, anxious not to add to Matt's anxiety. "Look, Matt, I liked it very much. The music is terrific, the dialogue is clever, everyone in the cast is excellent. It just seemed, well, that some of them weren't real sure where they belonged."

Craig, who had been busily finishing up his notes, hooted with mirth. "God, truer words were never spoken! The group scenes looked like staged games of bumper pool. Come back tomorrow, Zach. You'll see a remarkable difference."

Ashley's eyes flew to meet Zach's. If only he would. If only he'd be right there beside her every day, holding her hand. He seemed to read the message in her eyes, and his head shook, back and forth, just once. Was he saying no to her unspoken plea or answering some question in his own mind? She had to hold her voice steady when she said, "We're going backstage for a cup of tea. Would you care to join us?" Dear Lord. She should follow that line by putting her forefinger under her chin and curtseying. But it was certainly better than voicing her real desire. Take me home, undress me, make love to me....

"Sure, I'd enjoy it." His dark, dark eyes seemed hooded, remote.

The moment they entered the big room in the rear of the theater, Ashley knew she was in for a hard time. The chorus girls seemed to turn in synchronized motion to stare at Zachary. Acquisitive lust glared like a beacon from each and every orb. She wanted to stamp her foot, to yell, "Buzz off, he's mine!" But he wasn't, was he? He was unfettered and thirty-three. And he was a walking dreamboat. She wondered what any one of these girls would do if Zachary were to say, "Come live with me and be my love?" What a dumb question. She knew darn good and well what they'd do! Despite her previous misgivings, Ashley was spurred to step a little closer to him and slide her arm through his. After all, they *were* friends!

Zachary looked down at her, one eyebrow raised. "What's this? A change of heart?"

"Just a friendly gesture."

"I see. I have a few friendly gestures I'd like to make, too. How broad-minded is this group?"

"They're show people. It'd depend on how well the scene was played." Oh, Ashley, her conscience carped, you're stoking the fire!

"What do you think? Would I get a round of applause?"

"If you took off even one piece of clothing, you'd get mobbed. Haven't you noticed the expressions on the girls' faces? Carnal. All of them." She gazed up at him possessively. "I'm simply trying to protect you."

He smiled, his eyes narrowing. "Aha, so that's it! This sudden wave of affection is brought on by jealousy. You don't want me, but you don't want anyone else to have me, is that it?" His voice was teasing but had a slight edge.

"Who says I don't want you? That's never been an issue."

"Umm, maybe. But you don't want me quite *enough*." He looked around the room, obviously noting for the first time that, indeed, he was the object of all female attention. Even Agnes, the seventy-two-year-old dresser, was gaping. "I do believe I've been playing my hand wrong. I didn't realize your competitive instincts extended beyond music." He glanced around. "Not bad, not bad at all. Now look at that blonde. *Very* well-stacked. A regular little honey. Wonder if she'd like..."

"Zachary, dammit, stop that! It's not even funny when you're trying to be funny."

"Who says I'm trying to be funny? I just realized I've walked right into a bonanza! I could start with the sopranos and work my way through to the altos."

"Zachary..." Her voice had dropped about an octave. It was very near a growl. His smile grew bolder, and he deliberately raised one eyebrow at the blonde. He probably *knew* how devastating that made him look! Ashley tightened her grip on his arm.

"Ashley—" he stepped away and gently removed her hand "—please. You're cramping my style. If I don't get started, I'll never get clear through the chorus line."

Ashley knew he was just trying to give her a bad time. She also knew he was succeeding. Why hadn't she kept her darn mouth shut? She was sure he'd never have noticed all the come-hither looks if she hadn't pointed them out—well, at least *fairly* sure. "Do you want some tea, or are you going to stand there being a sex object?"

"Let's face it. There are worse fates."

"Zachary..." She was making a fool of herself and he was enjoying it immensely. And of course he hit home with his taunt. She knew how infinitesimal their chances were of getting together. Yet the mere thought of one of these hot-blooded show girls laying a hand on him brought out murderous impulses she'd never known she had.

"You actually do seem to be bothered by this, Ashley. Now, I'm a reasonable fellow. Say I pass up this delicious smorgasbord. Just what are you willing to offer as a substitute?"

"Tea."

He shook his head. "Uh-uh. Not nearly good enough." His eyes slid over her, smoky, enticing. "You're not even *beginning* to negotiate."

"Just what do you think we're holding here, an auction?"

"Could be." That one eyebrow went up again, and what could only be described as a licentious smirk appeared on his lips. "Who's doing the bidding, you or me?"

At that moment, Craig walked to the middle of the room, raised his hand and called, "Quiet!"

The interruption, Ashley steamed, was just in time to save Zachary from a kick in the shins.

It was amazing how fast the chattering stopped. Craig put down his tea mug and picked up his clipboard. "I want the full company onstage to go over my notes about act 1. As soon as we're through we start act 2." The area was vacated with amazing speed. Even the gawking chorus girls quickly disappeared.

Zachary watched the exodus with interest. "I have to admit, this is a hardworking group. There isn't much horsing around, is there?"

"Can't be. There's too much to accomplish in too short a time as it is. From here until the Boston opening it gets steadily worse."

"That hardly seems possible." The teasing tone had disappeared. Ashley wanted it back. If only there wasn't this constant friction between them; they had such fun together when they were relaxed and easy. "How about this evening—any chance for a romantic dinner? Or do you have rehearsals every night?"

She was becoming far too accustomed to a lump in her throat. It seemed to have taken up permanent residence. "Yes, I'm afraid we do."

"Why the weird hours? Can't rehearsing be done in the daytime, or don't show people wake up before noon?"

This was the only subject she could recall ever bringing out that snide tone in Zachary's voice. Unfortunately, the subject was very, very important. "Most of them spend the mornings taking lessons or working out or practicing. It's a terribly competitive arena."

He nodded. "I'm sure it is. Why *do* you have rehearsals at night? I'd like to understand."

"It's the decision of the individual director. Actor's Equity is very specific. They allow an eight-and-a-half-hour workday with seven hours of actual rehearsal. A lot of directors start at ten in the morning and run till one or one-thirty, then come back at three and work till seven. Craig has found that working in the morning and having a long lunch puts a lot of the cast in a stupor, so he starts in the afternoon at two, breaks at five-thirty, and then works again from seven till eleven. It does make for better rehearsals, but it doesn't leave much time for a social life."

"It certainly doesn't. I'm not sure this line of work ever leaves much time for a social life. Any kind of social life."

Ashley's hands balled into fists. How could their playful mood have vanished so swiftly? This back and forth, up and down swing was more than she could handle. "Dammit, Zachary, how in heaven's name could you expect something of this magnitude to be put together in less than two months without total, all-out commitment? If you really can't stand it, then why don't you just say so? You draw close, then retreat. You get me all hopeful again, then give me the deep-freeze. What are you trying to do, drive me crazy?" They were over in a corner of the room by themselves, but even so, Ashley had to turn away to hide the tears that had filled her eyes. "Maybe you can play this on-again, off-again, game, but it's too much for me. The pressure I'm under here is tremendous and getting more so by the day. I just . . ." Her voice broke.

Zachary put his arm around her and drew her close. "You're absolutely right to be mad. I confound myself. It isn't deliberate, I assure you. I'm neither a sadist nor a masochist." He tilted her chin up, forcing her eyes to meet his. "I'm a man so deeply in love that he's lost his rationality."

She leaned her forehead against his chest. "Oh, Zach, we've both got the same problem. What are we going to do?"

He stepped back and his arms dropped to his side. "I don't know, honey. I'm beginning to feel like a loose cannon on a rolling ship deck. But one thing is clear: you've got to be free to concentrate on your job. I'll stay away and leave you alone until you get to Boston."

Her chin dropped to her chest. "That's the most sensible thing either of us has suggested, and it makes me feel sick. I don't want you to stay away all that time." Out of the corner of her eye she saw Matt and Hans, the conductor, hovering near the door. Everyone else was gone. She had to go, but she couldn't bear to leave Zach, especially with the specter of three weeks of separation ahead.

Zach turned his head to follow her gaze. "They're waiting for you, aren't they?"

"Yes."

"You'd better go. We'll have to take it one step at a time."

"If only..."

"This isn't the time for if onlys. We'll have to wait till a later date for that sort of thing."

Ashley could tell, by the look on his face, that he was as afraid as she that time for "that sort of thing" might never come. Zachary had gotten his first full dose of a play in rehearsal. She wondered if there was any other kind of work that got so frantic. She wanted to throw herself in his arms, to cry, "Zachary, Zachary, don't leave. Or take me with you. I'll do anything, go anywhere, just let us be together!" But she did what she had to do. She kissed him on the cheek and went to meet Matt and Hans.

And Zachary did what he had to do. With heavy heart, he left the theater and took a cab to the airport.

Ashley's days and evenings raced by at a mad rate. She and Matt never stopped revising, rewriting, rearranging, and there were endless consultations on scenery and costumes and publicity. Zachary called every few days or, rather, nights. Often the phone was ringing as she let herself into the apartment. The phone calls became her lifeline to sanity. She'd forgotten how tired a person could get and still manage to function. Of course, with all the weariness and worry and problems ran the high voltage of excitement as the move to Boston got closer and closer. Even Matt was beginning to think they had a winner.

One night, after a particularly grueling session, Ashley staggered in the door, locked it behind her and kicked off her shoes. She could barely wait to put on her nightie and fall into bed. She was about halfway to the bedroom when the phone rang. At once, her spirits lifted. It had to be Zach. No one else called her at this hour. She ran to the desk and picked up the receiver. "Is this who I hope it is?"

"That depends. If you were hoping for Robert Redford, I'm afraid not."

"Why should I want Robert Redford when I can have you?"

"You can, you know."

She frowned in confusion. "Can what?"

"Have me."

"Gift wrapped?"

"Sure. What color ribbon do you want? And where?"

It was amazing, how one small innuendo from him could bring every molecule of her body to rapt attention. "Oh, don't tease. You're too far away for me to get to."

"Not for long. What is it now, just a week and a half?"

"Ten days. I'll be there in just ten days."

"I can hardly wait. Will I be able to pick you up at the airport, or do you have some other arrangement?"

She sank onto the couch. "If you weren't at the airport, I'd probably expire, right there. The only thing is, don't be too upset if I don't see you. Just come over and lift one of my eyelids."

"Pretty tired, eh?"

"That's putting it mildly. And now the real craziness begins. Rehearsals will be constantly interrupted for costume fittings. You have no idea how disruptive it is to have gaping holes in the ensemble."

"I remember that ensemble. Pretty nice. It's amazing how they all happen to be about the same height and every one good-looking."

"See how boring it would get to go from one to the other? You wouldn't be able to tell the difference before long. But I must admit that appearance plays a significant part in who gets chosen."

"Oh? You mean to tell me they don't get in on talent alone?"

"Unfortunately, audiences do see them as an ensemble, and just one 'interesting face' over a poor figure and spindly legs kills the whole image."

"Unfair. Life is definitely unfair to those who are not endowed with good looks."

"You have nothing to worry about."

"Nor you." She could hear him heave a sigh. "God, I miss you. I suppose your schedule will be even more hectic when you get here."

"I'm afraid so. Although, at this moment, I don't see how. There just aren't any more hours in the day unless I eliminate eating and sleeping."

"You poor thing, you must be exhausted." His voice was warm and sympathetic. She wanted to curl up in his arms and have him smooth her hair and say "poor thing" over and over. On second thought, if she were curled up in his arms . . . "Ashley? Have you fallen asleep?"

She laughed. "No. I was just fantasizing a little."

"About what?"

"If I put it into words, I'll get myself too worked up to sleep."

"Oh, that kind of fantasy. If you put it into words, neither of us would get any sleep. Speaking of slumber, you'd better get some. I don't want you getting sick. I intend to claim *some* of your time here in Boston, even if I have to come for breakfast."

"Maybe instead of breakfast?"

"Ashley . . ."

"Okay, okay, I'll be good. I probably wouldn't have enough energy to be bad, in any case." She wrapped both hands around the receiver, hanging on to the connection as though it were part of him. "I love you."

"Oh, honey. I love you, too."

They had, by unspoken agreement, begun to leave it at that. Simply 'I love you,' without any 'what next?'

Before the plane had come to a complete halt at Boston's Logan International Airport, Ashley undid her seat belt and stepped quickly into the aisle. Matt, who was seated beside her, looked up in surprise. "Hey, Ash, what's the rush? Did I miss something? Did someone just threaten to blow up the plane?" Before she could answer, he continued, "Oh, that's right. I'd forgotten who was meeting you. Don't run him down coming off the ramp!"

"Okay, wise guy, back off. I'm just tired of sitting in the airplane, that's all."

"Oh, yeah, sure, that's understandable. We've been cooped up in here for a whole hour." His mouth curled up at one corner, giving him the expression of a mischievous pixie. "Here, don't forget your purse." As she turned to head up the aisle, he called, "Will I see you at the hotel?"

"Don't hold your breath."

She could hear his teasing laughter all the way to the door. She scurried down the enclosed ramp and was the first passenger to step into the terminal. Damn. Where was he? She walked a little faster, her eyes scanning back and forth, searching for the one face she needed to see. Then he was there, standing just outside the roped-off area. His face broke into a huge grin the moment he spotted her. Ashley had to contain herself to keep from breaking into a dead run. She hitched the strap on her purse to a firmer position on her shoulder and tightened her grip on the carry-on satchel so she could quicken her step.

Then she was in his arms, and the world, a capricious sphere that had been off-kilter for three weeks, settled back into a smooth orbit. Zachary's arms clasped her to him, and his lips reached hungrily for hers. Every part of her heaved a vast sigh of relief, as if she'd been infused with a heady dose of life-restoring elixir.

"God, it's good to see you." His eyes were alight with sparkles of happiness.

"I know. I feel like an exile who's just been allowed to come home."

He put his cheek next to hers and whispered, "Yes, exactly. That's it exactly."

Ashley had dropped both her bag and her purse to the floor in order to throw her arms around Zachary, and several people had stepped over and around them, casting irritated glances her way. She disentangled herself from Zachary's arms and bent to retrieve them.

"Here, let me take that," he said, reaching for the bag, reserving one free arm to put around her. "Do you have checked luggage?"

"Oh, yes. Quite a lot of it. I've never been one of those people who can travel with two changes of clothes."

"I think I can forgive you that flaw."

"Don't be too hasty. Wait till you see how much stuff has to be carried."

When they'd taken her three suitcases and one hanging bag from the carousel, Zach ran his fingers through his hair and grimaced. "I didn't anticipate this."

"Well, we could try for a porter. Or I can carry at least two of them."

"No, that's not the problem. Wait till you see my car."

By that time, other members of the show group had clustered around, and they took time for hellos and how-are-yous. Then, with help from Matt, they transported her baggage outside.

Zach set down two of the heavy suitcases. "Matt, I'd like to offer you a ride to the hotel, but we already have a little problem here. I didn't think ahead. I'm driving a Mercedes sports coupe and it already looks like I'll be making two trips—one with Ashley and one with her luggage."

Matt laughed. "Yeah, this kid doesn't exactly travel light. Go ahead and get your car. I'll wait with Ashley."

When Zach drove up to the curb, Matt was gone and so were two of the larger cases. As he jumped out, he asked, "Have you been robbed, or is this some sort of disappearing trick?"

Ashley smiled. "I may pack too much, but I do pack efficiently. I had Matt take the stuff I don't need for a couple of days to the hotel."

Zach's face clouded. "I take it that means you're not staying with me very long."

They had managed to pack the luggage into the small space, and Ashley slid into the seat, fighting the rise of apprehension his question evoked. "I really can't, honey. As I told you, this is when everything really goes berserk. I'll need to be right there with the others."

He nodded. "That's reasonable. Disappointing, but reasonable."

She glanced at him in surprise. "You're not upset? What a relief!"

He turned his head just long enough to send her a loving smile. "I've decided to make an attempt at being reasonable myself. Not only reasonable, but involved."

"I hope you mean with me."

"Of course with you. But also with the play. If it wouldn't distract you too much, I'd like to look in on some of the evening rehearsals, get exposed to all that's required to prepare for opening night. Since I'm in love with a show biz woman, I should try to understand what it entails. I promise to stay out of your way."

"Zachary, do you mean it?"

"Yes." He reached over for her hand. "I want to try, darling. To see if perhaps this monster I've been so leery of isn't a monster after all."

Ashley's fingers wound tightly with his. For the very first time, she felt true hope surge in her heart. What Zach was suggesting was a chance, a real chance, that there might be a happy ending to their story. If he could take that first step, to understand and appreciate the demands of her career instead of simply becoming irritated by them, then further steps became possible. As they headed into the tunnel that carried the traffic below the harbor into Boston, she experienced a wave of anticipation. And it was not centered on the potential reviews of her show.

Zachary turned onto his side and propped himself on one elbow. He brushed a few wisps of hair from Ashley's face and ran his fingers over her cheek in a gesture of infinite tenderness. "Umm. You know, I like living here on cloud nine. Wonderful atmosphere."

Ashley, so sated with pleasure that her body was immobilized, barely managed to open her eyes. "Oh, yes, I agree. Absolutely the best address in town." She yawned. "Excuse me. It isn't the company, I promise."

"I bet you're bushed. Luckily, the housekeeper stocked the refrigerator so we can eat right here. In fact, if you'd like, you can snooze until dinnertime and I'll serve you supper in bed."

Her eyes really opened at that. "Wow, what an offer! That's right, you did tell me you'd learned to cook."

He chuckled. "I'm afraid I won't be able to take much credit for this meal. The food came from Bildner's, which is a great little market on Charles Street that caters to the Yuppies. Which means a hefty array of ready-to-serve dinners that bear no resemblance to the frozen variety."

"Yuppies, eh? Now, I might be classified as one of them, but not you. Uh-uh. I'm surprised they even let you shop in the store. Or is that why you send your housekeeper, so no one will know it's for a fancy dude on Beacon Street who *started* at the top?"

"Listen, how do you think those outrageously expensive little markets got started? Before Yuppies there were always fancy dudes and dudettes from Beacon Street." He leaned down to kiss her nipple.

Ashley was amazed to feel a shock of excitement run through her. "Good grief, my body's still responding. And here I thought nothing whatever could possibly catch its attention."

He moved his fingers across her breasts, gently squeezing each jutting tip. In response to her gasp, he moved his hand slowly toward the beguiling triangle he'd so recently been in intimate contact with. "My, my. Just look at that. Instant reaction. Why are you squirming, my love? Is there something you want?" His devilish fingers tantalized her reawakened passion, and his lips and tongue returned to her nipples to augment the sweet torment with teasing kisses.

"Oh, Zachary, this may be the absolute end of me."

He lifted his head. "Should I stop?"

"Ummm. Don't you dare. That I'd never survive. Oh Zach..."

They ate dinner at a card table set up in front of the leaping fire in the brick fireplace. Ashley had forgotten how lovely his town house was, with its high ceilings and spacious rooms furnished with richly polished pieces that held that special patina of centuries of care. She glanced around, appreciating anew the rich hues of the huge Oriental rug stretched out over dark, gleaming floorboards. Like its owner, the house projected that special aura of class—undefinable, really, but easy to spot. It was something that couldn't be bought or imitated or, her persistent mind pointed out, married into. That thought provoked a brief wave of awed inadequacy, which she quickly banished. She'd long ago won her battles over childhood feelings of inferiority, and they had no place here with Zach. He had made that abundantly clear on the one occasion she had voiced them. They had enough barriers to surmount without letting her imagination build more.

The more
you love romance . . .
the more
you'll love this offer

FREE!

Mail this heart today! (See inside)

Join us on a Silhouette® Honeymoon
and we'll give you
4 free books
A free manicure set
And a free mystery gift

IT'S A
SILHOUETTE HONEYMOON —
A SWEETHEART
OF A FREE OFFER!

HERE'S WHAT YOU GET:

1. Four New Silhouette Special Edition® Novels — FREE!

Take a Silhouette Honeymoon with your four exciting romances — yours FREE from Silhouette Books. Each of these hot-off-the-press novels brings you the passion and tenderness of today's greatest love stories . . . your free passports to bright new worlds of love and foreign adventure.

2. A compact manicure set — FREE!

You'll love your beautiful manicure set — an elegant and useful accessory to carry in your handbag. Its rich burgundy case is a perfect expression of your style and good taste — and it's yours free with this offer!

3. An Exciting Mystery Bonus — FREE!

You'll be thrilled with this surprise gift. It will be the source of many compliments, as well as a useful and attractive addition to your home.

4. Money-Saving Home Delivery!

Join the Silhouette Special Edition subscriber service and enjoy the convenience of previewing 6 new books every month delivered right to your home. Each book is yours for only $2.49 — 26¢ less per book than what you pay in stores. And there is no extra charge for postage and handling. Great savings plus total convenience add up to a sweetheart of a deal for you!

5. Free Newsletter!

You'll get our monthly newsletter, packed with news on your favorite writers, upcoming books, even recipes from your favorite authors.

6. More Surprise Gifts!

Because our home subscribers are our most valued readers, we'll be sending you additional free gifts from time to time — as a token of our appreciation.

START YOUR SILHOUETTE HONEYMOON TODAY — JUST
COMPLETE, DETACH AND MAIL YOUR FREE-OFFER CARD

Get your fabulous gifts
ABSOLUTELY FREE!

MAIL THIS CARD TODAY.

PLACE
HEART STICKER
HERE

GIVE YOUR HEART
TO SILHOUETTE

Yes! Please send me my four Silhouette Special Edition novels FREE, along with my free manicure set and free mystery gift as explained on the opposite page.

NAME _____
(PLEASE PRINT)

ADDRESS _____ APT. _____

CITY _____ STATE _____

ZIP CODE _____

235 CIC R1WV

Prices subject to change. Offer limited to one per household and not valid to present subscribers.

SILHOUETTE BOOKS "NO-RISK" GUARANTEE

— There's no obligation to buy — and the free books and gifts remain yours to keep.

— You pay the lowest price possible and receive books before they appear in stores.

— You may end your subscription any time — just write and let us know.

START YOUR
SILHOUETTE HONEYMOON TODAY.
JUST COMPLETE, DETACH AND MAIL YOUR
FREE-OFFER CARD.

If offer card below is missing, write to:
Silhouette Books, 901 Fuhrmann Blvd., P.O. Box 9013, Buffalo, N.Y. 14240-9013

DETACH AND MAIL TODAY!

BUSINESS REPLY CARD

First Class   Permit No. 717   Buffalo, NY

Postage will be paid by addressee

Silhouette Book Club
901 Fuhrmann Blvd.
P.O. Box 9013
Buffalo, NY 14240-9933

She took a long sip of the cold white wine, setting down the cut glass goblet with care. "My compliments to the chefs at Bildner's. That was delicious."

"They do a nice job, no question." Zach put down his fork and stood to throw another log on the fire. "Warm enough?"

"Oh, yes. There's nothing quite like a roaring fire, is there?"

"Nope. As long as the roaring's confined to the hearth."

"Oh my, yes." She leaned back and looked around. "I love your place. Everything looks so... used." She laughed in embarrassment, covering her mouth with her hand. "Oh dear, that is not the way I meant it at all."

"No, no, don't apologize. After all, not everyone can splurge on elegant new furniture; some of us just have to live with the hand-me-downs."

She put her elbow on the table and supported her chin in her palm as she gazed thoughtfully into the multicolored flames. "Funny, isn't it? There's such a vast difference between family antiques and hand-me-downs. Yet, in truth, it's all used furniture."

"Maybe it depends on the manner and length of use. John Steinbeck wrote that the best legacy a man could leave was to dig a big hole, throw all his junk in it and bequeath the piece of land to his great-grandchildren with instructions for excavation. That way they could open an antique shop and make lots of money."

Ashley laughed. "Good idea."

He studied her face, serene now in the firelight. It had lost most of the signs of strain that had been there when he met her at the airport. "Tell me. How's the show coming along?"

Her eyes moved to his and a tiny frown of uncertainty appeared. "I guess it's all right."

"All right? That's not nearly as positive as your last report."

"I know, it's just..." Her fingers fiddled with the stem of her glass. "Oh, Zach, I'm so scared!"

"Scared?" He hitched his chair closer and put his arm around her. "Why? I thought everything looked very encouraging."

"I don't know, it's just that opening night is almost here. And that's so frightening."

"Ashley, you're shaking! Here, come over to the couch." He pulled her to her feet and led her to the deep-cushioned sofa, where he sat down and pulled her into his embrace. "Now tell me what this is all about."

"You don't know what it's like, Zach. It's like putting bits and pieces of yourself out there on the stage, scene after scene, and waiting for the audience to give a thumbs-up or thumbs-down. The responses are never the same as they were in rehearsal. The laughs come at different places, so you have to sit through excruciating silence where you've expected reaction. And sometimes the songs you think will stop the show are all but passed over, and you have no idea why. You sit there and chew on your heart for hours till the play is over, then you go someplace and do the same thing until the reviews are in. It's just too awful."

"Honey," his arms tightened around her. "I had no idea! I saw none of this before, when we were first together."

"No, of course not. It was three weeks after the opening. By that time all the New York reviews were written and we knew we had a hit. The tickets were sold out for months and everyone was on high." She shrugged helplessly. "I'm sorry to sound like such a baby. I suppose people in other lines of work have their own terrors. It's just that this is, well, so intensely personal."

"Well, yes. I can see where it would be." He lifted her chin and looked into her troubled eyes. "I'm sure it will go well. And I'll be right there with you."

She slid her arms around him and held on tight. "Do you have any idea how much that means to me?"

He kissed the top of her head and laid his cheek against her hair. "Yes, I do. It must mean as much as it means to me to be needed. I love you, Ashley. I'll be there for you. I'll be there if it's a loser. And I'll be there if it's a winner."

Ashley relaxed in his embrace. She knew the importance of his words. In some ways, she was sure, it would be easier for him to help her through a flop than it would be to stand by her with a hit. "I'll need you just as much either way. Strange as it may seem, a smash isn't entirely easy either. Everyone gathers around when you come a cropper, but a hit leaves you very exposed."

"A little lonely on the top of the hill. Is that it?"

She tipped her head up to look at him and was warmed through by his expression of understanding and sympathy. "That's it exactly. I am so lucky to have you, Zach. So very lucky." His lips came to hers, and their sweet touch went a long way toward calming her fears.

Chapter Eight

Matt and Ashley stood in the side aisle of the Colonial, staring at the stage in stunned silence. Matt shook his head in despair. "It looks like an explosion in a junkyard."

Although she knew Matt was caught in his own preopening angst, Ashley could find no cheering words to say. He'd put his finger right on it; that was exactly what it looked like. "Dear merciful heaven," she moaned, "it looks hopeless. I think we'd better get out of here."

"Yeah. Let's go get drunk."

"Oh, sure, that'll help. All I need at this point is a hangover."

Craig was standing at the edge of the stage, gesturing toward a backdrop that was hanging upside down at a precarious angle. When he spotted them, he jumped down off the stage and strode in their direction. "Hi there. Did you see Hans? He was looking for you."

Matt nodded gloomily. "Yeah. We saw him."

Craig grinned, enhancing his expression of sunny contentment. "Good. He's very pleased with the orchestra. One thing about Boston, there're some awfully good musicians here." He waved toward the stage. "Everything's coming along fine."

Ashley and Matt followed the hand gesture with wide-eyed disbelief. "You're kidding!" The retort was a perfectly timed duet.

Craig's eyebrows went up. "No, I'm not. It's all coming together." He took a closer look at them and shook his head. "You two, you're too much. Bad enough that Mat gets suicidal, but you, Ashley?"

She frowned, becoming a bit defensive. "I'm being perfectly rational. How can you possibly say it's all coming together? Look at that mess! In case you hadn't noticed, the drop is wrong side up, that 'Cronin's Market' flat is listing to one side, the scenery's lying all over the place—and just look at the lights!" She made a wide, encompassing sweep of her hand. "They're hanging every which way! How can this place possibly be ready for rehearsal by tomorrow?"

Craig patted her on the arm. "Relax, my dear. Gregory and Joe have it all under control." He looped one arm through Ashley's and one through Matt's, and led them to the foyer. "I suggest you both avoid this place today. It's obvious that neither of you can stand much more stress." His voice had the subdued tone of a doctor counseling a paranoid patient.

Matt nodded as he let himself be ushered from the scene. Just as they were going through the door, there was a loud crash, followed by an enraged bellow: "Damn it all to hell!"

Craig said firmly, "Don't even turn around." They both obeyed. Once they were safely cut off from the bedlam of the auditorium, Craig faced them squarely. "Now. Is something specific bothering either of you, or is this a simple case of preopening jitters?" He glanced from one to the other. "Or, rather, *two* cases of preopening jitters?"

Ashley and Matt looked at each other and shrugged, then looked at Craig and nodded.

"Well, today's Monday. Maybe that's part of the problem right there. Like Garfield, I don't much believe in Mondays."

Ashley tried to force the expression of distress from her face. Craig had been working just as hard as they, and look how optimistic he was. She and Matt were professionals, they shouldn't allow themselves to get completely undone this way. She pulled in her tummy and took a deep breath, willing calmness into her mind. Just as she opened her mouth to say something pleasantly sanguine, the theater manager sighted them through the glass door and came rushing in, his face alight. "Good news! It's close to a sellout for the preview on Saturday night!" He clapped Matt on the back and smiled at Ashley. "Better hope it doesn't lay an egg!" Chuckling at his own pun, he swung back through the door.

"Oh, God." Matt sank into a straight-backed chair, managing to sag into its unyielding frame. "We're through, finished. The shortest run of any two playwrights in Broadway history."

Ashley gave him a consoling tap on the shoulder. "Buck up, Matthew. Look at the bright side. Most people never even have a *brief* shot at fame."

Craig let out a snort of disgust. "Will you guys knock it off? You're going to get *me* in the pits, and that's not easy. Listen, you'd better buck up, because by Wednesday afternoon all the principals will be frayed from spending two days dashing back and forth between Hans and me. They need to see confidence on our faces. One look at you and they'll all refuse to go on! And I think poor Kelly is developing a grand case of advance stage fright. This *is* her first big role. Why don't the two of you take her to a piano somewhere and let her run all her songs till she could sing them through a paralytic seizure, just in case she has one?"

Ashley frowned. "We thought we ought to rewrite the second verse of the 'Forever' song. We're worried about it dragging."

"Honey, do me a favor. No more rewriting until after Saturday. Let it play once as it is. None of us really knows how things will go over until their first exposure to an audience. You know damn well what'll happen. There'll be at least one total surprise and a few minor shocks."

"Yeah," Matt groaned. "Like a Tuesday-morning closing."

Craig chuckled jovially. "Can't happen, Matt, tickets sales are high through the whole three-week run. That's not to say it'll necessarily open on Broadway, but . . ."

"Craig!" Ashley hit him on the arm. "Don't say things like that!"

"I have to get to work and so do you. Will you give some time to Kelly? If you can pull your chins off the floor, you're very reassuring people to work with. I'm sure it'd do her a lot of good."

Matt looked at Ashley and raised his eyebrows. She nodded. "Okay," he said. "And we'll promise to leave the music alone until after the run-through with the orchestra. Sometimes a few glitches show up there."

"Fair enough. Now, I have to go talk to Claire about the costumes that got lost. . . ."

"What!"

Craig ignored the double-voiced cry of anguish and walked back into the auditorium.

Matt and Ashley, chins still drooping, got their coats on and headed down the street for the hall where the principals were rehearsing with the conductor. When they stepped onto the crosswalk, Ashley drew her scarf closer about her ears. "Brrr."

"I second that." Matt was hunched forward into the icy February wind. Several feet of snow had dropped on the Boston area during December and January, and a deep freeze had kept it from melting, so great ridges of dirty slush rimmed the side streets, waiting for the road crews to find time to remove it. It made walking a bit hazardous. "Who needs winter, anyway? I think I'll move to California."

Ashley let out a hoot. "What happened to your spiel about New York being the hub of the world?"

"Me? I said that? I don't believe it. New York's a foul place. Muggings and degenerates and crummy air. I want to head for the wide open spaces."

"You mean like L.A.?"

He gave her a reproachful glance. "Like Palm Springs. We wouldn't be freezing our tails off in Palm Springs!"

"We also wouldn't be waiting for the opening night of our very own musical."

"Yeah. Think how relaxed we'd be."

Ashley had to smile, picturing how radically his mood would swing at the first sound of applause. She'd only seen Matt like this twice—before the openings of their other two musicals. Of course she had to admit, she'd been this way twice, too. "Matt, is Amy coming for the opening?"

He stopped, turning his full attention on her. "Oh, God."

"Oh, God, what?"

"I forgot to invite her."

"Oh, Matthew, you didn't! Why that lovely woman doesn't feed you to the crows is a mystery to me."

His arms flailed out in woeful appeal. "What the hell's the matter with me? My bloody mind has stopped functioning!"

She laid a restraining hand on his arm. "Calm down, friend. You'll be back to normal by late Saturday night." She hesitated a second, as she faced the ever-present possibility that their show really could lay an egg. She swallowed hard, fighting waves of apprehension she didn't dare mention. "I suggest you get to the nearest phone and rectify your omission."

"Is that a fancy way of telling me to eat the crow before it gets a shot at me?"

"Exactly."

When they reached the rehearsal hall, Matt headed for the telephone while Ashley went in search of Kelly. She found the girl hidden behind a stack of empty crates. She was sitting on a small stool, hunched over, her shoulders shaking with muffled sobs. Ashley hurried to her side and laid a hand on her shoulder. Kelly jumped as though she'd been stabbed. "Oh!"

"Kelly, for goodness sake! What's the matter?"

Kelly looked up at her with great round eyes flooded with tears. "Nothing." A wail followed the word and the sobbing recommenced.

"Hey, come on. Nobody cries that hard over nothing. You can tell me, I'm a perfect clam. Nothing you say will go beyond this spot."

Kelly had a terrible time getting herself under enough control to talk. "It—I—he—" The staccato recitation was cut off by a loud hiccup.

Ashley glanced around. "Is there a water fountain or anything around here?"

Kelly gave a weak wave in the direction of a nearby door. Ashley managed to find a sink with some paper cups. She filled one and brought it back to Kelly. "Now. Drink this and take a few deep breaths. You shouldn't cry that hard. It's bad for your vocal chords."

Kelly managed a very meager smile as she took the cup and, in a few gulps, downed its contents. "I don't know if I can go on. I'm so scared!"

Ashley pulled up a crate and sat beside her, thinking of the other night when she'd made the same lament while Zachary held her in his arms. "That's perfectly natural, Kelly. It's a pretty scary prospect. But that passes. You know when?"

The girl wiped the tears from her face and looked at Ashley with reddened eyes. "When?"

"The first time you hear the audience laugh or applaud. All of a sudden the fear just vanishes."

"But what if they don't applaud? What if they sit there with their hands clasped in their laps?"

"Kelly, you've heard how the cast responds to your singing. Why would other people be so different?"

"Well, Sammy told me that the cast was just being kind. He keeps advising me to pull my volume back because my voice shatters when it gets loud, and he says—" she choked.

"Go on."

"That...that I'm playing in the big time now and I can't get away with amateurish performances."

Ashley was pushed upright by the strength of her outrage. Sammy Kirk. Why that little jerk! He was trying to cripple Kelly so she wouldn't steal the show from him! It took great effort to keep the anger out of her voice. "Kelly, haven't you noticed something about Sammy?" She saw the puzzled frown on the girl's face and kept going. She'd have to temper her words. She couldn't afford to say what she was really thinking about the leading man; but she intended to come very close to doing so. "Haven't you noticed that Sammy tends to be rather...egotistical?" Kelly gave a very brief nod. Obviously she, too, was exercising caution. "Well, some performers are so afraid someone else will take too large a cut of the glory that they try to undermine the competition's confidence." She leaned forward, bringing her face closer to Kelly's. "Are you getting my message?"

Kelly's large blue eyes were filled with a combination of hope, uneasiness and the faintest trace of dawning resentment. "You mean someone would really do that on purpose?"

Ashley was always saddened by the spectacle of dying innocence, but in this case, it had to be slain. "I hate to say it, but yes, someone might do just that. Let me assure you that no one in this or any other cast would cheer the delivery of a song just to be kind. Actors might do that sort of thing at a testimonial dinner for some old coot on his way out, but never at an ordinary rehearsal for some youngster on her way up.''

"Really?"

"Trust me. Now, I have a suggestion for you. Matthew and I would like to work through all your songs with you, so you feel absolutely sure of them. Personally, I think you've got them all knocked already, but *you* have to be confident. Then, I'd like you to ask Lyle Baker for his honest opinion of how you're doing."

"Lyle Baker? But he's . . . he's almost a legend in the theater! I'd be so afraid . . .'' Her eyes, once again, held real terror.

"I'll tell you what he is. He's absolutely honest and absolutely reliable. He'll tell you just how he feels, and if he sees any problem, he'll offer to give you all the time you need. And Craig will, too—I hope you know that."

"I was going to ask him, but Sammy said . . ." she stopped.

"That you shouldn't bother him, maybe?"

She nodded.

"Uh-huh. You, my dear, have been bushwhacked. Here comes Matt. Let's go up to the practice room and get to work." She held out a hand and helped Kelly up. "And when you go back into rehearsal, don't be shy about letting that voice of yours punch holes in Sammy Kirk."

It was the first real smile Ashley had seen on Kelly's face for some time.

That night, while Ashley was describing the hysterics of the day to Zach, she told him about the problem with Kelly. "I told her I'd keep it to myself, but of course telling you is almost the same thing." They were cuddled on the sofa in front of the roaring fire, a scene that Ashley had begun to equate with homeyness.

Zach frowned. "That's a rotten thing for Sammy to do. Why don't you can the little slime?"

"Zach, one thing you don't do, unless you have suicidal instincts, is fire your biggest star five days before opening night. It does make for an interesting dichotomy, however. For the show's sake, I hope he wows the audience. From a personal standpoint, I'd like to see him fall on his face."

"I know what you mean. We had a guy in our firm a couple of years ago who brought on the same opposing reactions. He was positively brilliant in the courtroom, but such an insufferable pain in the gizzard that even the large fees he brought in didn't keep us all from wishing he'd take a dive."

"What happened to him?"

Zach's smile was definitely smug. "He became progressively more arrogant. One day, during a partner's meeting, I flipped. In extremely graphic terms, I told him what he could do with himself." Zach's smile broadened. "He resigned."

"Didn't your partners get mad at you? I mean, if he was that good..."

"As a matter of fact, when I returned from a late afternoon appointment that day, there was a bottle of iced Dom Perignon on my desk, with tulip glasses. They all came in and we drank a toast of thanksgiving." He lay his head back against the piled-up cushions. "You know, as the years accumulate, and I become old and sage..." Ashley hooted. "I'm more and more convinced that life's too short to deal with the jerks of the world. Unless you have no choice at all."

Ashley leaned her head against his shoulder. "Um-hmm. I shall try to remind myself of that next time we're casting a play."

"Shall I tell the members of my family to boo when he comes onstage?"

She sat up. "What? When are they coming?"

"Saturday night. I got a large block of tickets for them."

"A large block? How many are there?"

"Well, let's see. Mom and Dad and Emily..."

"Oh, gosh. Emily! It'll be so good to see her!"

"Yes, she says the same about you. And of course Jared and Diane."

"That's his wife, I trust."

"Yep. And Aunt Julie and Uncle Roy. And Diane's parents. And my great-aunt, Sarah, and Aunt Phoebe and Uncle Seth, and..."

"Zach, you're scaring me to death! What's the grand total?"

He did some mental figuring. "Twenty-six."

"Twenty-six! And they're all related to you?"

"In one way or another, yes."

"How come I never knew you had so many relatives?"

"If you'd hung around long enough for the wedding, you would have."

The remark was as lightly tossed out as the review of the relatives, but it brought on a familiar wave of remorse. At moments like this, Ashley could think of nothing that would surpass the joy of being Zachary's wife, of knowing that this evening was just one in an endless string, that they would sit like this, winter after winter, held in each other's arms.

He ran his hand over her hair. "Why the heavy silence? Did I say something wrong?"

She shook her head. "No. I was just wishing I *had* stuck around for the wedding."

He took her chin in his fingers and turned her face to him. "Were you really?"

"Yes."

"I'll offer you another shot at it. Anytime you say."

Their eyes met and held. Every instinct pressed her to throw herself into his arms and say, "Yes, yes, yes!" Sometimes, she could swear there were two distinctly separate people in her head. One of them wanted, above all else, to be this man's wife, to run his home and bear his children and devote herself exclusively to the joy of sharing his life. But that other person flatly refused to vacate her skull. Like Shakespeare's shrew, she gave no quarter, giving shrill reminders of how much of herself would be sacrificed in that bargain.

Zach leaned forward to kiss her on the tip of her nose. "Let it alone, honey. I shouldn't have brought it up. Your mind's on overtime as it is; I didn't mean to introduce any heavy issues." He pulled her back into his embrace, canceling, for the moment, an issue that neither could afford to address until a later, more relaxed time. "On another note, my folks would like to entertain you and some of your friends. Whenever the pressure eases up enough to allow an evening of frivolity."

Ashley let go of the issue of marriage gladly. Zach was right, this was not the time. "That's really nice of them. I hope they know it'll have to be on a Monday night after the opening. Even then, we'll have to see how much fixing and changing needs to be done."

"Yes, they understand that. But why don't you give some thought to whom you'd like to have included. They're anxious to meet Matt, of course. And Emily, being as starstruck as she is, will have a few requests, I'm sure." He grinned at her. "Maybe we should invite Kelly and not invite Sammy."

She returned the smile. "Wouldn't I love to see him snubbed! But no. I'm afraid petty revenge will have to be foresworn. It ranks somewhat lower on my wish list than having a hit show."

For a few minutes, they sat silently gazing into the fire, absorbed in their own thoughts. Finally Ashley said, "You're very quiet. What're you thinking about?"

"I was wondering how that would feel."

"That what?"

"Having a hit show. It must be extraordinary, being in a theater with everyone applauding your work. Laughing and crying and clapping. Experiences like that happen to very few people. Very few."

"I know. I've been awfully lucky."

"You're awfully talented."

She looked at him, her face serious. "I won't be coy and say, 'Who, me?' But there're any number of people just as talented, who've worked every bit as hard as I have, who never make it. There's a definite luck factor, no question. It doesn't reduce the thrill of success.... It just makes me that much more grateful."

"I can't quarrel with you. I'm sure there's a luck factor in everyone's life; but Ashley, most people's lives are far more mundane than yours." He watched the flickering flames leap and stretch on the hearth. "You know, I once read an article about what the author called 'peak experiences.' He described them as exceedingly rare moments, perfect little particles of time—an instant or an hour, it doesn't matter. But it's when the person feels emotionally lifted beyond himself. Suddenly everything seems absolutely superb, and there's a sensation of pure exhilaration. His point was that they're few and far between for anyone, and some people go through a whole lifetime without having any. Yet I should imagine you've had a number of them."

"Funny. When you said 'peak' I immediately pictured someone standing on the top of a mountain."

"Well, that was one of his examples. But I have the feeling that with you it's more likely to be linked with standing in a theater."

She frowned, concentrating on the question. "There's one that comes immediately to mind because it was so incredible. I doubt there'll ever be another quite like it."

"When was that?"

"Actually, it was exactly as you said: I was standing in the theater. It was a couple of weeks before I first met you. *Bright Side* had just had its Broadway opening. There was a preview performance on Saturday, and the official opening on Tuesday. It was amazing, both Saturday and Tuesday nights, the audience jumped up at the end and gave the show a standing ovation. Then we went to Sardi's to wait for the review, biting our fingernails to the quick; and, God, when they came in they were unbelievably good! It was wonderful, of course, but through it all, my senses were...I don't know, kind of dulled, sort of hazed over. I suppose because of the sheer enormity first of my apprehension and then my excitement." She sat up, lost in thought, her face alive with vivid memory. "On the Friday night after the opening, I was standing in the back of the theater. I think it was the first time my mind had calmed down enough for me to really *hear* the reactions of the audience. All of a sudden it struck me, as it honestly hadn't till then, that I had a hit show on Broadway! Me, Ashley Grainger! Up there on the stage my lyrics were being sung, and my lines were being spoken, and the audience loved it! I'll never forget the feeling. I'd dreamed about having that happen all my life, but never really *believed* it would. It was about as 'peak' as you can get." She sighed, then repeated, in a tone very near reverence, "I'll never forget it."

Zachary watched her, her eyes alight and face aglow with remembered joy. The experience she'd recalled was, in every aspect, unique. It brought to mind his sister's comment, when they were skiing in Stowe, that Ashley would have to be crazy to give up her career for the roles of wife and mother. It would, he had to admit, be asking a lot, maybe entirely too much. So what then? He liked to think of himself as a modern man of the eighties, flexible and adaptable to new ideas, new life-styles. But in truth, every factor of his upbringing had equipped him far better for traditional patterns. He had simply assumed that when he married his career would take precedence, that he and his wife would settle down in the Boston area to live their lives and raise their family. He was chagrined to realize that never, in all the time he and Ashley had spent going over and over the demands of her career and finding them incompatible with his, had he actively considered the idea of making major changes in his own work. But how could he? He was the senior partner of one of the most prestigious law firms in Boston. He had a thriving practice that was important and lucrative. The Jordan family had been well placed in Boston society for generations. In every way, he belonged here.

He looked at Ashley's lovely profile as she stared into the fire. She'd had none of the family advantages he'd had. She had made it completely on her own in one of the most competitive businesses in the world. So how could she be expected to turn her back on her accomplishments and walk away? And Emily had been right on that subject, too. In Ashley's case, the only place to ply her trade in the big league was New York City. He rubbed his eyes. God, the whole thing seemed so hopeless. But now that they'd come back together, the prospect of parting once again, this time for good, loomed as more insuperable, more ludicrous than any of the other impossible possibilities.

"Zach, is anything wrong?"

He jumped. He'd been so lost in thought that he hadn't noticed Ashley studying him with concern. "No, no, nothing. I was just thinking about what you said. It must have been quite a moment." He cupped her cheek in his palm, acutely aware of the smoothness of her skin, the green glints in her lovely eyes. "You mentioned that one of the high points for a cast is the first time they hear the orchestra."

She looked perplexed. Small wonder, he'd veered sharply off on a new track.

"Yes?"

"When will that happen?"

"Wednesday afternoon."

"I'd like to be there, I'd like to be in on it."

Ashley's eyes lit up with eagerness. "I'd love to have you there to share it with me. It's really a thrill. Do you think you could manage it?"

"Do you start at two?"

"Yes."

"I'll see if I can rearrange my schedule. My first appointment that afternoon is with Jerry, but maybe we can have a working lunch and I can have the others changed."

She slid her arms around his waist and hugged him. "That would be wonderful, darling, please do try."

He laid his cheek on top of her head. "I will, I promise." He would. He'd try.

Ashley sat scrunched down in the middle of the last row, watching the stagehands adjusting the flats. Impossible as it seemed, they had straightened things out enough to run through the play on Tuesday afternoon. On Tuesday evening, they'd had the technical rehearsal, where the actors just stood in their places and mumbled their lines, so lighting and staging cues could be set. That was both exhausting and boring, and by the late end of the night, everyone's nerves were thoroughly frazzled. She hoped today's rehearsal would run smoothly. Her eyes, for the dozenth time, darted over to the side door. She prayed Zach would make it.

She had moved over to the Ritz Carlton Hotel, where Matt and Craig and Jerry were staying, on Tuesday morning. The pressure was mounting to tie up loose strings and corner stray lyrics, and she needed to be there with the others, available for consultation as the inevitable crises erupted. The degree to which she missed falling asleep in Zachary's arms was overwhelming. She wished the show could play Boston for two years, that the transfer to Broadway was unnecessary. The demand on her time would now be constant, and she wanted to have her time free to spend with Zach. God, how had she managed to get herself to this point of no return once again?

She squinted down at her watch. One forty-five. The members of the orchestra had begun to amble in, and the familiar sound of instruments being tuned heightened her anticipation. Hearing the orchestra for the first time might be pure thrill to the cast, but it was a mixed bag to the composer and the lyricist. Just as she began to chew on one edge of a fingernail, Matt slid in to sit beside her, his face set in a grim mask of dread. Matthew's peak moment of fear occurred when, for the first time in front of the entire company, the orchestra launched into the overture. All those notes he'd so laboriously written for the various instruments, heard, so far, only in his head, were about to become living sound.

Ashley reached over and took hold of his hand. "Don't panic. We may just survive this."

"Doubtful. Very doubtful. God. Why did I ever get into this business? Why couldn't I have followed my father's advice and been an accountant?"

A picture of Matt sitting at a desk with pen and green eyeshade leapt to mind. She had to laugh. "Do you even know how to add?"

"Of course. I'm very good at math. Mathematics and music have similar structures. You should know that."

"Umm-hmm. That's why I'm a lyricist."

"Here comes Craig. We're gathering on the life raft. If we go down, we go down together. Hi ya, Craig, have a preserver."

"A what?" Craig, his usual chipper air noticeably missing, sat beside Matt.

"Never mind. The hour draws near. Saturday night will be upon us before we know it. I wonder what an ex-composer can do as an alternative way to make a living."

"You can stand in the unemployment line right behind the ex-director."

Ashley clapped her palm against her forehead. "Stop it, you guys. At least give the show a sporting chance!" At that moment, she saw Zach enter the theater. "Ohh." She exhaled a long sigh of delighted relief.

Matt followed the direction of her gaze. "Thank heavens. I thought someone had punctured your balloon." He and Craig stood up. "Hi, Zach. Slide in, you can sit on Ashley's other side and hold her other hand. But you can't have this one. At the present it's my lifeline. I'd hold Craig's hand, but it'd make him awfully nervous."

Zachary grinned at them as he edged past. "Why is the air palpitating? Could this be a case of group nerves?"

Craig nodded solemnly. "You better believe it. Good thing these seats are solid or they'd shake to pieces. Nice to see you, Zach. Maybe you can disperse a little calm in this direction."

"I'll see what I can do." He leaned over to kiss Ashley as he sat down. "How about you? Are you quavering, too?"

"Oh, my, yes." Her fingers wove through his and held on tightly. "I'm so glad you're here."

Zach leaned forward. "So how things are going?" A collective groan answered his question. "That bad, eh?"

Craig replied, "Nah, not really. It's a tense time, because once the orchestra comes in, you know you're on the final run. It's nervous making. Hell, before we turn around it'll be Saturday night and the whole show will be laid right out there, naked, for everyone to check over and vote on. I guess most of the seats went for a big charity group."

"Oh, Lord," Matt moaned, "They're probably the kind of people who'd like to see a punk rocker fried for breakfast. They'll boo his first success and it'll be downhill from there."

"Yeah." Craig rubbed his forehead. "And wouldn't the 'dear shits' love that!"

"The dear what?" Zach turned to Ashley with a puzzled look on his face.

She grinned. "'Dear shits.' It's a term used for all the agents and actors and other show biz folk who turn up for out-of-town openings. They always wish you the best of luck, which means they hope you bomb. I don't know if this is true, but someone told me one agent used to appear at the openings with a script and a flashlight, so he could read during the second act if it wasn't good."

"They sound like the sort one loves to hate."

Craig nodded. "The other side of it is that if the show's a winner, they are genuinely enthusiastic and full of praise." He shrugged his shoulders. "Strange business, Zach, no doubt about it. But, boy, I can't think of any other that can touch it."

"I take it you like your work."

"Nothing like it. Nothing in the world. I'll be at it until they cart me off in a box or I can't get a job."

"Hey." Matt's hand convulsed in Ashley's. "Here comes Hans. Oh, God."

Hans's arm rose, baton in hand, and silence dropped like a cloak. The musicians straightened, all attention. Then the music started, filling the theater with the thrilling sound only a full orchestra can produce. Everyone in the cast crowded to the front of the stage to listen, grouped in their silence as the tunes of the first act took their turn in the medley. When Hans held the final chord, then dropped his hands, the entire company burst out in cheers.

Zach glanced over at Ashley. Her face was pale, and there were tears running down her cheeks. He leaned over to kiss her, then said, "Matt, it's wonderful. It really is."

Matt had scooted down in his seat, his flesh a sickly ashen color. "Too much horn. Dammit, Robbins, you put in too much frigging horn!"

Craig whispered, "Hush up, Matt, it's starting."

Zachary grew progressively happier that he'd come as the show wound on. The excitement and the enthusiasm were infectious. Each song, heard with the orchestral accompaniment, was met with oohs and aahs and rewarded with enthralled applause. Ashley's face now had a smile on it, and Matt had straightened up in his chair. His color had not only returned but been heightened by a flush of pleasure and an upturned mouth. Craig was sitting forward on his seat, socking one fist into the other hand after each song or bit of dialogue, muttering, "Hot damn, that's it! That's it!" When Uncle Hermie launched into the "Don't Count Your Money" song, a surge of proprietary pride rippled through Zachary.

Ashley leaned over and whispered, "Not too bad for your first shot at lyric writing."

Zach grinned. "You helped it along just a little." All he'd done was plant an idea, but it was still kind of exciting, a small sliver of the pride of creativity.

When the run-through ended, the whole cast crowded onto the stage to clap and cheer and yell, "Author, author!" Matt and Ashley stood up and walked to the front of the auditorium, accompanied by Craig. Zach insisted on staying where he was. This was their moment, and he was more than content to be one of the observers. As he watched the joyful scene with Ashley and Matt and Craig and Sonja and Hans and all the other creators of this musical play, he was struck by the camaraderie, the exultant high they were all sharing. Through his empathetic happiness, there was a prick of envy. Craig's words came back to him: "There's nothing like it in the world." It was special, no question. And Ashley was a special, elite member of the special group. For just a brief instant, Zach felt very lonely. Then he shook himself impatiently and went up to add his congratulations.

The big night was here. Zachary joined Ashley and Matt and Amy Johnson, who had flown in from New York that morning, for an early dinner in the Ritz dining room. All the waiters came by, one after another, to wish them luck, and the manager had a couple of bottles of wine sent to their table. The air around them was electric. Craig and his wife, Amanda, stopped by their table to say hello before meeting a few close friends. Jerry joined them for one drink, then dashed off to have supper with the Sanderses and the two men and their wives who were on the verge of investing in his future comedy.

Ashley was in a state that bordered on hysteria, laughing a little shrilly, talking too rapidly, jumping at the slightest noise. And Matt was in worse shape than Ashley.

Amy patted Matt's hand. "Calm down, now, you'll choke on your food."

Matt dourly answered, "It's better than being publicly executed."

"Matt, even if they don't like your play, they don't draw and quarter you."

"You wanna bet?"

Ashley turned to Zach, her eyes so crystal-brilliant that Zachary was a little afraid that if she blinked, they'd shatter. "Zach, did I tell you your parents sent me a beautiful bouquet of roses?"

"Yes, you did. Twice. And Emily sent you a bottle of champagne. Emily is far more enthusiastic about champagne than roses."

Ashley blinked, and Zach sighed with relief. They didn't shatter. "Twenty-six relatives?"

He nodded. "With instructions to clap loudly."

Amy grinned at him. "I swear, being with these two tonight is like sitting beside a couple of sticks of lighted dynamite. I hope you know, Zachary, that you and I will have to sit through the show without them. They'll both pace through the whole thing."

"It will be my pleasure to have your company." He meant it. Amy was a gem. And he couldn't imagine anyone who'd be better for Matt. She was even-tempered, gentle, and had a good sense of humor. "Where did a guy like you find this nice lady, Matt?" He was glad he and Matt had become easy enough with each other to make that sort of teasing jibe.

"I won her in a lottery. I had my choice of her or a weekend in Newark." The smile he sent in Amy's direction was the tenderest Zach had yet seen from Matt. "I'd marry her, but I can't afford any more alimony."

Zach chuckled. "You don't have very high expectations where marriage is concerned."

"Hell, no. Can you imagine a woman staying with me once she finds out what I'm really like?"

"You have a point."

The conversation had stayed flip all evening. It was clear that it wasn't the time for anything profound.

The maître d' appeared at the table. "Mr. Robbins, you wanted me to alert you when it was time to leave."

Matt stared at him in horror. "Oh, God."

The man's smile didn't waver. "Good luck."

"Thanks."

Amy had been right. Ashley and Matt barely lasted through the overture before they both got up to go to the back of the theater for what Amy had labeled the Stew Room. The theater was packed. Zach's group of relatives, who had stopped in the lobby just long enough for a quick hello were seated a few rows behind. The applause was thunderous after many of the songs, and laughs, though subdued, were constant. Amy leaned over to inform him that preview audiences were often more sober than most. She'd obviously been involved in this long enough to develop a familiarity with the process.

At the intermission, Ashley and Matt were surrounded by what Zachary could only guess were the "dear shits." They were gushing over the musical, and their tones, as Craig had predicted, were warm and enthusiastic. By the end of the play, it was obvious that the audience had loved it. Zach joined Ashley, who looked as if she'd swallowed a five-hundred-watt bulb, and listened to one rave after another. When they finally escaped the crowd, they joined a group in Craig's suite for a celebration drink. Craig stood in the middle of the room and said, "Allah be praised, we're golden tonight! Now, here's to the big one on Tuesday!"

With cries of "hear, hear" all around, they drank.

Ashley clung to Zach's arm as though she'd fall flat on her face if she let go. He asked, "How're you doing?"

"Good. Real good. Oh, Zachary, if only the critics like it!"

"Were they there tonight?"

"No. That'll be the Tuesday night ordeal."

Tuesday came so quickly Ashley would have sworn both Sunday and Monday had been canceled. She and Matt had worked nonstop on one of the songs in the first act that wasn't working, and had once again revved up to a condition resembling St. Vitus's dance. She tried to stay seated beside Zach, but she just couldn't do it. All too soon, she was at the rear of the theater, walking back and forth, back and forth, in counter motion to Matt. It was another full house, and this group was more overtly approving than the Saturday-night audience. Laughter rolled over her in great, healing waves, and the applause at the end of the first few songs began to calm her fears. When the newly revised song was performed by Kelly, the audience went nuts. They clapped until Kelly, her face aflame with joy, gave them an encore. And at the end, everyone rose to their feet, calling out "bravo" as they beat their hands together. Matt appeared at her side, and in answer to demands from the audience, they went up on stage for a bow. Ashley felt she could have soared out above the crowd into the cold night air with nary a shiver.

Zach watched the woman he loved, standing on the stage among the stars and the chorus and the dancers and the directors. Her smile threatened to split her face. He kept clapping, along with everyone else. He agreed with their reaction. It was a fine show, fun and upbeat and full of marvelous music. As he stood there, something new and unexpected happened. A deeply spawned, visceral feeling of pride rose in him. Ashley was, indeed, extraordinary. And she loved him as much as he loved her. He glanced around him at the joyful faces, realizing how much pleasure her talent provided to so many people. The pride grew and blossomed.

And Zachary called, "Bravo!"

Chapter Nine

Ashley went home with Zachary that night, or rather, the following morning. By midnight, the euphoria over the audience reaction to the show had been superseded by the agony of waiting for reviews. Somewhere in the wee hours, euphoria returned to reign supreme. Zachary realized two things as he unlocked his front door and held it open for Ashley. First, he hadn't been up this late in years, and second, he couldn't remember when he'd had more fun.

Ashley's face was sore from so much smiling. She wavered as she stepped inside and Zach's hand shot out to steady her. "Hey, lady, what's this? A little too much champagne?"

She laughed, a tinkling ripple of joy. "Not champagne, happiness. I'm giddy on happiness." She rose to her tiptoes to bestow a kiss on his lips. "Can you *believe* those reviews? I should send a thank-you note to the critics. Those guys can be rough; Boston's known to be a very picky town."

"Then that should make you all the more proud. It was fantastic, honey, it really was. Of course, I do think the highlight of the show was my song."

She giggled again, delight shining in her eyes. "I see you've become awfully possessive. Matt and I were getting some credit until tonight, but now I notice you're taking it all." Uncle Hermie had stopped the show with the "money" number. The song and the dance were perfect vehicles for his superb showmanship.

"Listen, that's one thing I learned from the 'dear shits' on Saturday night. How to grab a big chunk of the credit."

"Like who?"

"For one, that agent, what was his name? Oh, yeah, Crocker. Actually, the name would fit him better if he dropped the last two letters. He was telling Craig that he was the one who suggested the idea to you and Matt about the immigrant kid whose uncle gets him into the country, teaches him English and makes him into a rock star."

"That jerk. He never had an original idea in his life, and if he did, I'd instantly discount it."

"I figured him for a phony. But he wasn't the only one. From listening to all the comments, it's amazing you and Matt had the nerve to put your names on the musical."

They were in the bedroom, and Ashley went straight to the drawer in which she'd left some clothes to get her nightgown. "Well, Matt and I are pretty cheeky, you know. We just pick up everyone else's ideas and make them ours." She laughed. "They all want to be part of a success. It would've been a different matter entirely if the show had flopped. Those people are experts at distancing themselves from failure. They'd all have sworn they hadn't even talked to us for a couple of years, just to make it clear they had nothing to do with it."

"Doesn't that kind of get to you, to have types like that in your business?"

"Why? There're jerks in every business. For every cipher in my field, there's a hardworking, down-to-earth person to offset him. You must have the same problem, Zachary. There are an awful lot of real sleaze balls in the legal profession. But you can't go around apologizing for your line of work just because others abuse it."

"You've got me there." His mind had veered far from the topic. Ashley was stark naked, about to put on her night-gown. His voice dropped to a seductive tone. "Ah, you're wearing your most becoming outfit. That luscious skin of yours sure fits you nicely." He crossed to her and ran one finger up her arm, down her chest, across her breasts, stop-ping to circle each nipple. He chuckled at her gasp, a low, sensual sound. "You know, I turned on the electric blan-ket. You'd probably be warm enough in the raw." His eye-brow rose suggestively. "And if you aren't, I'll help raise the temperature."

She put her hand behind her and let the nightie drop to the floor. "Umm, I feel it going up already." She pushed closer to him, moving her body against his. "Strange, something else seems to be coming up, too."

"You have some wonderfully naughty instincts."

"You have a wonderfully responsive..." his mouth got the last word, directly.

She wound her arms around his neck. "You're being aw-fully slow getting those clothes off. Hurry up, I want to make wild love to you."

He ran his hands over her soft smooth body. "I cer-tainly—" he kissed her lips lightly "—won't fight that. Give me two seconds to shave, so I don't whisker burn this vel-vety skin." He kissed her deeply for good measure before heading for the bathroom.

"Zachary..."

"Yes?"

"Be sure you don't lose anything while you're gone."

He gave a decidedly lascivious laugh. "Don't worry, there's no danger of that."

When Zach emerged, Ashley was in bed, lying on her side, with the covers pulled up under her chin. He turned out the light and slid in beside her. "Honey..." He curled his body around hers, burying his nose in her long, sweet-smelling hair. "I have something for you." There was no answer. "I'm ready to be wildly seduced. In fact, I'm prepared to be more than cooperative." He was still met by silence. Zachary eased his arm under her head and, with his other hand, turned her face to him. "Have you decided to play hard to get?"

Ashley was sound asleep, her breath deep and even. Zachary, fighting pangs of frustration, sighed, pulled her closer into his embrace and settled down beside her. "Poor baby. You've had quite a day." So had he, and it wasn't long before he, too, gave way to slumber.

It was close to two weeks later that Zachary's parents had their Monday night party in Ashley's honor. Ashley, who had been working with Matt practically nonstop on revisions, came from the hotel by taxi, accompanied by Matt and Craig. When they drew up in front of the town house, Craig said, "That was fast."

"I told you we could walk. You guys are so scared of using your feet." Ashley slid out of the cab after Matt.

Craig grunted. "You can get mugged just as easily in four blocks as four miles."

"Now Craig, this is Boston, not New York, and we're in the best section of town."

Craig paid the tab and crawled out into the cold night air. "Humph. Where do you suppose the discriminating muggers hang out? They want a crack at the rich dudes."

Matt shook his head. "You're not in your usual cheery mood, friend. Bad way to go to a party."

"Oh, I'll get over it in a few minutes. I had to speak to Sammy again. He's still trying to tuck it to Kelly. He can't stand the ovations she's been getting. If he weren't essential to the show, I'd love to lock him in a closet somewhere and forget him."

Matt grinned. "Yeah, the one back in the corner of that wind tunnel we rehearsed in the first couple of days. No one'd go near it for weeks." They'd reached the top of the stone steps. "Hey, dig all the brass. Someone must keep real busy shining it."

Ashley nodded. "The servants. The Jordans have family money and family antiques and family servants who stay for a lifetime." She shivered.

Matt put his arm around her. "Cold?"

"No, nervous."

"You? Why, because you're making a visit to the far right of the tracks? You don't need to worry, babe. You're famous. It buys just as much acceptance as all that family stuff. And you're riding high right now, the special ornament on the top of the cake."

"I suppose."

"Don't suppose, believe. Besides, Zachary doesn't give one small damn about all that stuff. You know that very well."

She looked at him with interest. "I never thought I'd see the day. You and Zach are becoming downright chummy."

"Nice guy. In fact, two nice guys. No wonder we like each other."

Craig cleared his throat. "How about canning the TL's and ringing the bell? It's cold out here."

Matt started to press the buzzer, then stopped and looked at Craig quizzically. "What's a TL?"

"Something my sister used to drive me nuts with when we were kids. I don't remember what it stood for, probably 'trading lies.' She'd come up and say, 'I have a TL for you,' which meant someone had said something nice about me.

But before she'd tell, I had to think of a compliment some-one had paid her. Drove me nuts."

"Then why didn't you just tell her to buzz off?"

"Could you pass up hearing a compliment when you were a kid?"

Matt thought for a second and answered, "Hell no. In fact, I still can't." He pushed the doorbell.

The door swung open almost immediately. A tuxedoed butler stood before them. "Good evening." He stepped aside to let them in. "May I tell Mr. and Mrs. Jordan who has arrived?"

Ashley took a peek at the mischievous expression on Matt's face and stepped quickly forward. "Yes—"

Before she could go further, the butler smiled. "Why, it's Miss Grainger. It's been a long time. Welcome."

She managed a shaky smile. She could feel two sets of curious eyes burrowing into the back of her head. "How nice of you to remember, Charles. Yes, it has been several years."

"Let me take your coats, and I'll announce you." He looked at Matt and Craig, his eyebrows discreetly lifted.

Ashley jumped in once again. "This is Craig Clarke, the director of our show, and this is Matthew Robbins, my musical collaborator."

"Welcome, Mr. Clarke, Mr. Robbins. I'll take your coats and see you in."

As he turned to hand the coats to a uniformed maid, Ashley hissed at Matt. "I see that look in your eyes, Mat-thew Robbins, you behave yourself."

"Hey, babe, don't sweat it. I'll be so polished they'll put me out front with the brass."

"That's what I'm afraid of. The brass." She frowned at his quirk of a smile, and turned back to Charles.

"Would you like to take the elevator or the stairs?"

"Elevator?" Matt's eyes lighted up. "There's an eleva-tor in this place?"

"Yes, sir. Right over here."

"Hey. Me for the elevator."

Ashley shot him a withering look. "Heaven forbid you should walk if you can ride."

"My sentiments exactly." Matt, with an openly curious Craig beside him, stepped into the small, ornate elevator. Ashley, not wanting to complicate the arrival, reluctantly got in beside them.

Charles reached in to push the button for the third floor. "Have a nice evening."

Matt's grin split his face. "Boy, this is shattering the hell out of my concept of Yankees. If this is keeping it close to the bone, there must a lot of prime rib in the cooler."

Craig punched his arm. "Keep your eyes open, Matt. Might learn something about real class."

"Listen, I'm not easy to intimidate. I've got a pretty fancy place myself."

"Yeah, but their furniture won't still have the price tags on it."

"Listen, you two. Cut it out. Straighten your ties and dredge up any old Emily Post rules you remember."

"Emily who?"

Ashley scowled at him again for good measure. Matt had that twinkle in his eyes that made him potentially dangerous.

When they got out of the elevator, Zach was there to meet them. "Hello. Glad you're here." He kissed Ashley, his lips lingering for a tiny trace of a second longer than might have been deemed proper, then turned to Matt and Craig.

Matt put up his hands. "Just a handshake, if you please."

Zachary broke into laughter. "Don't worry, friend, that's all you'll get from me."

Ashley frowned. "Don't encourage him, Zach, he's in one of his moods. He'll probably do something embarrassing before the evening's over."

"Let me know when the time comes, Matt. I don't want to miss it. Craig, welcome. Come in and meet my family. They've been anxious to see you."

The parlor was a huge room with high ceilings, two glittering chandeliers and tall windows richly draped with brocade. Even Craig, who'd been in a lot of fine homes, said, "Wow. This is really something, Zach. When Ashley said your folks lived in a condominium, I pictured something quite different. This is real old-world elegance."

Zachary nodded. "Actually, this is officially called a town house. It belonged to my great-uncle. When he passed on, Mom and Dad bought it from the estate. They were lucky it worked out. These places are becoming impossible to find. Most of them do end up converted into several condos."

Ashley's eyes moved around the room as she followed Zach. This place had a more ornate aura than their suburban home. She'd been a guest there several times in the past, when she and Zach were together. That house had enough of the sprawling, country feel to dissipate any sense of grandeur. But here, in the more confined quarters, the elegance was more pronounced. Deep-piled Oriental rugs of a quality that retained their beauty through the generations covered the dark, shining floors. The furniture had that dense, layered gleam peculiar to beautifully maintained antiques. Ancestral portraits shared wall space with authentic Audubon prints and tastefully selected paintings—originals, of course.

There were about fifty or sixty guests standing in small groups chatting, sipping drinks out of sparkling crystal glasses while a string ensemble consisting of a harp, two violins, a cello and a viola supplied a discreet musical background. The men wore dark suits so similar they could have been in uniform, the women tasteful dresses in classic styles. Ashley could see Craig taking it all in, imprinting the scenario on his memory, and she knew, instinctively, why. If he ever had to stage a scene of top-drawer refined civility, this was the ultimate model. Ashley, despite Matt's buoying assurances, still experienced a wave of Cinderella syndrome: hoping her gown wouldn't revert to rags in front of these highly refined people.

To augment that tremor of uneasiness, here and there, easily spotted in the group, were her theatrical colleagues. Sonja and Hans and Sammy and Kelly and Lyle and Buzz and Claire, plus a few others, each displaying the touch of shabbiness or "today" fashion or flamboyance that stamped their individual style. Talk about two different worlds! And behind it all, lodged firmly in her mind, dwelled vivid etchings of yet another milieu: the homespun, paycheck-to-paycheck environment in which she had grown up. In her heart Ashley knew there were real differences between them, gaps wide and deep enough to make the transition difficult to impossible. Could she and Zachary, even without the problems that had been discussed, truly find a sturdy bridge by which to move freely back and forth?

She pulled her rambling mind to attention as they approached Mr. and Mrs. Jordan. Zach's mother, much to Ashley's surprise and pleasure, opened her arms. "Ashley, my dear. We are so very proud of you."

Ashley stepped into the embrace, warmed by the genuine sound of approval in the woman's voice. "Thank you. That means a lot to me."

Mr. Jordan took her hand in both of his. "My, my, what a triumph you've had! It isn't hard to see what has kept you so busy the past few years." He patted the back of her hand. "We've missed you, Ashley. It's a great pleasure to have you here."

She looked at him, her eyes widening, for an instant, with wonder. The words seemed to be spoken from the heart. Had she, by nursing her own insecurities, built obstacles to their affection? "I've missed you, too." And, even as she said it, she knew it was true. She'd not only missed Zachary, she'd missed his family and their gracious way of life and their never-wavering courtesy. There were many admirable qualities here worth savoring and copying. Not the least of which was an unbending code of good manners.

She felt a tap on her shoulder and, upon turning, saw Emily, her face split in a huge smile. "Ashley!" This embrace was easy and natural. "I didn't get a chance to see you after the play. God, it was marvelous! It's so exciting to know someone who's really famous. Especially when it's so well deserved!"

"I should get you to write our reviews." Ashley was so glad to see her old friend.

"I don't know how they could have come out any better than the ones you got." She tipped her head toward Matt and Craig. "Are you going to introduce me?"

During the introductions, Jared and Diane appeared, and there was another round of compliments and thank-yous. From that point on, the evening raced by, full of meeting new people, accepting congratulations and the wearing ritual of small talk. Ashley found herself the center of attention, along with Matt. They were surrounded all evening, answering questions, describing work rituals, receiving the somewhat awed homage paid to stars of the theater. Ashley, on several occasions, caught Zachary watching, his face unreadable, one thin line between his brows.

But the two incidents that stuck fast in her mind had nothing to do with *her* career or with its inevitable side issues. During the evening, Ashley met Graham Sawyer, a man of advanced years who had, he proudly informed her, been the senior partner of the law firm before he'd retired and Zach had assumed the position. He was a handsome old man, tall and straight and white-thatched. The first thing he did was apologize for the fact he hadn't seen her play.

"My ears have gone into semiretirement. Entirely, I might add, without my permission. It does no good whatever to attend the theater, unless, of course, it's mime. But I understand it was superb."

"It got a good reception, we're very pleased. I'm sorry you weren't able to come. It must be very frustrating to lose your hearing."

"Maddening, child, maddening. I have yet to find any socially redeeming features about growing old. That statement is usually countered by the overworked saying that it beats the alternative, but I have, as yet, met no one who can give me firsthand assurance of that."

Ashley was charmed by the elderly gentleman. The complaint was heavily laced with humor, as though he'd long since quit taking life too seriously. "I must admit, neither have I." They shared a moment of laughter.

"I understand you are the young woman with whom our Zachary was so enamored a few years back. I must say, the lad has good taste."

"Why, thank you."

"And so, I dare say, have you. Zachary is an extraordinary man. One of the few true gentlemen of the younger generation."

"I have to agree. He is extraordinary."

"Of course, being special, as you must know, has its cost. Zach, for instance, is being pursued by the pols. They want him to run for public office. I do believe he is seen as a viable contender, in the future, for the governor's office."

Ashley stared at him in shock. "Really? He's never said a word about that."

"Oh? Then perhaps I shouldn't have, either. Personally, I have mixed feelings about the possibility. He'd be a boon to the world of politics but a dire loss to the firm. One doesn't replace a man of Zachary's caliber."

She nodded. One certainly didn't. "I'm sure that's true."

"Well, it has been a delight to meet you, my dear. I wish you great success in your theatrical endeavors." He bowed his head graciously and walked away.

Ashley's eyes followed him as he moved across the room and stopped to join a small group. She had the distinct impression there had been a message in his words. In a subtle, courteous manner, he'd informed her that Zachary was needed where he was. Well, she thought, he's needed elsewhere, too. But where, Ashley? The question immediately presented itself. Would she want Zachary to take premature retirement to follow her about, making her reservations and tending to the busywork of her life, the way the husbands of some stars did? No. Because then he'd no longer be the Zachary she so loved. Damn. Everywhere they turned, obstacles rose to display themselves, to prevent their forgetting that, as the old song said, they lived in "two different worlds."

The other incident was more distressing and caught Ashley entirely by surprise. At one point in the evening, she caught sight of Zach, standing beside a lovely young woman with blond hair, his arm around her shoulder, his head inclined toward her as though he couldn't bear to miss a word. Ashley knew who she was, because Emily had pointed her out. Her name was Joan Hudson, and she was, in every way, one of "them." Her parents were lifelong friends of the Jordans, and Joan had been in love with Zachary most of her life. She was eminently qualified to be his wife. As Ashley watched them, heads close together, laughing and talking, she was assaulted by a vicious stab of jealousy. She was forced to face a grim scenario. If she didn't marry Zach, eventually someone else would. Maybe even that tooalluring bluestocking now monopolizing his attention.

She was galvanized to the spot by the dreadful speculation. What would she do if Zachary married someone else? She'd repeatedly pushed the possibility from her mind so effectively she'd almost succeeded in blotting it out. But now she couldn't. He was one of the most attractive men she'd ever met, both physically and mentally. He was handsome, rich, successful, charming and incredibly nice. And he was thirty-three years old. His yearnings for a wife and children were bound to escalate rapidly in the near future. Suddenly, Ashley felt terrified. She couldn't lose him, she couldn't! The thought of some other woman becoming Mrs. Zachary Jordan was unbearable!

Then her eyes moved across the room to where the "theater folk" had clustered together, their expressions intense as they talked. She had no doubt about their subject. It had to be the show. At that moment, Ashley felt as divided as East and West Germany. One side of her dreams and longings and aspirations drawn inexorably to the right, the other side pulled with equal force to the left. The problem was, both sides wanted Zachary, and each side recognized the near-impossibility of reconciling the differences. It appeared that either decision would cost half of herself. She felt sick. Sick and confused and terribly afraid.

Ashley was supposed to return to the hotel that night, so she and Matt could get an early start the following morning at the endless revisions and corrections that were part of any out-of-town tryout. But she made an arbitrary decision to go home with Zach. An awful mental picture had seared itself on her brain of Zachary leading that cool, elegant Joan-person into his bedroom, taking her into his arms . . . it was too much for her. She had to cancel, entirely, the unlikely but threatening scene.

All the way to his house, she snuggled close to him, her head on his shoulder, her hand possessively clamped on his thigh. Acute awareness ran rampant in her, increasing sensory reactions, augmenting sensual response. The hard, bulging muscles of his thigh rippled beneath her hand as he braked and accelerated. The subtle scent of his after-shave tickled her nostrils. When she raised her head to gaze at him, the sheer beauty of his features pricked her ardor. She ran her hand up his leg, smiling at the low moan of response when she reached the V of his body. Excitement built in her like a surging tide.

The car swerved slightly. "Ashley, what are you trying to do, get us killed?" His voice was a growl, hazed over by arousal.

"Just tend to your driving, don't mind me," she teased. She could feel her blood speeding through her veins as she gently touched him, barely restraining herself from doing things that might send the car careening off the road. She nuzzled her face in his neck.

"Ashley..." Her name came in a gasp as she nibbled his ear, her hot breath fanning the sensitive area.

When he had pulled the car into the garage and pushed the release to close the door, he turned off the motor and reached for Ashley in the same movement. "You vixen."

She smiled at him seductively, her yearnings far from sated. "Are you complaining?"

"Oh, no. Crazy I'm not. But now it's your turn." He grabbed her shoulders in his steely grip and brought her mouth to his, covering it with emphatic ownership, his tongue plundering, demanding, inciting. Every inch of Ashley responded. She pulled at his tongue and followed it with her own, wanting all of him. Her breath escaped in a heated rush when he undid the buttons of her dress and his fingers slipped inside her brassiere to torment the throbbing peaks of her breasts. "You have far too many clothes on."

She started to undo his tie, but he pushed her hands away. "Uh-uh. Just lie back, give yourself entirely to me."

His head dropped forward, kissing her breasts through her lacy bra. The gentle touch of his teeth, the relentlessly firm warmth of his tongue, his lips pulling on her nipples though the taut fabric, filled her with the agony of ecstasy. Her hands began to push at Zachary's coat, struggling to remove it, but his hands came up to stop her.

"Not yet, my darling." Before she could react, he was out of the car and had come around to her side. "Come along, wench. My sword is poised, ready for the attack." He leaned down and pulled her out of the car. She gasped as the cold air cut through her open blouse to her still tingling breasts. But before she could register a complaint, he had swept her into his arms and carried her through the back entry into the house.

By the time they'd reached the living room, he had maneuvered his arm tightly around her so his fingers could just reach her nipple. She squirmed with desire at his touch. "Not fair," she moaned. "I can't stand any more ecstasy, I may perish of it."

"What? After that blatantly lascivious attack on the most private sector of my personage, you dare say 'no more'? There are penalties to be paid for such conduct." He lowered her to the soft fur rug that was laid out in front of the fireplace. "I intend to lay my prize on top of the prize my grandfather brought back from Africa." He was on his knees beside her, and bent to kiss her lips as he laid her down. "Are you absolutely sure you can stand no more?"

"Zachary, no more teasing. Oh please, touch me, kiss me, take me." She'd already wriggled out of her coat and dress. His fingers struggled with the hook at the back of her brassiere, then, with a grunt of impatience, he yanked it free. She was in no mood to mourn a torn bra. He slid out of his own coat, his eyes seeming to sear her skin with the heat of his desire. Then his strong hands eased her back and his lips went to her upthrust, pulsing nipples. She would explode, she knew she would. Hot licks of lust swept through her, turning her into a blazing inferno.

Zachary's hands were busy again, pushing down the slip and the panty hose and the bikini in one movement. He took them off and threw them aside with her other clothes. She lay stretched out on the fur, naked and quivering under his demonically clever touch. He leaned over her, his lips taking command of hers, their mouths grinding together in hungry response, each to the other. But each time she tried to undo his shirt, or push at his jacket, he thwarted the effort.

"No. I want you just this way, naked to me, at my disposal." It was richly, excitingly decadent to lie there nude, stretched out for his use, while he remained fully clothed. His hands roamed every part of her, his fingers dipping into crevices, tormenting each erogenous particle of her flesh, his lips and tongue locating and tantalizing the hardened nubs of her desire. He played her like a gifted musician would play a tautly strung harp, until she twanged with pulsating fervor.

Ashley flung her arms above her head, arching to his touches, giving way completely to the unimaginable pleasuring of her body. He brought her to the edge of orgasm again and again, then tarried, holding her on the torturing brink until finally she cried out. "Oh please, please!"

With a satisfied groan of victory, he completed his conquest. With his tongue and his fingers, he pushed her beyond the confines of ecstasy. Then beyond that limit, until she sank back, snuggling onto the fur, exhausted.

"Ummm." She gave a deep sigh and closed her eyes. "I could go to sleep right here."

"Sleep?" he asked incredulously. His finger crept into the most private sector of her personage, and she wriggled in animal pleasure, her back tickled by the fur. "See there?" His voice rumbled, low and excruciatingly sexy. Shock waves of wildfire jolted her deep inside. "Are you sure you want to sleep?" He stood and loomed over her, one foot on each side, his eyes dark as midnight as they looked down at her, his black hair tousled on his forehead, his chiseled features accentuated by the one shaft of light that shone from the hallway. Whatever the game they played, she wished it would never end.

"Why do you insist on keeping all those clothes on?" she asked plaintively. "I want to see your body."

"If you want them off, why don't you see to it?"

With a smile of impure lust, she got to her knees and reached to unbuckle his belt. Unzipping his pants, she pulled them down to his ankles.

"You should have started with the shoes." The wicked grin on his face gave him the remaining aspect of a marauding buccaneer.

"Why? Now I have something very appealing to look at while I undo the laces." She mentally became the subservient captive ministering to her master's designs. When she had one foot bared, he lifted it and tucked it into her lap. The toes were unmerciful as she untied the other shoe. When he had kicked aside his lower garments, she stood to undo his tie and shirt, while all the while their bodies rubbed together, whipping their need to a roiling tumult.

When Zachary, too, was naked, they sank to the rug together, arms and legs encircling each other in the frenzy of their fiery passion. Lips, fingers, palms, tongues, every instrument of excitation was used, again and again, back and forth, from one to the other: a total, unrestrained giving of pleasure to pleasure, love to love. Nothing seemed too much, nothing withheld or restrained, two bodies joined in a frenzy of smoldering, mutual need. When Zachary entered her, Ashley cried out in gratification, calling his name aloud.

They were molded together, one undulating form, writhing in the ritual dance of passion. When she was halfway arched, on the edge of the precipice, he stopped the movement and lifted his head, holding her in the heat of his gaze. "Say you're mine, Ashley. Say you belong to me!"

She looked deep into those dark wells of enchantment, sinking in their beguiling tide. "Oh, yes." It was a hoarse whisper. "Yes. I belong to you."

"And I to you. Remember that. Remember this. You and I are part of each other." With a husky moan, he sank into her once more, initiating the irresistible rhythm that would carry them both beyond ecstasy.

Chapter Ten

For Ashley, days and nights melded together, fused by the common denominators of constant work, magic moments stolen with Zachary and the growing excitement of the upcoming move of the show to Broadway. The Boston run was coming to a close. The show had played to packed houses full of enthusiastic audiences. They had a hit, and the word was out in New York. Although their Broadway opening night was still two weeks hence, seats had sold out for the first couple of months and were still selling at an astonishing rate.

Each Boston performance was followed by adjustments: in pace, lyrics, music, stage movement, lighting, costumes...the list went on and on. It was honing time, sharpening the musical to a biting edge of excellence. Ashley swung between radiant happiness, caused by the state of euphoria that she and Zach lived in, and steadily growing dread of being evicted from that state when she left Boston.

The day for departure inevitably arrived. The entire company was caught up in the madness of the move. The set had to be struck and prepared for transport, costumes sent ahead for any necessary repairs and cleaning, lighting boards and all the special Fresnels, spots and strips carefully packed...and always more to do. Tempers were short, due to both the frantic confusion and the usual sadness that reigned when a troupe left the scene of a triumph. An out-of-town hit, though the best of omens, did not guarantee a hit on Broadway.

Ashley stood in the middle of her baggage in the hotel room, her mind messily rummaging about, attempting to arrange itself in orderly process. She was so preoccupied with the prospect of moving away from this magic city, home to her lover, that details of packing, sorting and readying herself for departure seemed monumental chores. When the knock on the door came, it had an aftershock, like the knelling of a bell of doom.

She opened the door and tried for a smile. "Hi, honey."

Zachary's expression mirrored hers: forced cheerfulness layered over grim acceptance. "Looks like you're all packed."

"Yes, I think I have everything."

"Want to check through once more before we go?"

"No. If I've left something they'll send it." She grimaced. The one thing of true value she was leaving couldn't be packed up and sent. Her eyes kept swinging back to Zachary, wanting to engrave every aspect of him on her mind's eye, to be called up and viewed in the lonely days ahead.

"I guess we'd better go. The traffic will be fierce in the Callahan Tunnel at this time of day."

Ashley had already called a bellhop, and he appeared at the door. Time to go. Her heart was steadily sinking. By the time they reached the airport, it would be beating in her feet.

They drove in comparative silence, broken only by monosyllabic comments of no import. They had said their goodbyes the night before, passionately, sadly, sweetly, hopefully. Their capacity for farewells had been wrung dry. When Zach pulled up in front of the Eastern terminal, he pushed the gear to neutral and pulled on the hand brake. "I'll open the trunk and check your luggage."

Ashley was fighting a losing battle with tears. "Are you coming in to wait with me?"

He looked at her, his dark eyes clouded with sadness. "No. I said goodbye to everyone yesterday, and I don't want to stand in the middle of the group and try to make small talk."

She nodded. "I understand." She couldn't quite make herself open the door, and Zach was obviously having the same problem. She felt her control give way, felt the tears start to roll down her cheeks.

He took out his handkerchief and wiped the tears from her face, then handed it to her. "We're not parting permanently, darling." He ran his fingers across her cheek. "It just feels like it."

She leaned into his embrace. "I love you."

"I love you, too. That won't change when you get on the airplane."

"Promise me you won't marry Joan while I'm gone."

He pulled back, looking at her in amazement. "Who?"

"Joan. The blond girl at your parent's party."

A spark of humor lit his eyes. "Dear God, where did that come from?"

She shrugged, trying to make light of a subject she'd worried about ever since that party. What in heaven's name had made her say it? She tried to lighten her voice, to turn it into a joke, as it should be. "She was hanging all over you. And Emily says she's been in love with you for years." *You darn fool,* she told herself. *There's nothing that catches a man's interest like knowing a woman admires him.*

At that, Zachary laughed, kissed her and reached for the door handle. "Emily has an outrageous imagination." He grinned at her. "And it seems yours isn't far behind. Joan's an old friend. I've known her as long as I can remember; we share a lot of memories. But friendship and love are two different things."

Ashley shakily returned his smile. All very well for him to say. But love did sometimes grow out of friendship. And the thought of Zachary and Joan Hudson sharing a lot of memories did nothing for her peace of mind. The luggage got checked, and she took her small carry-on bag from Zach. There was nothing left to do but turn around and walk through the door. Why did it feel like she was preparing to walk the plank? "I guess it's time."

"Yes."

"I'll call you. And you call me."

"Of course."

"I hate this. I don't want to go."

"You could stay." But his eyes acknowledged the impossibility of her doing so.

"I wish I could." She stepped forward and lifted her face to his light kiss. "Goodbye, Zachary."

"I'll see you soon."

"Oh, yes." Her throat closed, allowing no more words to pass, so she forced her feet to turn and walk through that damned sliding door. She looked back only once. Zachary had already gotten into his car. She watched it pull away from the curb, then headed in the direction of the New York shuttle.

It was a week later that Zach, busily at work at his desk, answered his secretary's buzz to be told, "A Mr. Robbins on the line; are you in?"

"Yes. Definitely." Matt? God, was something wrong with Ashley?

"Hi there, Zachary. I like your secretary's voice. Is she as cute as she sounds?"

"In a word, no. How are you, Matthew? Is everything all right?"

"Sure. Smashing. One more week to go for the big night. You're coming, I trust."

"Of course. Wouldn't miss it. So, is this just a social call, or do you have need of a lawyer?"

"Not at the moment, but one never knows. Listen, Zach, I've got sort of a weird and wild favor to ask."

"Ask away." Zach liked Matt more and more as he grew to know him. He strongly suspected that beneath that flip exterior was a very sincere and sensitive man.

"Well, as soon as we get through opening night and have been either praised or pasted by the press, it'll be only a couple of weeks before I could sneak away for a nice long holiday."

Zachary frowned, unable to make a connection between Matt's vacation and this call. "That sounds great. But so far it sounds like you should be talking to a travel agent."

"All in good time. You see, I want to take Amy with me."

"I don't blame you. Amy is about as nice a companion as could be found. She's also of legal age. So far I see no need for legal services."

"I don't need a lawyer. I need a friend."

Zachary sat back, surprised by the sudden tone of soberness and touched by Matt's turning to him for friendship. "I would be honored to fill that role, Matt. What can I do for you?"

"Be my best man."

"What?"

"Yeah. Amy and I are getting married. I don't want to take my girlfriend with me, I want to take my wife."

Zachary pushed at his chair, tilting it onto the back legs. "That's terrific, Matt. When and where is this auspicious event to be held?"

"In Las Vegas."

"Las Vegas!"

"Yeah. It's the fastest. And it seems like an appropriate place for a guy like me to get married. I mean, talk about a gamble!"

Zach chuckled, then stopped, frowning in thought. Something very bothersome had just occurred to him. "Matt, I hope I won't offend you . . ."

"Uh-oh."

"I just . . . well, to tell the truth, I'm a pretty hidebound cuss in some ways. When the minister says something about not taking the marriage vows lightly, that's the sort of thing I take very seriously."

"Okay, Zach, whatever's on your mind, just spit it out. One of the things I admire about you is your honesty. So I promise not to get mad if you want to turn me down."

"It's not that I wouldn't be pleased to be your best man, Matt, really. It's just, well, if you're going into this marriage with a cavalier attitude, you know, maybe it'll work and maybe it won't, but why sweat it . . . I couldn't, in all conscience, be part of the ceremony. For one thing, I think Amy deserves far better than that."

There was an extended silence at the other end of the phone. Zachary squirmed in his chair, feeling like a stiff-necked party pooper. Sometimes he got caught up in his own rigid ethics when more flexibility was called for. He didn't want to hurt Matt's feelings. He wished he could call back the words, but it was too late for that.

When Matt answered, his voice held a sincerity and conviction Zachary could swear he'd never heard before. "Zach, I appreciate your saying that. I really do. Believe me, I want this one to last. I'm not as carefree and thoughtless as I sometimes appear. I married twice in a row when I was a young hotrod on the prowl. Neither of them had a chance; I married girls who were gorgeous and party-loving and empty-headed. That's why I've stayed single for ten years, to give myself time to grow up. Amy's special, as you say. I don't want to be alone anymore, and I sure as hell don't want to grow old by myself. Amy keeps me in touch with important things. She keeps me in touch with myself. I love her, Zach, and I want this to be till death do us part.'' He gave an embarrassed laugh. ''Listen to me, waxing poetic.''

Zach had to swallow hard to dislodge the lump in his throat. ''Thank you for sharing that with me, Matt. And I'd be extremely honored to be your best man. When are you planning to go?''

''I think this weekend might be our last chance to get away for a couple of days.''

''Had you thought of waiting until later, when you have more time?''

''Yeah, we thought of it. But, I don't know…we're ready now. Does that make any sense?''

''Lots of sense.'' Zach sighed. He was ready, too. But his story, thus far, didn't promise such a happy ending. ''Is Ashley going?''

''Sure. Naturally. She couldn't be my best man, so she'll be Amy's maid of honor. Hey, maybe you two should quit horsing around and make it a double. I understand they give a special rate.''

''Don't I wish we could. I'm afraid Ashley and I have a few things to settle first.''

''Yeah. I suppose. But you belong together. It doesn't take twenty-twenty vision to see that.''

They settled on times for departure and return, and discussed other details before hanging up. After Zach had replaced the receiver, he sat very still for awhile, gazing thoughtfully out the window. Damn. It wasn't going to be easy, watching someone else get married while he and Ashley stood by in their unaltered singleness.

Amy and Matt stood before the justice of the peace in the small, tasteless chapel. The four of them had looked it over before the ceremony and pronounced it a fine example of early tacky. They were all in a holiday mood, ready to laugh at the slightest excuse. It seemed a good ambience for a wedding.

Zachary's eyes kept meeting Ashley's as the vows were spoken and the rings exchanged. A silent question hovered between them: "Why can't we just do this, and try to work it out from there?" There were times, he thought, when too great a dedication to personal responsibility seemed an onerous burden.

As soon as the ceremony ended, Zach and Ashley stepped forward to kiss the bride and groom. Zach held Amy's shoulders, looking down at her with genuine affection. "Well, you did it, kid. I'm not sure whether to congratulate you or offer to have it instantly annulled."

"No way. It took me a long time to get this guy to the altar. Now he's stuck with me. And I mean *stuck*."

Zach gave her a hug and a kiss. "Good luck, Amy. You deserve the very best."

"That's what I got."

He smiled. "Yeah. You did at that."

When he turned to Matt, they stood, grinning foolishly at one another until, at the same moment, they moved forward to give each other a bear hug, complete with backslapping. Ashley watched with tears in her eyes at the display of affection between her best friend and the man she loved. She and Zach had come a long way since the first round of their love affair. If only they could find a road smooth enough to make the rest of the journey!

They'd flown to Las Vegas on Friday evening, and they flew back to New York on Sunday. During that brief time, as well as having the wedding, they'd dined and danced and played the slot machines and sat in the intense heat out by the pool—and laughed and laughed and laughed. All four of them were geared to having fun, set in a sort of lull-before-the-storm mentality. Ashley and Zachary clung to each other, sitting close, holding hands, walking with arms entwined. They both felt somehow threatened by the newlyweds, as though they were witnessing an improbable dream.

When they reached New York, Zach continued straight to Boston. He'd postponed a great deal of work while Ashley was in Boston and couldn't afford any more lost time. They wouldn't see each other until opening night, ten days away.

Matt and Amy, acting every bit the part of newlyweds, dropped Ashley off at her apartment, then drove off in the taxi, giggling and hugging.

Ashley walked into her empty apartment, and took her bags to her bedroom to unpack. She held herself together until her clothes were put away and she'd taken a shower and fixed herself a cup of tea. But as she sat in the spacious living room, all by herself, she was overcome by loneliness. She stretched out on the couch and gave way to a flood of tears.

"Where the hell is Hans?" Craig stamped down the theater aisle, his hair rumpled, sticking out every which way from too much pulling.

Ashley sat in a seat on the aisle, going over a list, checking off the things that had been done, groaning over the number of items still remaining. "I think he went out to grab a bite of lunch, Craig. What's up?"

"He wanted a better cue-in for the interlude after Lyle's exit in the third scene. How the devil does he expect me to work with him if he's off running around?"

"The poor man does have to eat, Craig."

Craig dropped into a seat in the row ahead of Ashley's. "Yeah, I know. I'm getting frazzled."

She looked at him sympathetically. "I can't imagine why."

Craig let out a short laugh. "Running out of time for repairs. We soar or get shot down tomorrow night."

She studied him anxiously. "Placing any bets?"

"Sure. Bound to be a hit. They loved us in Boston." Lack of total conviction rang through his tone. He shrugged. "Hell, why should you and I try to con each other? We'll all be shaking in our booties until the ballots are in."

"True. No sure things in this game." They looked at each other helplessly for a second, then Craig got up and walked hurriedly out the side door. Ashley sat still, ignoring her work, focusing inwardly on a peculiar phenomenon. She was having the exact same reaction now that she'd experienced right before the opening of her first on-Broadway show. A pervasive numbness, as though none of the proceedings had much of anything to do with her. Funny. She'd expected it to be different this time, less remote, more personal. After all, she was already a bona fide Broadway playwright, with a short but solid record of success. Why did she still feel like an outsider, looking through the window, hoping to be admitted to the warm inner haven of acceptance? Perhaps the mental distancing was a protective device her mind had invented to offset too calamitous a disappointment.

Her mind seemed to deal with a number of things that way. It persisted in canceling out nagging doubts and fears concerning Zachary, insisting on dwelling instead on the delightful memories held over from Boston and Las Vegas. It was better that way, as long as she could make it work. They were, she was all too aware, careering toward the point where they could no longer brush aside all the cloying questions, when decisions would have to be made. The prospect scared her to death. She shook her head and returned to her list. Enough, for the moment, to worry about tomorrow night. The rest of her life would have to wait.

The house was packed. Every inch of official standing room was filled. Ashley and Matt sat huddled together in the back row, inclined forward in preparation for the rising and pacing to which they would soon yield. Ashley kept looking around, nervously anticipating Zachary's arrival. He was involved in two extremely important cases, one in San Francisco and one in Chicago. She'd known he couldn't get there until the last minute, but fate had thrown another monkey wrench into the timing. March, doing its "lion" number, had produced an unseasonal blizzard, making hash of the airplane schedules. She wasn't sure which was making her more nervous, the impending opening of the curtain or the possibility that Zachary wouldn't make it.

Matt tapped her arm. "Here comes Hans. Oh, God, I've got to get up." Ashley nodded and swung her legs to the side so he could squeeze past.

The round of polite applause faded out as Hans bowed to the audience, turned to his orchestra and gave the downbeat. The first number in the overture was a rollicking, brassy tune that brought a spatter of applause. Ashley scrunched down in her seat, experiencing the onset of intense anxiety. Would it work? Would they like it? Should she have changed that one verse of lyrics that still bothered her? Could she survive a flat-out failure? Where, oh, where, was Zachary? What if he didn't get there? Oh, Lord, what if he was circling in a plane, his life endangered by the storm?

The curtain was just parting when Zachary quietly slid into the seat next to hers. She had a hard time restraining herself from collapsing in his arms. "Oh, darling," she whispered, "I'm so relieved you're here!"

He leaned over to give her a quick kiss on the cheek. "Me, too, it's bad out there."

Any further conversation had to be curtailed. The show had started.

At the end of the first act, Zachary stood quickly and came back to Ashley, who had been driven from her seat by the persistent jump of nerves. She waited for him, then started toward the door that led backstage. Zachary took her arm. "Where are you going? Don't you want to mingle with the patrons in the lobby? Hear the comments?"

"Oh, no. No, I really couldn't stand it."

"Ashley, honey, what are you so nervous about? The audience loves it."

She stared at him, eyes round with apprehension. "Are you sure? They hardly applauded the 'Poor Me' number, and it doesn't seem like they're laughing very much."

"They're laughing. I think they cut it off so they won't miss the next line."

When they'd reached the safety of the backstage area, Ashley sagged against a wall. "I don't know why I get so crazed. I'm sorry. It must seem so silly to you."

He pulled her into his arms. "No, not at all. I can't imagine anything tougher than sitting there with all those people who are about to publicly approve or condemn over three years of your hard labor. Why wouldn't you be unstrung?"

"Oh, Zachary." She leaned against his sturdy chest. "It's so wonderful to have you here with me. I honestly think I could keep my chin up through a flop with you beside me, holding me up."

He kissed the top of her head. "I honestly don't think you'll have to. Besides, no one has to hold you up, love. You're a very strong, self-sufficient woman."

She closed her eyes, soaking in the warmth of his embrace, storing up the comfort and the strength that traveled from him to her. Was she really the way he described her? And how did he feel about that? Most men wanted to be essential to their women. It was a subject that probably needed exploring, but she certainly wasn't up to it now. Further comment was cut off, in any case, by the appearance of Matt.

"Hi, you two. Zach, glad you made it." Matt's words leapt forth at machine-gun speed when he was revved. "Have you seen Amy?"

Ashley shook her head. "She may be in Kelly's dressing room. They took a real liking to each other."

Zach looked puzzled. "That's right. Where was Amy during the show?"

"Eighth row center, sitting with some friends." Matt gave a sheepish grin. "She refuses to sit with me anymore 'cause she says she ends up alone. Which is true." His feet were shuffling, ready to move. "Gotta go find her, see if she can paste me back together."

Zachary shook his head. "I don't believe you two. Everyone in the audience must have sore hands from clapping, and you're acting like they booed the whole first act."

"Zachary, old buddy, you said it yourself. Don't count the money till the money's in the bank. Same thing holds true here. Never say 'hit' until the reviews are in. It's murder." With a wave of his hand, he was off.

Zachary glanced around, then said, "I thought your parents were coming tonight."

She frowned, disappointment showing on her face. "They were, but this darn storm interfered. They're not the most enthusiastic flyers, even in good weather. The predictions for heavy snow stopped them cold."

"That's a shame. It must have been a real letdown."

She nodded. "Yes. But I have to admit, if I had to choose between their making it, or you, I'd have chosen you." She gave him a big hug. "My folks will see the show later, and it won't make that much difference. But I needed you here tonight."

Ashley insisted on waiting until the audience was seated and the house lights out before sneaking back to their seats. Zachary was getting just enough used to the paranoia that he simply followed her lead, holding her hand tightly to lend support.

When the curtain came down at the end of the second act, the audience rose as though strung together, clapping, cheering, calling "Bravo!" Zachary, caught up in the general enthusiasm, didn't feel Ashley tugging at his sleeve until she gave it a yank and hissed, "Come on, Zach, let's get out of here!"

If her mood was strange during intermission, it had moved beyond that to unfathomable. She was remote, withdrawn and gave every appearance of being in a trance. When they were once again cloistered backstage, Zachary took her by the shoulders and asked, "Are you all right?"

"Fine. Just fine." Her eyes, glazed and unfocused, moved about restlessly. "We should find Craig and Matt, see what they're going to do."

"I thought everyone was going to Sardi's."

"Matt will, for sure. Craig? I don't know. Maybe we could find someplace quiet. Get a drink and something to eat."

"Ashley..." he bent closer and waved his hand back and forth in front of her eyes. "Are you in there?"

"What?" She stared at him as though not entirely sure who he was. "In where?"

Zachary took her by the hand. "Come on, Sleeping Beauty. Let's go find your pals and go to Sardi's. You're certainly not going to hide out somewhere and let this experience slide by."

"But . . . what if the critics hated it?"

"We'll burn them in effigy and you can feign unconsciousness from smoke inhalation and I'll carry you out. You'll get the sympathy of the American public, which should keep the show running an extra year or two."

"You're not taking this seriously!"

"You're right. That's because you're taking it far *too* seriously. You'll have to read the reviews eventually, no matter where you are. And what if, by any mammoth stretch of the imagination, they happen to be good? How would you feel then about being somewhere quiet, cut off from the fun? Come along, Ashley. I've never been involved in a

Sardi's first-night panic. Surely you wouldn't deprive me of that!''

It was the first smile he'd seen all evening. And the last he was to see for several hours.

The mood at Sardi's was comprised of the special form of hysteria that comes of nerves stretched taut, high expectation and corrosive apprehension. Voices were pitched high, laughter was sharp-edged and staccato, drinks were downed with frantic rapidity. Zachary had never seen anything like it. The waiting in Boston had been a subdued, held-breath variety that hadn't prepared him for this raucous anxiety. Ashley continued to act as though someone had set her down, hypnotized her and walked away, forgetting her entirely.

He finally quit trying to pull her out of the mood once Craig assured him she'd return to the living once the papers arrived. "Don't worry about her, Zach, she's withdrawn into the 'holding room.' It happens to a lot of actors.''

"But Ashley's a writer, not an actress.''

"So? Just means she has more of herself at risk. The reviews should be in pretty soon now.''

"You seem calm. How do you do it? You have a lot at stake, too.''

"I've been in this game a long time, Zach. You develop a pattern. The last days before the opening I'm a wreck, but at this point? Hey, the first showing is history, nothing can be changed. The critics have probably finished their summations. It's go or no go. Out of my hands.''

Zach was developing a growing admiration for many of these people. Their dedication, persistence, and plain hard work was unexcelled in any other profession he'd observed and, indeed, unequalled in most. He watched Craig move through the group, chatting, encouraging, joking, buoying up spirits. He wasn't at all sure he'd be that composed under the circumstances. His eyes went back to Ashley. Poor honey. The suspense must be agonizing. He'd acknowledged, earlier on, the ambiguity of his feelings and accepted them as normal, in fact, inevitable. He hoped for raves for Ashley's sake, as well as for all the rest of them. From a strictly low-down, selfish standpoint, he couldn't help facing the fact that a hit would move Ashley more firmly into this world of show business, which meant, inexorably, farther from his "normal" world.

Suddenly a young man came rushing into the room, his hair and coat covered with snow, of which he seemed entirely oblivious. "*The New York Times* is out!"

Zachary had to stand back to avoid being trampled in the stampede. He found himself holding his breath, his eyes fastened on Ashley, who still sat frozen in her chair. At that moment, all secondary considerations disappeared, and he was left with a single hope: that the review would be lavishly laudatory, that his love's face would lose that expression of stunned anxiety and be transformed to pure, undiluted joy.

The young man riffled the pages until he obviously found the theater section. He and several others, straining to see, read silently for a few seconds, clearly too fearful to communicate. Zachary considered himself a rather contained man emotionally, but what happened next brought tears to his eyes. The young man's face lighted up, his eyes round. His smile was mirrored by those around him. He climbed up on a wooden chair, raising his voice to a semi-yell. "*For those who have feared the demise of the American musical comedy, who had come to expect nothing better than tired reruns or plotless, tuneless production extravaganzas, take heart. Robbins and Grainger, aided by the magic touch of Craig Clarke, have given us a great glittering gift of a show, full of singable songs, laughable lines, and even, here and there, tear-jerking poignancy.*"

A great cheer went up from everyone in the room. Zachary moved to Ashley's side. Her whole face had become a blazing beacon of joy. As the reading of the review continued, extolling the outstanding performance of Lyle's Uncle Hermie, the solid portrayal of the rock star by Sammy and the brightest new performer of the decade, namely Kelly...she slowly stood up and snuggled into Zachary's embrace.

When the reading ended, the young man threw his arms above his head, waving the paper. "I've got a steady job!" Laughter, the kind full of uncontrollable glee, rolled around the room. The other reviews followed suit, with nary a naysayer among the critics. Jubilation reigned supreme, and Zachary, thoroughly entangled in Ashley's unbridled happiness, rejoiced with the rest.

As the party began to really crank up, Zachary pulled Ashley off to one side. "Ashley, I'm afraid I've got to go. It's crucial that I get on the red-eye special to L.A. so I can make my meeting in the morning."

Her mouth fell open in astonished distress. "But Zach, you *can't* leave now! I couldn't bear it!"

"Honey, I told you, four or five days ago, that it was the only way I could get here for opening night. This is a very big merger and it's vital for me to be there. As it was, I had to bow out of an important discussion to catch the plane east."

"Oh, damn, I'd forgotten! How could I have forgotten something like that?"

He smiled. "You've had some pretty important things on your mind."

"Couldn't you take an early morning plane?"

"It'll be early morning by the time I get there. I'll barely make it in time as it is. I'm praying the plane will leave on schedule."

A glimmer of hope came into her eyes. "Maybe you should call. With this storm, the airport may be shut down."

"I already called. The snow has stopped, and the plane is there now. They expect to leave on time."

"But Zachary..." It was a wail of protest.

His expression sobered, just a little. "Ashley, don't make this any harder than it already is. I'd love to stay with you, I'm sure you know that. But I can't. My job is important, too."

She caught the next protest just in time. She was being unfair. He had told her of the commitment. It wasn't his fault she'd forgotten, it was hers. She gulped, then went into his arms. "I'm sorry, darling, it's just that I hate the idea of your leaving me. You've been wonderful to make such an effort to get here. I hope you know how much it meant to me to have you here."

He tipped her chin up and kissed her lightly on the lips. "I do know. And it's meant a great deal to me to share this triumph with you. Congratulations, Ashley. You've accomplished something extraordinary." He gave her one more kiss and a lingering hug, then was gone.

As Ashley watched him go out the door, a major portion of her balloon of delight deflated, leaving her with the morning-after fatigue that follows too raucous a night.

She got a ride home with Craig and his wife. Everyone else, including Matt and Amy, were still going strong. She kissed them both goodbye and walked into her building, smiling her thank-you to the doorman's congratulations. In many ways, New York was like a small town. Rumors and current news circulated with uncanny speed.

Ashley unlocked her door and entered the large, empty apartment. The silence was cacophonous. She felt flattened by loneliness. She'd once read a book by Alan Jay Lerner that had explained how he retreated into himself after a flop, so was quite content to be alone; but how important it was to have someone you love to share a hit, in order to thwart the awful loneliness of success. When she'd read it, she hadn't understood at all. To her mind, failure would always be harder to deal with, alone or not alone. But now, here in this luxurious container of excruciating silence, she knew what he meant. It all seemed a fading memory, not quite trustworthy: the unimaginable pride of accomplishment, the euphoric release of pent-up anxiety, and the thrill of shared delight all vanished into the abyss of soundlessness.

The lapse into sadness had the extra weight of guilt. How could she be so ungrateful, how could she ask for more, when she'd just been handed a large chunk of the world?

As she stood, staring out over the city that had just given her acclaim, she felt an unbearable, overwhelming, crushing need for Zachary. Had he become her *sine qua non,* without which there was nothing? And, if so, what did her future hold?

She was still there, in the big, still room, when the sun rose.

Chapter Eleven

Hi, Zach." Ashley sat on the edge of her bed, cradling the phone with her shoulder while she plumped up the pillows to lean against them. These telephone conversations with Zachary grew more lengthy as their time apart expanded. She'd seen him just once, for a day and a night, in the last two and a half weeks. "What's it like in San Francisco today? Our weather is frigid; I'm beginning to lose hope that spring will ever come."

"Actually, it's fairly brisk here. You know San Francisco—it can be pretty chilly if there's any wind."

"No, as a matter of fact, I don't know San Francisco. I've never been there."

"I think it's very negligent of you not to have seen San Francisco. It's a wonderful city. Almost as nice as Boston."

She laughed. "If it's as good as all that, I'd better hop on a plane today."

"I wish you would. I miss you terribly."

She swung her legs up on the bed and sank back on the pillows. "I miss you, too. I'm learning the meaning of 'wilting on the vine.' I think that's what I'm doing."

"I'd better get back soon, so I can pluck you before that happens."

She giggled. "A retort comes instantly to mind, but I'll let it go."

"I should hope so. How's the show going? Still standing room only?"

"Oh, yes. It seems impossible that it's been running for almost three weeks. The bugs have just about been worked out, so for the first time in I can't think how long, we're beginning to relax. Matt and Amy are taking off for a late honeymoon next Monday. They're going to Aruba to lie in the sand. Doesn't that sound heavenly?"

"It sure does. You and I should go somewhere, too, as soon as I get this wrapped up."

"That would be wonderful, Zach."

"Then let's plan on it. As soon as my schedule is predictable, we'll book space. Start thinking about where you want to go."

She was suddenly full of anticipation. Nothing in the world would sound as good to her as the prospect of going somewhere far away with Zachary. Well, maybe one thing: Going far away with Zachary on *their* honeymoon! "I'll run out today and get scads of brochures. Oh, Zach, I can't wait!"

"It'll give me extra incentive to push ahead on this deal. We can't have you withering away there in the big city."

"Actually, lest you think of me as a complete stay-at-home, I should tell you I'm about to take off on a trip too."

His tone immediately changed. "You are? Where?"

Ashley smiled, pleased by the trace of possessive concern in his voice. "I wish I could name someplace at least minimally exotic.... Mom and Dad are finally coming to New

York to see the show this Friday; I'm flying back with them on Sunday to spend a few days."

"That's a good idea. It's been quite a while since you've been there, hasn't it?"

"Almost ten months. It's scary how fast time disappears when you're preoccupied with work."

"I know. Downright frightening…. Ashley, I have to go. I've got to get to another meeting. Take care of yourself."

Each time they reached this point—the ending of the connection—she felt an awful emptiness begin to gather inside. "Talk to you tomorrow," she said softly. "I love you."

"Love you, too." She hated that tone in his voice, the one that said "I have to say goodbye, I'm in a hurry."

When she'd hung up the phone, she got up and headed for the bathroom to take a shower. Actually, she didn't have much time, either. She was meeting Matt and Amy and Craig and his wife for dinner before they went on to the theater. It struck her that this could well be the last time for this ritual. The pattern was changing. The need to attend every performance had ended, Craig was negotiating to direct another play. Sonja had already begun work on new choreography. Claire had left for London to consult on costuming a period comedy and Buzz had two offers to light other shows. It was a sad time, in many ways. Rather like watching your family split up. Families were much on her mind lately. In fact, all close relationships. Mainly, of course, one in particular. She reached into the shower stall to turn on the hot water. She was very glad she had somewhere to go tonight, so she wouldn't be by herself, closed in with her own thoughts.

The first morning Ashley awoke in her parents' home, it took her a few seconds to orient herself. At first she felt misplaced. Then, as she gazed around the familiar room, much as it had been when she'd moved out over a dozen years before, the feeling changed to one of comforting familiarity. Tempting smells of perking coffee and sizzling bacon offered major incentives to get up and start the day. She sat up and stretched, sliding her feet into the slippers on the floor. She was excited at the prospect of visiting with her family and seeing old friends.

It didn't take long for her to shower and dress in jeans and a shirt and sweater. She tied her sneakers, then headed downstairs.

Her mother stood by the stove, her dark blue cotton dress covered by a white apron, turning the bacon, then lifting it out and placing it between two sheets of paper towel. Such a nostalgic sight. For a moment, Ashley felt as if she'd never left. Doris Grainger looked up from her chore as her daughter entered. "Good morning, dear. Did you sleep well?"

"Umm-hmm. Very well. The only thing that bothered me was all the silence."

Her mother laughed. "I can well imagine. How on earth you sleep through all that New York racket is beyond me. Want some bacon and eggs?"

"Sounds great. Can I help?"

"No thanks, dear. I'm so used to having my kitchen to myself that someone else fussing about just confuses me."

"Where's Dad?"

"Out in the garage, trying to fix that old snowblower. Foolish thing never starts up when it's needed. Honey, maybe you could pour the orange juice, then call him. These eggs will be done in a jiffy."

When the three of them were seated around the table, Mr. Grainger said, "Isn't this nice, having our daughter at home with us? You should stay on for awhile, Ashley. Do you good to breathe some clean air and go to bed early. Could stand to put a little meat on your bones, too. You're awfully skinny."

She smiled at him. "Daddy, I'm skinny on purpose. That's the fashion."

"Fashion. Humph. Bunch of anemic-looking people running around in New York. Bunch of strange-looking ones, too. Doesn't seem like a healthy atmosphere for a young woman."

"Now, Daddy, let's not start that again. New York has some perfectly nice, normal inhabitants. And it's where I happen to work. It's been very good to me, and I like it just fine."

Doris broke off a piece of toast and spread it with some of her homemade strawberry jam. "Well, you've made quite a name for yourself. You have a lot to be proud of." Ashley chewed a little faster so she could swallow and say thank-you. Praise for her career from her parents hadn't been frequent. But before she could say anything, her mother changed the subject. "We were certainly disappointed to miss Zachary."

Ashley took a sip of her juice and replied, "He was sorry to miss you, too. He said to be sure to give you his best."

Ashley could almost smell the question that was coming. "Honey, your father and I, well, we sort of wondered what the situation is with you and Zachary. I mean, do you think he's at all interested in marriage now, or was that chance lost?"

That chance lost. Ashley stared down at her plate, taking her time chewing her bite of bacon. Her mother and father had only the best of intentions. They would have no idea how much it hurt her to realize that, to them, everything she'd accomplished—the acclaim, the wealth, the fame; having a hit show on Broadway; having people stop her outside the theater for her autograph; being recognized and, as Matt would put it, fawned over, in the restaurant she'd taken them to for dinner—paled beside the loss of the opportunity to marry someone like Zachary Jordan. There was more than the decor of her old bedroom that hadn't changed. Why did it make her want to cry? After all, she didn't feel so hot about losing that opportunity either. It was just, well, it would be awfully nice, just once, to hear one of them say: "Zachary's a wonderful man. But how could you bear to abandon that marvelous career after you've worked so hard to get where you are?"

"He's still interested, Mother, but don't start sending out invitations. We still have all the same problems we had before, so we're taking it one day at a time, to see if there's any solution."

Her father put two slices of bread in the toaster and pushed the lever. "Just seemed to us that, well, you've had a chance to do all you wanted to do. Might be a good time to move on. After all, nature does have a way of taking away options. You might regret not having a family."

She looked from one loving, concerned face to the other, overwhelmed by her inability to find a reply. Of course she'd regret that. She'd regret not marrying the man she loved. She'd regret missing the showers and the wedding and buying a house somewhere in suburbia. But why couldn't they understand what it would do to her to give up her career? Why was it supposed to be so damned easy to discard something of that magnitude simply because she was born female instead of male? She had to swallow hard to halt the rise of bitterness. "We'll just have to see how things work out, that's all."

The dulling of both pairs of eyes bespoke their disappointment. Their only daughter was still driven by the fire in her belly. She could read the question on their faces. When in the world was she going to stop all that nonsense and settle down? She put down her fork. Her appetite was gone.

Ashley forced a note of cheerfulness into her voice. "I thought I'd go over to Jim and Audrey's house a little early. Audrey said I could come over and play with the baby before everyone shows up for lunch."

At the phrase, "play with the baby," two sets of eyes lighted up, sparked by hope. She had a terrific urge to stamp her foot and shout "Get off my back!"—but she knew it would be less than useless. Their values were so set that nothing was going to change them. A woman's main function was that of wife and mother, period. And, she knew, they were prompted only by their love for her and concern for her happiness. Those were hard motives to fault.

Her mother smiled indulgently. "That's a good idea. You haven't seen little Kathy for a long time. You won't believe how she's grown."

"She must be adorable."

Her father nodded. "She is that. I'm afraid she'll be spoiled rotten, with two sets of indulgent grandparents. Time for her to have a little competition for our attention."

She was *not* going to get back into that! "Well, I imagine Jim and Audrey will be thinking about a little sister or brother for Kathy pretty soon." Ashley jumped up, cup in hand, and went to the stove. "Either of you want another cup of coffee?"

"Yes, dear, thank you. Wasn't it nice of Audrey to invite some of your old school friends over to see you? That should be quite a reunion."

Ashley nodded. "It sure will. Do you realize it's been six or seven years since I last saw Edie, or Joanne, and longer than that with Helen."

"That's right, she's been living out in Wyoming, hasn't she? Did her husband get a new job back here?"

Ashley couldn't resist. "Oh, no. They're getting a divorce." She lifted her eyebrows in a show of sympathy. "Not all marriages work out, you know."

It was fun to see her old friends. They oohed and aahed over Ashley's fabulous success story, and Ashley relaxed into the role of visiting celebrity, enjoying the attention without chastising herself for doing so. Matt would say she was learning. But that subject was soon exhausted and Ashley was relieved to have it finished.

During lunch, they roared over tales of shared high school high jinks. But before long, the conversation moved on to the things that were clearly foremost in their minds. Husbands, babies, new houses, a few tidbits of gossip. As the afternoon wore on, Ashley felt increasingly cut off. Their lives were so drastically different from hers. She glanced around the neat, comfortable house that her brother, the doctor—the one with an acceptable fire in his belly—had provided for his family. It was homey, tasteful, inviting. She'd had a wonderful time playing with little Kathy; and there was no denying the maternal urges she awoke.

Ashley couldn't help projecting herself into this scenario. How would it feel to live like this, as one of the women, getting together to gossip and compare notes on being a wife and mother? She sat quietly, listening and observing and trying to imagine herself in the circle. It was appealing: no stress, no craziness, no all-night writing sessions, no terrifying first nights or mind-boggling hitches to iron out, no...excitement. The word was there, unbidden. Damn. In any case, she reminded herself, life as Zachary's wife would be different from this. But would it really? In the ways that mattered? She was back at the beginning, with too many unanswered questions.

The gathering broke up with lots of hugs and vows to get together again soon and lots of promises to come to New York and see Ashley's play, which she knew wouldn't really happen. Ashley was left with the old homily, "You can't go home again." She had changed, moved on. Her life wasn't necessarily better or worse, but it was certainly different. And no matter how nostalgic she felt about this beguiling life-style, it wasn't hers. She was far more at home in her madcap New York surroundings. God, growing up was hard sometimes.

When she arrived back at her parents' house, her mother's eyes were shining with delight as she announced, "Zachary called you, just a half hour ago. We had a real nice chat. Such a nice man! Oh, he left a number. Said he'd be there for a couple of hours." She bustled over to the telephone table to get a notepad. "Now you go right ahead and call him, don't worry about the cost!"

Ashley took the pad, smiling at her mother's undisguised enthusiasm. "Thanks, Mom. I'll put it on my charge." Her mother's lips pursed. Charging anything was suspect. But her face quickly relaxed into the pleased expression. Clearly, as long as her daughter returned the call, all else could be forgiven.

The moment Zachary's voice sounded on the other end, all of Ashley's discomforts disappeared. "Hi, Zach. I'm glad you called."

The low rumble of his voice wound through her, an instant balm. "I needed to hear your voice. I'm lonely."

She blinked, amazed to feel the wetness of tears. "Me, too. Very lonely."

"With your whole family around?"

"Yes." It was fruitless to attempt an explanation. She'd discuss it with him later, when they were together, and when she'd had time to try to sort it out. "How are you doing? Can you come back soon?"

"I'm flying out tomorrow."

"That's wonderful!" Relief flooded through her. "Can you come to New York? If not, I'll meet you in Boston."

She could hear the pleasure in his voice. "That's a very nice offer, but I can stop in New York. Ashley, another business matter has come up."

"Oh?" Relief was suddenly clouded by dismay.

"One of my clients has asked me to attend a special party celebrating the reopening of his hotel. I helped iron out a very messy problem between him and his former partner. He bought the partner out, did some massive remodeling and has just reopened. He wants to celebrate."

"That's very nice." Ashley tried to keep the disappointment out of her voice.

"There's one little addendum: This hotel's in Cancun, Mexico, which has a delightfully sunny climate. I hear it's a terrific place to unwind, lie on the beach, snorkel, swim, screw around...."

"Zachary! Are you saying what I hope you're saying?"

"I just might be. I see no reason why we can't both go to this party, then stay for awhile. Say a week?"

She could feel her face light up in an all-encompassing smile. "I'd love it! When can we go?"

"The sooner the better. Would your parents be too upset if you left tomorrow? I need to get an Ashley-fix before I go home to pack."

"Believe me, my folks will be very understanding as long as I'm going somewhere with you."

"Very wise, those two. Here's the plan. I've booked us through Miami to Cancun on Friday morning. I'll get to New York on Tuesday afternoon, so I can go home Wednesday to pack and sort out business details while you do the same. Then I'll fly back and stay with you Thursday night, and we'll leave from La Guardia Airport at 9:00 a.m. Friday. Does that sound okay to you?"

"Okay! It's wonderful! Perfect! Marvelous!"

"Does that mean yes?" He was chuckling.

"Yes, yes and yes. I have nothing but yeses to say."

There was a very brief pause. "All right. I won't take advantage of this opportunity to slip in a tougher question. In fact, why don't we vow to leave all the toughies alone for awhile and just have a thoroughly relaxed, pleasurable vacation?"

"Let's do—I'd like dealing with nothing tougher than what to eat for breakfast, whether to go swimming or sailing...."

"So be it. See you tomorrow, love."

Ashley was right. Her parents didn't object at all to her leaving them to join Zachary.

* * *

The moment they entered the lobby of the Mendez Hotel, Ashley could feel herself begin to relax. The Spanish architecture, with its soothing combination of stucco and tile and large potted plants, created a wide-open feeling, enhanced by great stretches of glass visually connecting it, in every direction, with the outdoors. The colors were pastel, soft and cool. Everyone was very casually dressed and there was a noticeable lack of rushing. Looking straight through the lobby, Ashley could see a ribbon of white sand and the gleaming blue of the ocean beyond.

They had scarcely stepped inside when a voice called, "Zachary! *¡Mi amigo!*" A tall man with brown skin further darkened by the sun and a brilliant smile that split his face and creased it with pleasure hurried forward to clasp Zach in a hearty bear hug.

"Carlos, how good to see you." Zachary returned the hug, then stepped back to take a good look at the man. "You look terrific—much better than the last time I saw you."

Carlos laughed, his eyes crinkling up with appealing humor. "*Sí.* I was one unhappy man then. Now, you can see, it is much different."

Zach turned to Ashley. "Carlos, meet Ashley Grainger. Ashley, this is my friend, Carlos Mendez."

Ashley's hand was being pumped in a joyous burst of enthusiasm. "I am very happy to meet you. You are, Zachary tells me, very famous."

She grinned. "Maybe not all that famous, if he had to tell you. I'm delighted to meet you, *Señor* Mendez."

"*Por favor*, Carlos. What is it you say? A friend of Zachary's is also a friend of mine?" Ashley had no time to reply before he went on. "He saved my hotel...and so he saved my life! I am most grateful!" He held up his hand and snapped his fingers, calling to a bellhop for assistance. "Come, we take you to your rooms. You must get into something cool."

Ashley followed the others, enjoying the obvious affection and esteem in which Carlos held Zachary. They got off the elevator at the tenth floor, the hotel's top floor, and walked to the end of the corridor. Carlos unlocked the door and handed Zach the key. "Here you are, *mi amigo*. Stay as long as you are able, with my compliments."

Zachary, after a brief hesitation, smiled and clapped Carlos on the back. "Thank you, Carlos. It's extremely generous of you. Ashley and I are both badly in need of a rest."

Carlos beamed his pleasure. "Ah, then our island is the right place. Sleep, swim, take in the sun, eat and sleep some more! You Americanos run too fast. You must learn to take time. What is the word?" He frowned in concentration, then his face creased again in the wonderful smile. "Stroll! That is it. Stroll instead of run. You last longer." The bellhop had placed all the bags inside and, with Carlos's nod of permission, left them. "Now, I go. I will see you tonight at the party?"

"You will see us."

With a deep bow to Ashley, Carlos headed back down the hall and turned the corner to the elevator.

They watched until he disappeared from view, then entered the room or, as it turned out, rooms. Ashley gave a little gasp as they looked around. "I do believe, my love, that your friend has given us the penthouse suite."

"I do believe you're right. I was wondering whether to protest the extravagant gift, then decided it would offend him if I did." He indicated the rooms with an expansive gesture. "Like I told you—stick with me, kid."

Ashley wandered through the sumptuous living room, with sliding glass doors leading onto a wide balcony overlooking the ocean, into a large, elegant bedroom, which, in turn, led to an elaborate bath and dressing area, complete with whirlpool, sauna and a shower with more heads than a centipede had legs. "Gotta hand it to you, Mr. Jordan. You have the right kind of friends."

Zachary joined her, catching her up in a light embrace. "And there's more. There's another bedroom and bath on the other side of the living room, with the same layout, and there's a refrigerator full of cold drinks and a telephone nearby for room service."

"Gadzooks, we could hole up for days."

"Exactly what I was thinking." He turned her to him. "Do you believe that we're actually here, away from all outside pressures, for eight whole days?" His eyes took on a wickedly sensual gleam. "I have a terrific idea; why don't we unpack our suitcases, and then use the shower in this bathroom, the whirlpool in the other, toss for the sauna and try both beds to see which one we'll sleep in?"

She slid her arms around his waist. "I think that's an excellent idea. After all, we want to be fair."

"Oh yes, that we do."

The reception was on the tiled patio outside a large ballroom. They heard the music of the band as they walked around the lovely oval pool, holding hands and smiling happily at the star-bedecked night. Soft lights shone out of the room, and flaming torches surrounded the terrace. Zachary put his arm around Ashley and leaned to whisper, "This is the last time I share you with anyone for the next eight days."

She raised her face to his, tantalizingly close. "Promise?"

"Promise."

They crossed the patio to greet Carlos and offer their appreciation of the beautiful suite. From that moment on, Ashley experienced a phenomenon she hadn't encountered for some time—almost total anonymity. In this setting, Zachary was the star, and, with the exception of two Americans who were somewhat acquainted with the musical theater, she was simply the woman with Zachary. She spent the evening smiling sweetly as they were introduced to Carlos's friends, listening to repeated rave reviews about Zachary's prowess in the legal field. On several occasions, she was addressed as Mrs. Jordan and was amazed at how good it felt to be taken for Zachary's wife. She mentally relaxed into the role, pretending, in her heart, it was so. It was a temptingly attractive part to play....

As she danced with Zach after dinner, held close in his arms, Ashley was enveloped in a happiness so encompassing, so complete, that nothing else seemed remotely important. How had she thought it mattered, any of the rest of it, as long as she had a love like this? She snuggled more closely and whispered, "I'm so happy. At this very moment, life feels entirely complete."

He rubbed his chin against her hair. "Yes. I feel that, too. Ashley, you're becoming as necessary to me as the air I breathe."

There was a long pause and Ashley was certain that he must be, as she was, recalling their vow to avoid serious issues. Just as well, she thought, because if he asked her to marry him right now, she'd say yes without hesitation. And how could she know for sure how much her answer would be based on lasting certainties and how much on the aura of unreality, the absence of obligations and the hypnotic beat of the music?

The song ended, and Carlos came to claim Ashley for a dance, ending, for the time being, any such speculations.

The days flowed into one another, each an extension of perfection. Ashley and Zachary bartered their way through the old town, honing their bargaining skills by buying colorful shirts and gauzy dresses and cheaply made jewelry, all of which they knew they'd never use, but had great fun purchasing. They had a fascinating tour of the ruins of Chinchen Itzi, managing to survive the trip with minimal sunburn. They danced at the local nightclub and ate fresh fish and drank Margueritas. They swam and snorkeled and sailed. And made love. The delicious sort of lovemaking born of having no demands on their time other than the complete enjoyment of giving and receiving pleasure. Each rediscovered the delight of the other's steady company, and as the end of the week encroached, they were both thoroughly convinced they belonged together. Which left them with only two unspoken questions: where and how.

Ashley stood on their balcony, watching the waves rise and curl. "Tomorrow. It doesn't seem possible." She glanced over her shoulder as Zach came outside to join her. "Couldn't we stay here forever?"

"I suppose we could. I could have some money transferred to one of the local banks, and we could buy a hacienda of our own and set up housekeeping."

"Wouldn't that be wonderful!"

His tone was sober. "I don't know. I've had several clients who tried to turn vacation magic into everyday reality. It was, in each case, a terrible mistake."

She leaned her head back against his chest. "Why does everything seem so much clearer, so much simpler, when you're away from home?"

"That's why people take vacations, to put aside their problems for a while and give themselves retrenching time." His fingers closed around her arms. "It's been so good, Ashley. I wish it *could* go on forever."

She turned into his embrace. "You haven't asked me to marry you since we got here. I was sort of wishing you would." The words seemed to have slipped past her screening process, bursting out without the restrictions of practical consideration. Now what, Ashley? she asked herself; if he does ask you, what do you say? She shivered, suddenly chilled.

Zachary watched the swift changes of expression on her face and knew what was causing them. The brief flood of hopeful joy her words had brought quickly ebbed, leaving him saddened. "I think we'd best avoid the mistake those clients of mine made," he said quietly. "I'll ask you after we get home, when you can look your life square in its workaday face. I don't want an answer you'll regret as soon as the plane touches down in New York."

She lay her cheek on his chest. "Why do you have to be so darned practical? Can't you just sweep me off my feet and drag me off to the justice of the peace? It'd be so much easier if I had no choice."

He chuckled. "I'd have to polish my armor plating and saddle my white charger."

She laughed. "That reminds me of the time Matt said you should have thrown me over your shoulder and carried me off into the sunset, and I told him that only happened in Western movies, and besides, if you had, he'd have had to find a new lyricist."

"And what did Matt say to that?"

"That I'd probably steal your horse and ride back to town in time to write the next show." The moment she said it, she could have bitten off her tongue.

Zachary stiffened, ever so slightly. "And there, as the bard put it, lies the rub." He stepped back, dropping his arms. Her whole body felt bereft. "We'd better get going. It's almost time for our dinner reservation."

She sighed. Suddenly it felt as if their vacation was already over. Time—the archcriminal of intrusion. But there was another, just as bad: reality.

Chapter Twelve

They were on a direct flight back to New York. Ashley moved closer to Zachary and lay her head against his shoulder. "I wish you didn't have to fly right on to Boston. It's going to be awful to kiss you goodbye on the plane and leave with you still sitting in your seat."

"I know. It's a hell of a way to run a love affair." In response to his tone, she lifted her head to look at him. He was frowning.

"If you weren't going to be so busy, I could come to Boston for a visit."

"That's tempting, but it wouldn't do much good. I'll spend a couple of days in the office catching up, then hit the road again. Have to see clients in Toronto and Chicago."

"Now, see? You're always talking about *my* schedule, and you have a pretty busy one yourself." She said it in a teasing voice but knew, the moment he replied, that it had triggered thoughts that were far from frivolous.

"Ashley, I've used up an inordinate amount of what should have been working time traveling back and forth to New York and taking days off to be with you. I do have a full professional life of my own that's been sorely neglected lately, and I'm a little young for retirement."

"I'm sorry. I didn't mean to question the importance of your career."

"I know you didn't. I'm just feeling a little edgy. It's hard, after being together constantly, to think about going back on that damned 'now and again' schedule."

They were teetering perilously close to a subject she wasn't at all eager to address. She seemed always to be the one with her defenses up. She was at the top of the heap in a profession she loved. Why was it automatically she who was expected to back away from her career to solve a conflict?

"You're awfully quiet." He took hold of her hand. "What're you thinking about?"

"About my going home to my place in New York and you to yours in Boston. And what we're going to do about it." There, it was said. Laid out on the bargaining table. Careful, she warned herself, he's an expert in the field of arbitration. God, she made them sound like a couple of antagonists struggling for supremacy.

"Yes. We can't dance around it much longer, can we?"

"I suppose not. But the alternative scares me to death."

"Is the alternative that certain?" He looked at her, his eyes deep wells of unreadable messages.

"No, that's not what I meant." Wasn't it? "Zachary, why can't we just keep on the way we are for a while longer, give ourselves time to figure something out."

"And what is time going to tell us that we don't already know? That it's a hell of a long way from Beacon Street to Broadway?"

"It's only an hour's plane ride." It sounded so feeble, that statement, so beside the point. It was. But she couldn't bear looking in the direction the real point led them.

"Ashley, we can't both hang in some sort of dating limbo forever. At least, I can't. I want to have a family. And I sure don't want to start one at the age of fifty. I know you're not as keen as I am about having children..."

"Zachary, I'd love to have children. It's just..."

"That it would interfere with your career?"

It was too late to hedge, to try to tiptoe around the issue to safer ground. She turned in her seat, facing him squarely. "If we lived in New York, it wouldn't interfere all that much. I'd be able to do my work and have a family too. But I don't see how I could do it from Boston."

He nodded. "You probably couldn't. And I have to tell you, I don't want a part-time family. I can't see having to make an appointment to spend an evening with my wife and flying to another state to visit my children."

She leaned her head against the backrest. "Oh, damn! It always comes back to the same place, doesn't it?"

"It seems to." He squeezed her fingers. "I told you I'd ask that special question after we got home. We'd better both give a lot of thought to what the answer should be. If there is one."

She closed her eyes for a moment, suddenly almost as tired as she'd been during rehearsals. More accurately, *she* had to give a lot of thought to the answer. Because from what Zachary had just said, if they were to marry she was the one whose life would change drastically. She opened her eyes and looked over at him, conscious of her fingers intertwined with his. "I love you, Zachary."

"And I love you. I want us to spend the rest of our lives together."

"Me, too."

"Why does it have to be so damned hard?"

She shook her head, unable to come up with a single reason.

The ride from the airport passed in a blur of swirling thoughts and feelings. When she reached her apartment, she thanked the doorman for helping her with her luggage, closed and locked the door and headed straight for the bathroom for a shower and shampoo. Maybe that would help refresh her flagging spirits.

When she came out, a towel wrapped around her wet head, she went to the kitchen to put on water for a cup of tea. It was then that she noticed the red light flashing on the answering machine on the small desk in the corner. Before listening to the recordings, she waited for the water to boil and then for her tea to steep. She found an unopened package of Pepperidge Farm cookies in the cupboard and took a couple of them, along with her steaming cup, to the desk. When she was comfortably settled, with a pencil and paper ready, she pushed the rewind lever, then Play.

"Ashley, this is Jerry. I know you're on vacation. Just thought I'd let you know we've already had inquiries about foreign performances of the play. No great hurry, but call me."

She wrote, "Call Jerry."

"Hi, babe. Welcome home. Amy and I are either coming back on April twenty-sixth or never, haven't decided yet. Got an incredible idea for a musical. If we return I'll tell you about it. Love ya."

"Send flowers to Matt & Amy on April 26th." She wondered what the idea was, and why Matt was thinking about business on his honeymoon. Her curiosity wasn't overly piqued. She and Matt usually made their way through quite a number of possibilities before a subject felt just right, and heaven knows she was far from ready to dive into another project.

She took a sip of her tea and a bite of cookie while the tape wore on. A few beeps, followed by a dial tone—people who still wouldn't talk to a machine.

"Ashley, hon. This is Audrey." Ashley straightened up. Audrey never called her; it was always her brother Jim who made contact. "This is Thursday. Get back to me as soon as you can."

Ashley switched off the machine and reached for the phone in the same movement. She dropped the receiver and bent to pick it up. Something was wrong. She knew it.

"Hello?"

"Audrey, this is Ashley. I just got home."

"Oh, Ashley, I'm so glad you're back. Uh, something's happened..."

"What is it, Audrey? Dad, Mother, Jim?"

"No. It's Johnny, honey. He's had a bad accident. Something about a net out of place when he jumped from a roof."

Oh God, no. Not Johnny. Not her brother. "Is it bad?"

"Yes." The word cut straight through. "Your parents are out there and so is Jim. Johnny's holding on, but nothing's certain yet."

Ashley could barely breathe. Johnny. Oh, God. "Where is he?" Her fingers shook as she wrote the name of the hospital and the hotel her family was staying in. "Audrey, thanks. I'm going to hang up so I can call the airport."

"Yes, of course. Good luck, Ashley, and give him my love."

There was a plane leaving at six-thirty, exactly two hours away. She booked a seat, called for a room reservation and flew into motion. Ignoring the stack of still packed suitcases, she threw some necessities into a duffel bag and called a cab. Before she had time to think twice about it, she was back in the air, heading west.

By the time they landed in Los Angeles, Ashley's nerves were poking holes in her skin. The accumulation of hours of flight and escalating tension had her as taut as a high-pitched bow string. The moment the engines were turned off, she grabbed her bag from beneath the seat and made for the door. It wasn't until she was in a taxi that she took a deep breath and considered her options. Even by California time, it was close to 11:00 p.m. The chances of her getting in to see Johnny were exceedingly slim, but she had to go to the hospital just to be near him, to try to find out how he was.

When she stepped out of the elevator on the fourth floor and saw the sign directing the way to the intensive care unit, her heart hung in her chest, feeling too heavy to beat. For as long as she could remember, she and Johnny had clung together, mavericks in their own ways, both of them creative, dramatic and just different enough to suffer the strange loneliness that was the price of being out of the ordinary. They'd used the telephone to insure that their closeness would never be damaged by the miles between them. The thought of a Johnny-less world seemed too dismal to be borne.

The nurse on duty was sweet and very helpful. She pulled Johnny's chart and scanned it, her face struggling to remain impassive. "His condition is...holding." Ashley's breath caught at the hesitation. She could read the sympathy in the other woman's eyes when she glanced up.

"Is there any chance I could just peek in at him? I'd be very quiet."

The nurse bit her lip, her eyes scanning the hall. "I'm not supposed to let anyone in at night, but what the heck. You've come such a long way, and I don't see what harm it can do. He's in a private room." Mumbling her thanks several times, Ashley followed her down the corridor, frightening in its stark whiteness. They stopped in front of room 435. "Remember, he's in a full cast, and he slips in and out of consciousness. Don't expect too much." Her eyes were gentle and her voice cautionary. Ashley got the message. He's in bad shape. Be prepared.

When she stepped inside the room, she had to stifle a gasp. Every inch of him was covered in white plaster except his face and his hands, and even they looked like survivors of a cat fight. "Oh, God."

The nurse patted her on the arm, then left her alone with the still form of her brother.

Ashley sat on the chair by the bed and reached for the limp fingers. Could this really be her brother, the one who had never been able to stay still more than a few seconds? Would all those awful tubes sustain his life? If he was to be too severely damaged, she said a silent prayer that they wouldn't. She knew Johnny wasn't afraid of death. She also knew how terrified he was of physical impairment.

She sat there for about an hour, holding his hand and praying, until the nurse came to tell her she'd have to leave before the resident made his late rounds.

When she got to the hotel, she left a message for her parents, telling them she was there, then went up to her room, undressed quickly and fell into bed. She was asleep almost instantly.

The shrill ring of the telephone awakened her. Still groggy, she fumbled for the receiver. "Hello?"

"Ashley, darling."

"Mom. Hi." She struggled to a sitting position and looked at the bedside clock. Nine-fifteen. They'd let her sleep in. Her parents were always awake by six.

"We're so glad you're here, dear. I'm sorry to wake you up."

"I'm glad you did."

"Well, we're about to go down to breakfast, and thought you might want to join us."

"Oh, yes. I'll get dressed as fast as I can. Shall I meet you downstairs?"

"Yes, why don't you? We'll sit toward the door, so you can see us."

She took a quick shower and dressed in slacks and a short-sleeved sweater. Taking time only to brush her hair and put on some lipstick, she grabbed her purse and headed downstairs. She saw them the minute she entered the restaurant. The terrible stress was clearly etched on their faces—her mother and father, and Jim, the favored one. She'd felt envy toward him all too often, probably natural in a sibling who never quite measured up to the one who always did. But none of that mattered now. When one of them was threatened, the family pulled together into a cohesive unit of love and support.

After they'd kissed and hugged and called the waitress over to take Ashley's order, they resettled themselves in the curved booth, asking minimal questions about when she arrived and how she'd managed to make it so quickly after getting back from Cancun. When the small talk was exhausted, only the one paramount question remained.

Ashley took a deep breath, steeling herself for the answer before she asked, "How is he?"

Jim's face was drawn with tiredness and unmistakable signs of anxiety. Her brother, the doctor, was worried. Knots formed in her stomach. "The most troubling injury is the skull fracture. As far as the rest of the injuries go, I've been assured they're not as bad as they appear to be."

Ashley listened in shocked horror as her brother, in his doctor's calm voice, chronicled the broken bones. How could anyone survive such trauma?

"Bad as it sounds, Ashley, all of those bones will mend, and with a relatively short period of physical therapy, he'll be all right. If, of course, they've succeeded in relieving the pressure on his brain."

It was too much for her. All her resolutions to maintain a stiff upper lip so she wouldn't add to her parents' burden dissolved in a flood of tears. Three sets of arms reached out to comfort her.

They finished breakfast and went to the hospital, forming a pattern that remained unbroken for three days. Breakfast, vigil at the hospital; lunch and a rest, more vigil at the hospital; dinner, a shorter stay at the hospital, then back to the hotel and to bed. Ashley talked to Zachary several times, keeping him up to date on the progress—or lack of it. Johnny drifted into consciousness now and then but seemed vague and disoriented, barely recognizing any of them.

By the fourth morning, the routine was almost automatic. So was the rhythm of fear that her heart picked up as they neared the fourth floor. Would he still be alive? As they got out of the elevator, a white-clad man started to enter, but was halted by Jim's "Dr. Caldwell! I'm glad we ran into you."

The doctor stepped back and let the elevator go. "Good morning, Dr. Grainger." He greeted their parents and acknowledged an introduction to Ashley with a smile. "Oh, yes. Johnny told me about you. He was hoping you'd be coming this morning."

Jim's hand shot out to grasp the doctor's arm. "*Johnny* told you?"

Dr. Caldwell's smile widened. "Yes. He has regained full consciousness and his reactions appear to be fully normal. I think it's pretty safe to give a good prognosis."

For a moment, there appeared to be danger of a mass collapse as Ashley's knees turned weak and her parents both sagged in relief. But the rush of joy quickly bolstered them.

"Thank God." Her father's face reflected the happiness they all felt. "Can we see him?"

"Yes, of course. It might be easier for him if you didn't all go in at once. He can't do any neck swiveling, you know." His chuckle was the best indication yet that the crisis was over. Ashley waited impatiently as her parents went in to visit. When they emerged, fifteen minutes later, their faces were wreathed in smiles. Her mother came over to report to Ashley and Jim. "He's fully alert. It seems a miracle. Even his sense of humor is intact!" She took Ashley's hand. "He's anxious to see you, dear."

She turned to Jim. "Do you mind if I go in alone? I won't stay very long."

He patted her on the shoulder. "You go right ahead, and take your time. Just the sight of you will be a tonic to him."

Ashley hesitated, chagrined for the moment at his automatic acknowledgement of their closeness. She was embarrassed to realize she'd never given much thought to how Jim must feel about being excluded from their tightly fused friendship. She sighed. There was a price to be paid for everything. Even being the favorite child.

When Ashley walked into Johnny's room, she had to bite her lip to keep herself from crying like a baby in relief. His eyes jumped right to her, open and alert. And he smiled. Never had a smile brought more sunshine into a room.

"Hi, sis."

She moved to his bedside on numbed legs. "Johnny. Haven't I always warned you to look before you leap?"

His grin looked incongruous in the middle of all that white. "You know me—never had enough sense to listen to warnings."

Ashley sank into the chair by his bed, fighting like mad to stop the tears that had risen to her eyes, and losing the battle. "Oh, God, Johnny." Further words were blocked by the constriction in her throat.

"Hey, lady, you'll run your mascara. Here, hold my hand. I'd take yours, but they've put me in bodily confinement." His face sobered as she took his hand and squeezed his fingers. "Don't cry, sis. I'm going to make it. The doctor thinks I'll be in good enough shape to go back to work in about six months, if I want to."

Her mouth dropped open in horror. "You're not thinking of going back to that madness, surely!"

He frowned for a second, then laughed. "Damn. I just tried to shake my head. Are you sure I'm not already dead, and they've made a mummy out of me?"

She had to smile. Her mother was right; his sense of humor was still in place. "You dip. You promised all of us you'd quit that stunt-man stuff before you reached thirty. You're already a year late."

"Yeah, yeah. Just like all the rest, making me feel over the hill when I'm still a young pup."

"Johnny..." Ashley's voice held all the concern she really felt. The thought of his returning to stunt work was intolerable.

His expression sobered. "Hey. Don't worry, hon. I'm out of it, I promise. I almost lost the whole package, and that's way too high a price to pay for holding on to a hazardous occupation just because you get a kick out of it. I happen to enjoy life, and it's time for me to take time for other parts of it." He grinned. "I might even give Leslie a call and see if she's still interested if I swear to reform."

Ashley rose enough to kiss him. "I love you so much, you crazy galoot. I don't know what I'd do if I lost you."

"Hey, sis, don't get all mushy. Only the good die young. At least that's what I've been counting on all these years. 'Course, after all this, I guess I'd better take another look at that moldy old saying."

"Will you miss the work terribly?"

"Yeah, probably. At least for a while. But, hell. There's lots more to life than rolling cars and jumping off high buildings." His eyes narrowed slightly. "Even, I'd guess, than writing hit plays."

"How did that get in there?"

He smiled. "I'd shrug, but I can't. I dunno. Been thinking a lot about you since you called that night. Just been hoping you wouldn't someday figure you'd passed up too much, that's all."

Her eyes dropped. "Funny you should mention that."

"Uh-huh. How was the trip to Mexico?"

"Wonderful. Oh, Johnny, I love him so damned much! But I still don't know what to do."

"Yeah, it's a tough one. Giving up a career like yours would be damned difficult, more so than mine. There're lots of stunt men in Hollywood. But top play writers and lyricists on Broadway? Uh-uh."

"You're the only one in the family who understands. Mom and Dad think the decision should be easy."

"Yeah, I know. But they can't live your life, you have to do that."

"Oh, damn. Johnny, what should I do?"

"Come on, sis, I can't live your life either." He raised his eyebrows in question. "How would it feel to cut it off with Zach again?"

"I don't think I'd survive."

"You may have just answered your own question."

She nodded. She may have, at that. "I guess I'd better go out so Jim can come in. He's obviously been a nervous wreck beneath all that professional calm."

"Yeah. Good man, our brother." With one last eye-to-eye agreement, Ashley kissed him again and left the room.

She stood outside the door and leaned against the wall, her mind churning. They'd come so close to losing Johnny, so awfully close! It pushed one thought to the forefront of her mind. People you love are the most important part of your life. Suddenly she was absolutely consumed by the need to be with Zachary, to be held in his arms, to be engulfed in his love.

With a sigh, she headed toward the waiting room, her mind miles away: in Boston, Massachusetts, to be precise. When she reached her destination and stepped into the room, she froze. Zachary was seated between her mother and father, talking earnestly to them and to Jim. As soon as he saw her, he rose.

"Hello, Ashley."

With a cry of thankfulness, she ran into his embrace, giving herself over entirely to the unbridled joy of seeing him there. He swept her into his arms, holding her tight, his cheek against her hair. "Oh, Zachary, I can't believe you're really here. I'm so glad to see you. I had no idea you'd come!"

He touched her cheek with his fingers, barely able to control his urge to kiss her hungrily. "I knew how scared you'd be, and I wanted to be with you earlier, but I got here as soon as I could."

She looked up at him, her eyes full of the gratitude she felt. "Thank you."

"You're more than welcome." He glanced around at her family and let his arms drop. "It sounds as though I arrived on a good morning. How's Johnny?"

"Wonderful." She shook her head and gave a confused laugh. "Terrible. I mean, he's still funny and lovely and completely Johnny with one major exception. He's immobile." Her eyes twinkled. "He asked me to assure him he hadn't already died and been turned into a mummy."

Jim hooted and stood up. "That's it. He's back with us, sure enough. If you'll excuse me, I'd like to go in and bedevil my kid brother." They all nodded assent and Jim headed for the door.

By the time Jim came back with all the lines in his face relaxed into a relieved smile and Zachary went in for a short visit, it was clear that Johnny was in need of some sleep, so they all headed back to the hotel for lunch and a rest.

Ashley rode with Zachary in his rented car, snuggled close beside him, her head on his shoulder, her hand on his thigh. Never within memory had she been so happy to see someone. Johnny's near miss had unnerved her to a point that made itself fully felt only now, when she knew the crisis was over and he would recover. The suspension of all that fear left her limp and unutterably grateful for Zachary's presence. "I'll bet Johnny was surprised to see you."

"Yes, that he was. Looks like he did a real number on himself." Zachary covered her hand with his. "This has been rough on you, hasn't it? I know how much you love Johnny."

"I'm just so thankful that he's going to be all right." And that Zachary was beside her. Her love of loves.

They had a nice lunch, full of the jubilance borne of the encouraging hospital visit. Ashley couldn't miss the heightened level of her parents' hopefulness. Not only was their son going to recover, but their daughter had brought this wonderful man back into their lives. Boy, talk about acceptance. As a potential son-in-law, Zachary had "approved" stamped all over him! But Ashley couldn't blame them. As a potential husband, she had to give him the same rating. She tried to focus on the factors in her life that had seemed too vital to let go of, but New York, the theater, the excitement of creating, the fun of seeing a show take form, all seemed so remote, so... nonessential. Her eyes moved to Zachary. But him? Essential. Absolutely essential.

"So, Ashley, dear, how long *are* you staying?"

She stared at her mother in confusion. "I'm sorry. What did you ask?"

Doris laughed. "My, you were a long way off! Zachary just said he'd wait till you returned east to go with you, and I was wondering when that would be."

Her eyes met Zachary's and she smiled. How considerate of him to once again put aside his business demands to be with her when she needed him. Had he been more willing to make sacrifices for their relationship than she? "I suppose there's no real reason to stay. We'll see Johnny again this evening. After that, well, it's obviously going to be a long time before he's up and around. It's easy enough to come back if he needs me. But, heaven knows, one thing my brother has no shortage of is friends! He'll get so much tender loving care he may decide to become a permanent invalid!"

So it was decided that they'd catch an afternoon plane the following day. Jim, too, had to get back to his patients. Her mother and father would stay a few more days.

That night they were all thoroughly pooped and went to bed early. Zachary, for the sake of appearances, had taken his own room. But very soon after everyone had retired for the night, Ashley heard a knock on her door. With her heart beating in anticipation, she went to open it, moving eagerly into her lover's embrace as he stepped inside and kicked the door shut behind him. All the awful anxiety of the last days dropped away; all the uncertainty of the last months seemed to disappear too. He was everything to her: home, family, acceptance, security, love. Her biggest need in life was to be with him.

She looked up at him, her heart in her eyes. "How can I tell you how much it meant to see you in that waiting room today? I love you so much."

"No more than I love you. That wouldn't be possible." He kissed her temple, very tenderly. "I can't believe how much I've missed you. I'd grown accustomed to your face. And various other parts of you." His hands ran over her as his mouth hungrily sought hers. She opened her lips to his questing tongue and curved her body into his, winding her arms tightly around his neck.

His head lifted, and his midnight eyes, opaque with desire, bore into her. "You have far too many clothes on." She raised her arms so he could easily slide her flimsy nightgown over her head, shivering slightly as the cool air brushed her flesh.

This moment, this pinpoint of time, held the extreme essence of happiness, the peak experience of loving and being loved. Eagerly, she unzipped the top of his sweatsuit and pushed it off, letting her hands enjoy the feel of his firm shoulders as she did. He untied the matching pants, let them drop, kicked them to one side. His mouth laid claim to hers once again, his strong fingers moving over her back, then sliding down to cup her soft round buttocks.

Ashley was submerged in the warm caress of their caring, happy beyond measure to be in the arms of this man she loved so totally. She ran her hands over the taut, sinewy muscles of his back, digging her fingers into the firm flesh, flushing with excitement at his low growl of pleasure.

With a deep moan of need, he lifted her off the floor and carried her to the bed, bending as he lay her down to search out the tips of her breasts with his tongue, sending quivering shock waves through her body. His hands roamed the silky skin of her hips and thighs as his lips pressed and pulled at her tightening nipples.

She ran her hand up the inside of his thighs to cup him in her palm, smiling at the gasp that escaped his lips. Her hand moved relentlessly, increasing the girth of his arousal.

His lips moved down to the satiny flesh of her belly, then beyond. Ashley cried out, her body convulsing with ecstasy. The delectable torment sent steaming blood rushing through her veins, pouring fuel on the flaming need of her desire.

With a cry she pulled him up to her, guiding him to close all gaps, joining body to body, love to love, binding them each to each. With one great, heaving shudder, they rose to a mutual fulfillment and the union was complete.

"Oh, Zachary," she breathed, overwhelmed by the dimension of her happiness.

He raised himself to his elbows and kissed her eyes and her cheeks and each lip, separately. Their eyes met and held, gleaming the wonder back and forth, a silent vow of faith. "Ashley." Her name was a whisper, a pledge.

She gazed up at him, so full of the marvel of their love she could think of nothing else, could care about nothing else. "You haven't done what you promised yet."

His eyes narrowed thoughtfully. "And what is that?"

"You said you'd ask me to marry you when we got back from Cancun."

He looked down at her, his blue-black eyes blazing trails to her heart. When he spoke, his tone was hushed, sober. "Will you marry me?"

"Yes. Oh, yes!"

There was a great sigh, a duet of joy, as they clung together.

They fell asleep, still interlocked in their oneness.

Chapter Thirteen

The following morning at breakfast, they announced their engagement to her parents and her brother Jim, which set off a positive eruption of enthusiasm. Hugs and handshakes and delighted exclamations abounded. Ashley, for perhaps the first time in her life, felt bathed in her parents' wholehearted admiration and showered by their unrestrained blessings. The applause for this, she ruefully acknowledged, vastly exceeded any she'd received for the seemingly inconsequential act of mounting a hit show on Broadway. At last, after all these years, she'd won their full approbation. It felt good.

When they said goodbye, her mother was still beaming like a floodlight, already making wedding lists and planning menus. Her father kept slapping Zachary on the back and jokingly calling him "son." Jim, a true product of his environment who firmly accepted the premise that a woman's place was in the home, hugged her several times, offering his sincere congratulations.

Before going to the airport, they stopped by the hospital to tell Johnny. He grinned at them, his eyes alight. "Hey. Now that's terrific. You two belong together, that's for sure." He winked at Ashley. "Get this guy to draw up a good marriage contract, sis, one you can both live with."

She and Zachary stared at him in confusion. "Marriage contract? Why would we want one of those?"

"Not for money, that's for sure. But you guys have to arbitrate a workable life-style. Might be challenging, but, hey, knowing you're committed to each other should brook all obstacles."

When they left him, Ashley and Zachary were still perplexed and, in truth, a little uneasy. They both knew what Johnny was referring to, and they knew it required discussion. But neither of them was ready to chance pricking their golden bubble of happiness.

About halfway to New York, Zachary, which great trepidation, asked, "Ashley, what about your career?"

She turned to look at him, savoring the sight of his handsome, aristocratic face, those fathomless eyes that promised such enchantment. "I know it'll have to be drastically limited, but that's part of my decision. Our marriage will take top priority. I don't see why Matt can't write the music in New York while I write the lyrics in Boston. There're always the wonders of the telephone and overnight mail."

"Were you serious about taking at least a year off?"

"Oh, sure. I can't imagine why either of us would want to start another show for a year or so. We need a rest." She leaned over to kiss his cheek. "And I need time to wallow in all this happiness."

Zach smiled and took her hand in his. "We can look for a house as soon as you'd like. Maybe even decide to build. And, before long, we'll probably want to think about a family."

The thought of a tiny, adorable baby of her own warmed her with gladness. "We'll have beautiful children! I hope they look just like you."

"No fair. I want a little girl who's the image of her mother." He frowned, a look of uncertainty crossing his face. "Ashley, what if you find it can't be done? That it's impossible, at any level, to have your career and raise a family at the same time?"

"Then Matt will have to find another collaborator."

"Are you sure?"

"Zach, I've thought about this for a very long time. Nobody can have everything. And I just simply couldn't endure our breaking up again. I'm sure I'll love being a wife and a mother. I can't imagine being married to anyone but you, and it's your children I want to bear. I can't remember when I've felt so completely sure and so completely happy. If my career has to go, then that's a price I'm willing to pay." The words flowed out easily, and felt right in the saying, and Ashley was aglow with certainty. Everywhere, that is, but for a tiny knot in the pit of her stomach.

They had to agree to limiting their contact to telephone calls for the next couple of weeks, since Zachary had become disastrously behind in his work schedule. Once again, Ashley had to leave him at the airport and head home by herself—but this time without that awful sense of aloneness. She was part of a whole now, only temporarily separated from her other half.

It took a good while to make her way through the mail and the phone messages, accumulated, as they were, since her departure for Cancun. When she called Jerry, they agreed to meet the following day for lunch.

When she entered the Pen and Pencil restaurant, he was there waiting for her. He kissed her and gave her a welcoming hug. "My goodness, Miss Ashley, you look brown as a Hershey bar and just as delicious."

She returned both the kiss and the hug. "Just goes to show what fresh air, sunshine and relaxation can do." She beamed at him. "Not to mention happiness."

They were seated quickly, and Jerry leaned toward her, his face one big question mark. "Tell me all about your trip. I've never endured such a dearth of gossip in my life. Matt off on a honeymoon and everyone else rushing in ten different directions. God, it's good to see you."

To her surprise, she felt quite teary. She'd had no idea till this moment how much she'd missed these people with whom she'd shared, on practically a daily basis, over a year of her life. "Did Craig decide to direct the Sheperd play?"

"Yes. Bless him, he's vowed to be available in time for Goulden's comedy."

"How is that coming?"

"Terrific. Joe Sanders has decided that his first investment on Broadway was clearly a winner, so he's taking a second plunge. He's brought in two of his friends, and believe me, that man has some nice rich friends! Poor Zachary, he's getting besieged with star-struck clients, not to mention a producer, a hoofer and a theater owner."

"Good grief, I didn't realize he'd taken on all those people."

"I think it started out with that old routine of a friend of a friend and just grew."

She grinned at him, unable to resist the perfect opening for her big news. "That's not all, Jerry. He's also about to take on a lyricist. As a wife, that is."

His face split in a huge smile. "Sweetie! Now that's good news! What a lucky guy!"

"I'm pretty darn lucky myself."

"I agree. He's a heck of a fine man, Ashley, congratulations!" He signaled the waiter and insisted on buying a bottle of Dom Perignon to celebrate her announcement.

Much to her relief, there were no questions about the possible implications of her marriage. For some reason, she just didn't feel like getting into that. Besides, she owed it to Matt to discuss it with him first. She told Jerry about their lovely vacation in Cancun and about rushing out to see her injured brother, and he responded with appropriate envy toward the first and sincere concern about the second. Once they were through the general catching up, the talk naturally turned to theater. "How's the show going? Still playing to full houses, I hope?"

"Hell, yes. Those are the hottest tickets in town. You're a genius, love; you and that crazy bastard you collaborate with. Broadway hasn't seen the likes of you two since Lerner and Loewe. I'm proud to be associated with you. I mean that."

A lump of mammoth proportions had formed in Ashley's throat. She was receiving one of the greatest compliments of her life. Why did she feel so strange, so...bereft? "Thank you, Jerry. Those are words I'll always treasure."

"You deserve them. Hey, you probably haven't heard the news. Hold on to your wig, sweetie, this'll blow you away!"

She leaned toward him, her eyes wide with interest. "Tell me, tell me. Don't keep me in suspense."

They had to wait for the waiter to open and pour the champagne and for Jerry to propose a toast to her wedded bliss. "Okay, speaking of romance, this one has to go down in the annals of time as one of the most unlikely."

"Well spit it out, for goodness sake!"

"Remember what a little twerp Sammy Kirk was all through rehearsal and how he picked on that sweet girl?"

"Kelly."

"Yes, Kelly. This one'll knock your socks off. They are now the most sickeningly lovey-dovey twosome who ever smarmed their way across a stage. They're getting married in two weeks, on a Monday, so they can have a one-night honeymoon!"

"You have to be kidding!"

"Oh, no, my dear. Love has bloomed, spraying its sweet nectar over all, stickying up the whole cast. And you won't know Sammy. The little son of a gun has become Mr. Wonderful. Sweet, considerate, kind. He treats Kelly like a newly exhumed treasure that requires tender care to guard its fragility. It's a real kick!''

"My God. Will wonders never cease.''

"Probably not. Now, let's order lunch and talk a little business so I can write off the meal.''

That night Jerry escorted her to the theater. It was like returning to see a beloved old friend. She inhaled the invigorating ambience. She consumed the applause like a glutton after a forced diet. During the intermission, she went backstage to have tearful reunions with the cast, fraught with emotion suitable to a three-year separation. She told everyone of her engagement and garnered their congratulations. She offered her own to Kelly and her unlikely beau, marveling at the change in Sammy. She felt engulfed in comforting familiarity and infused with renewed excitement about this show of hers, this baby of her creativity.

Jerry dropped her off at her place, promising to keep in close touch. She took the elevator to the third floor, reminding herself all the way of her mixed and multitudinous blessings. She couldn't talk to Zachary, because he was on a business trip where there'd be no chance to call for a couple of days. When she was in bed, lying in the dark, she rose to one elbow and looked out over the lights of New York City.

And she really didn't know why, but she cried herself to sleep.

Matt and Amy had extended their honeymoon trip, so the unsettling prospect of telling Matt about her coming marriage was postponed. She felt strangely adrift, caught between one country and another, trying to keep herself occupied until she arrived *somewhere*. At the end of the second week of her exile from Zachary, he called her very early in the morning.

"Good morning, my darling. I hope I didn't wake you."

"You didn't. Besides, you could call in the middle of the night. I wouldn't mind."

He chuckled. "It wasn't so long ago when that was the only time I *could* call you. It must feel good to be on a more reasonable schedule."

Ashley frowned. Did it? No. But he was right. It should. "Tell me you're coming to New York. Please." She hoped he hadn't heard that trace of desperation in her voice.

"That's exactly what I'm about to do. Why don't I pick you up about eight and we'll go to the Veau d'Or again. I'm feeling sentimental."

"Oh, Zach! That sounds wonderful! How long will you be here?"

"Let's see, it is Thursday, isn't it?" She tried to remember. Somehow the days seemed to be melting into each other. He laughed. "You can see how busy I've been, can't even keep the days straight." She hadn't been doing anything, and neither could she. "I have to catch a plane to Chicago on Sunday, so I can get together with my clients before our meeting on Monday morning. But that gives us a few days. Just think, before long we'll have every day and every night!"

When they walked into the Veau d'Or that night, Ashley was amazed to realize it had been less than four months ago that she and Zachary had met here, had rekindled their romance. And now look, they were engaged and destined to live happily ever after. They bid a cheerful hello to Charlie, the waiter, who insisted on seating them in his service area. "How about some champagne?" Zachary asked. "We certainly have plenty to celebrate."

She felt as though her smile must use up most of her face. "Lovely idea."

When Charlie had uncorked the champagne and poured it into two crystal tulip glasses, he asked, "Special event tonight?"

Zachary grinned. "Indeed. And by the time you come back to take our order, we'll be more than happy to tell you."

As Charles walked away, Ashley asked him, "Why didn't you just tell him?"

"Because—" Zachary reached into his pocket and took out a tiny box "—the prop wasn't in place." He opened the box and took out a ring. "I hope you like it, love. I had it made up out of two of my grandmother's rings." He took Ashley's hand and slipped it on her finger.

Ashley held her hand out in front of her, overwhelmed. "It's the most beautiful ring I've ever seen! Oh, Zachary, I love it!" A large square-cut diamond was surrounded by emeralds, all set in white gold. It was spectacular. "Thank you." Her eyes were full of tears. "It means even more to know it was made from stones your grandmother wore."

When Charlie returned, she stretched out her hand for his inspection, and they both grinned at his enthusiasm. He took their dinner order, then returned to tell them the champagne was on the house, an engagement present from the management.

The whole evening seemed magical and closely followed the pattern of that first night. Except that this time, after they'd made love, Zachary didn't leave. They fell asleep clasped in each other's arms, sure they'd been given permanent residence on that fabled cloud nine.

Zachary and Ashley decided they'd waited long enough—well over three years, to be accurate—for their wedding day, so they set the date for just two months in the future, on June 22. Her mother didn't protest the short notice; she was far too happy about the impending marriage to want it postponed. Zachary's parents appeared to be very happy for them, particularly, she sensed, because they'd been told of her intention to put their wedded life first.

The weeks skimmed by, one day running into the next, with scarcely enough time to *think* of all the things that needed doing, let alone get to the bottom of any of the endless lists. She went to Cedar Rapids to another reunion of friends. This one was a bridal shower, thrown in her honor, and included all her female relatives, as well as a good number of her parents' friends. This time Ashley felt a true part of the scene, sharing the same ambitions, the same motivations. She positively threw herself into the camaraderie, enjoying the unfamiliar sensation of being completely cast in a traditional woman's role. She talked about sheets and bedspreads, how to keep a cleaning woman and how to protect her husband from a diet too high in cholesterol. For the first time in her life, she felt like "one of the girls," and she reveled in the heightened sense of companionship. What in the world had made her feel so... separate... the last time she was there?

The one troublesome event in the steady stream of celebrations was when she'd had to tell Matt just what her marriage would entail. She'd put it off as long as possible, but when he and Amy had been home for a week, she knew it was past time. She asked him to come to her apartment. It was where they'd done so much of their work together, where they'd spawned so many exciting ideas, written so many songs, some of which were now played regularly on the radio and sold in volume on records.

When Matt came in, his face was aglow with the beam of a happy man, a condition that appeared to have taken permanent hold since his marriage. He headed straight for the piano bench and sat down. "You wanted to talk to me? What, have you finally come down close enough to earth to listen to my hot idea?" Matt, like Jerry, had been delighted at the news of her engagement and oblivious to the fact that it would interfere with her career. Probably, she thought, because neither of them could imagine life outside of the theater, and assumed she wouldn't either.

She sat down in the pink chair, aware that her hands were shaking. This was going to be so terribly hard; she grabbed hold of the opportunity to put it off a little longer. "It concerns a different matter. But why don't you tell me your idea? I've been anxious to hear it." The moment the words were out of her mouth, she knew they were a mistake. Thinking about a new musical wasn't going to help either of them.

But before she could change her mind and plunge into her explanation, Matt had started to play. He always liked to underscore his words with music. "Remember the old book by Robert Louis Stevenson, *The Strange Case of Dr. Jekyll and Mr. Hyde*?"

"Yes." Should she interrupt him and cut this off?

"I picked up a copy in that inn where Amy and I stayed. Hadn't ever read it, actually. I just remembered the story from that old movie they show on TV, which, of course, bears little resemblance to the book. Anyway, it blew me away. I mean, Ashley, the theme of that book is today, solidly contemporary. It's about a man who wanted so much to be entirely good, who wanted so badly to get rid of his faults and his weaknesses, that he kept working in his laboratory until he found a formula to separate his two sides, good and evil. That way old Hyde could go out and raise hell and Jekyll didn't have to suffer the guilt. Then, of course, the whole thing gets out of hand."

As he talked, Ashley grew more and more excited. Matt had already written a couple of tunes, and as he played them, lyrics jumped into place and the story began to build in her mind. Suddenly she jumped up. "No. Matt, I'm sorry, I can't afford to get involved in this, not right now."

His face was masked by disappointment. "Oh, yeah, that's right. I'm sure you don't want to think about a new musical till you get through the wedding. Tell you what, I'll ice it for a couple of months, okay?''

At that point, she had no alternative but to tell Matt, fully and truthfully, the limitations she'd promised Zach to put on her career. Including the possibility of ending it entirely. Her friend's face grew longer and longer during the telling, and her heart grew heavier and heavier. ''Matt, I know what a blow this is. If you want to consider another lyricist to work on this show, I would certainly understand.''

''Hell, Ashley, how can I do that? I mean, you and I, we're the perfect team. People just don't match up that well but once or twice in a lifetime.''

''I know.'' Her heart slid down a little farther, to somewhere around her waistline. ''But I love him, Matt, and I'm going to put that above everything else.''

He looked at her for a long moment, his eyebrows pulled together in an unbelieving frown. ''Babe, you know I want you to be happy. And I do think you and Zach are another perfect match. But it won't work, Ashley. Not this way. If you're telling yourself you can get a divorce from the theater, you're telling yourself lies. Hon, you're setting yourself up for another broken heart.''

''Matt, you don't understand. I've thought and thought about it, and this is the way it's got to be.''

''Okay, babe, I wish you luck.'' He stood up and took her into his arms, giving her a big hug and a kiss. ''The best of it.''

''Are you going to look for another lyricist?''

He studied her face for a minute, then replied. ''Uh-uh. Not just yet.'' She watched him as he left her apartment, his shoulders stooped.

It had been one of the most difficult things she'd ever had to do, but once she'd gotten past the painful job of telling Matt she was working her way out of the theater, she felt unburdened, free to throw herself wholeheartedly into the wedding preparations and the steady stream of parties. It was June 12 when Ashley took an airplane to Boston to attend yet another set of parties, including one more bridal shower, this one given by Emily. As she winged through the skies, she wondered what in heaven's name she could yet be given as a prenuptial gift that she didn't already have at least one of.

Taking advantage of the chance to get some rest, she sat back and closed her eyes. Within seconds, her mind began to wander. And, of course, it headed for home territory. Matt had been right about the theme of Stevenson's book being up-to-date. Look at the lengths to which people went in the effort to improve themselves. Thousands of books were sold every year—no, probably millions!—on how to be better-adjusted, how to deal with anger, how to be your own best friend, how to rid yourself of bad habits. If someone came up with a way to encapsulate all one's bad traits, so they could be let out just often enough to dispel their energy and would in no way reflect upon the person... Wow. But what would happen to a nineteenth-century Mr. Hyde if he were brought back, by mistake, to the present day? She grinned at the thought. The poor guy would have an awful time being evil enough to stand out! His surreptitious visits to the opium dens would be tame stuff next to the supposedly upright citizens who snorted, sniffed, smoked, injected and otherwise terrorized their own bodies with drugs! Now if a descendent of Dr. Jekyll's who was, in the family tradition, a doctor happened upon his ancestor's journal and, just for the heck of it, mixed the formula...

Ashley sat bolt upright, her eyes wide with alarm. What in heaven's name was she doing? She'd *sworn* she wouldn't get started on another project for a year and, even then, that she'd fit it neatly into her and Zachary's social schedule! Why, she should be taking this extra time to review the names of Zachary's relatives whom she'd be seeing again. Let's see, there was his Aunt Phoebe and her sister, Grace

Poole, and...Great Uncle Casper and...she closed her eyes again and promptly fell asleep.

When she saw Zach waiting for her inside the terminal at Logan, all stray thoughts vanished as she ran into his arms. "Zach, these days apart get longer and longer."

He hugged her so tightly her feet lifted off the ground. "They sure do; thank God they're almost over." He took her carry-on bag in one hand and her hand in the other.

"I can hardly wait! Oh, what time is it?" She glanced at her watch and answered her own question. "Just after noon. Good. Your mother and I are going into town so I can try on my wedding dress."

"Mom is delighted that you ordered the bridal gear at Priscilla's. I think she calls every day to make sure they're on schedule with all the bridesmaids' dresses, as well as yours. She's having the time of her life."

"That was fun, going shopping for my gown with her and Emily. It made me feel very much a part of the family already."

"You *are* a part of the family already."

Ashley noticed that practically every woman they passed looked covetously at Zachary. She was so proud to be with him, proud of his straight, authoritative carriage, his patrician good looks, the bright flashing smile that appeared so often on his handsome face. Being the wife of a man like Zachary Jordan should be enough for any woman! She squeezed his hand. "How wonderful, to be getting so close to our wedding day! Now, tell me again what I'm in for this weekend, and who I'll see that I should remember."

He grinned at her. "*In* for? You make it sound like an ordeal." He was teasing her. Why did his words make her feel guilty? "Well, let's see, tonight is dinner at the folks' place. Just the family. The *immediate* family. Then tomorrow's a biggee for you. Mom's having all the more elderly relatives over for a soiree—which really means another shower—in the afternoon. She'll review some of the names for you, but don't worry about it, no one will expect you to remember except Aunt Prissy, who got that nickname for good reason. Then, tomorrow night is the dinner party my partners are giving us at the Algonquin Club. And, of course, on Sunday afternoon it's Emily's shower.''

"Good grief, Zachary. What will we do with all that stuff? Your place is completely equipped already and so is mine.''

"And when you close your apartment, we'll have all that furniture to get rid of.''

At the words "close your apartment," she felt a sharp stab of anguish. She'd no longer have a home base in New York. It felt like she was about to have something amputated. "Where will we put my piano?''

Zach looked at her and frowned. "I don't know. It's so big. We may have to put it in storage until we settle on a house.''

Put her piano in storage? That would be like condemning a beloved pet to an indefinite incarceration in a kennel! "Well, at least we can be sure nobody will give me another one of those.''

Zachary laughed, not noticing that she said it without a smile. "We can always store some of the gifts in Mom and Dad's attic. The thing that'll really throw you is the number of thank-you notes you'll have to write.'' He chuckled. "But that shouldn't be any problem for you. After all, you're an author.''

She grit her teeth. She was the world's worst correspondent, which was one reason her phone bill was always sky-high. She hated and detested writing letters, cards or, especially, thank-you notes. She started to suggest he could help her with them but hesitated. It was probably another item on the endless list of "women's work.'' She hadn't yet finished the notes to all the people in Cedar Rapids, let alone those in New York. Of course with her New York friends, if she had time, she could just throw a big party and have giant placards made to hang all over the place saying "thanks for the gift!" Most of them were theater people who'd choose originality over conventionality any day.

Oh, well, somehow she'd get through all of it. She still wished they could have had a quiet, family-only wedding. With the size of Zach's family, that was quite enough. Her poor mother had been overwhelmed when she'd received the Jordans' wedding-guest list. They'd had to find a bigger church for the ceremony, since the one her parents attended was much too small. It had also become quite clear that a home-based reception wouldn't do for this crowd, so they'd arranged to rent a large room in the local country club, at which they were not members. Ashley had assured her mother that she and Zachary would cover the expenses. Although, she was sure, her folks would have gladly remortgaged the house to insure getting her safely married to Zach.

By Sunday afternoon, Ashley's smile felt stitched in place, and she wasn't sure how she'd summon another "ooh" or "aah" or "It's just what I needed!" She had described her wedding gown at least a hundred times in the last two days and effervesced over the convenience of a microwave oven and the sensibility of having at least one set of good sturdy pottery to use for everyday. By this time, she thought, they had to own at least eight sets, as well as more pieces of the fine china they'd chosen than anyone could use in two lifetimes.

When all the gifts were opened and the lunch and dessert were consumed and everyone had settled in to chat, Ashley grasped the brief opportunity to sit back and be quiet, to let her mind go blank. These were all such nice people, and most of them were also interesting and entertaining. Why was she feeling so... well, bored? It had to be the natural comedown from her hectic pace of the past couple of years. She'd never been very comfortable with too much time outside the work mode. Somehow the art of relaxing was one she'd never quite mastered. She'd just have to apply herself to a more steady demand on her social skills.

As she sat, a pleasant smile and attentive expression glued in place, her unruly mind once again strayed. She could picture the scene. Young Dr. Jekyll—the fourth? the fifth?—in his private laboratory that he had at his house for a few of his pet research projects, reading the original Jekyll's journal and, laughing at the foolish old myth, mixing the famous formula. An onstage explosion that knocks out the doctor. Then, out of the mist, appears Mr. Hyde. Not the ghoulish creature of the movie, but Mr. Hyde as he'd truly be if the doctor had created him as a part of himself, particularly the more "wicked" part of himself. Handsome, debonair. Probably fully dressed in a tuxedo. He'd walk to the front of the stage, give his top hat a couple of haughty taps and sing...

She had it. The lyric. Her eyes flew around the room. Everyone was completely engrossed in conversation, with the exception of Zachary's ancient grandmother, who'd fallen asleep in her chair. Her smile firmly in place, Ashley nodded her excuse to her immediate neighbors and headed for the bathroom. Once safely inside, she sat on the closed toilet lid, took her ever present spiral notebook and pen out of her purse and started to write:

What a delightful surprise.
Before your very eyes
Every man's dream of what he'd like to be...
Me!

She was into it now. The words jumbled up in her mind, impatient for their turn to be set on paper. She wrote as fast as she could, speeded on by the rush of adrenaline through her bloodstream, covering page after page.

Dimly, through the creative medley in her head, she heard a faint tap on the door. "Ashley, dear. Are you in there?"

She sat bolt upright, instantly aware of the passage of time. She looked at the large number of pages folded back after she'd written on them. "Ah, yes, I am." She tried to sound like someone with a stomach disorder as opposed to a weakness in the head.

"I just wanted to make sure you were all right." God. It was Zachary's mother!

"I'm fine. Just a little upset stomach." Hastily, she shoved the notebook into her purse, and unlocked the door, forcing a wan smile to her face. "It's so kind of you to be concerned."

Mrs. Jordan, who had been the soul of kindness and friendliness ever since the engagement, looked genuinely worried. "Can I get you anything? We have several medications that might help."

"Oh, no! Thank you, but I think it's over. Just nerves, I'm sure." She waved her hand in a gesture of dismissal, managing to fling her unlatched purse to the floor, where it disgorged its contents.

Before she could stoop to get them, Mrs. Jordan had picked up the various pieces. She handed the purse to Ashley, waiting until she had it open to give her the lipstick, the comb, the pen and . . . her eyes, quite naturally, saw the hastily scribbled notes. She was obviously embarrassed at having read the top page, which was complete with a time signature and key change. "Oh, my dear." She handed the incriminating notebook to Ashley, then put a consoling hand on her arm.

Ashley was mortified. How was she to explain *this*? "It's just that, well, Matt came up with this brilliant idea, and my mind does go off on its own tangents. . . ."

Mrs. Jordan put her arm around Ashley's waist as they started to walk back toward the parlor. "You shouldn't feel a need to apologize for your extraordinary gift, dear. Most people would give anything in the world to have your talent. Be proud of it."

"But, I promised Zachary..."

"Be very, very sure you don't agree to any terms my son has made that are going to cost you too much."

Ashley stared at her, at a complete loss for words. Finally she was able to speak through the tears that were forming in the base of her throat. "I love him, Mrs. Jordan. I can't bear to lose him again."

The older woman stopped and turned to her. "True love, Ashley, should never have too high a price. Especially if only one person has to pay it."

Ashley could no longer blink back the tears. "Mrs. Jordan, would you please..."

She held up her hand. "I would never discuss what happens, of necessity, in a bathroom." With a smile, she kissed Ashley on the cheek. "Dry your eyes, child. It's time to say goodbye to all these tiresome guests."

That evening, as she and Zachary sat slumped on his big, comfortable sofa, she lay her head on his shoulder and sighed. "I'm exhausted."

He chuckled. "I'll bet you are. It's a real strain, trying to be continually nice for three straight days."

Ashley nodded. "I'll say. It's all the smiling, I think, that does me in. I'm used to spending a lot of time alone when I'm working or with one other person who's working with me. I've never mastered the art of small talk." She straightened her head, her eyes lighting up. "Wouldn't that make a cute scene, Zach? Have a large group of people at a cocktail party and do a whole number incorporating all the silly subjects that are covered over and over at a gathering like that?"

There was a deadly silence. Then Zachary said, in a tone edged with impatience. "Lord, Ashley. Do you have to put *everything* on stage?"

She wilted back into her former position. "It's sort of automatic. I'll work on it." She foraged around in her mind for a more acceptable subject. "Everyone has sure been nice to me. I really like your relatives. They're all so interesting and every one of them has seemed genuinely pleased about our marriage.''

''Why wouldn't they be? Look what a gem I'm getting!''

She smiled and snuggled closer. ''Your mom is wonderful. I'm so glad we've had a chance to get better acquainted. And of course Emily. She's even more fun than I'd remembered.''

''Yes. Emily's special. She's a real fan of yours, you know.'' He pulled back suddenly, looking at her intently. ''Speaking of Emily, I almost forgot something. She said you left the party for almost an hour. That Mom found you in the bathroom, 'indisposed.' How're you feeling?''

She stiffened. ''Oh, I'm fine. Just one of those...stomach bouts. You know.''

''Well, take it easy for a few days. There's a lot of flu going around. Funny, Mom usually becomes a mother hen when someone's under the weather. I'm surprised she didn't slap you into bed.''

''She was awfully kind. She really seemed to understand....''

''Understand?''

Ashley gulped. She was getting flustered, she'd better slow down and think. ''You know, too much rich food, all those desserts...''

Zachary watched her, his eyes narrowing in concern. ''Ashley, is something the matter? You seem terribly, well, uptight.''

Oh, Lord, what did she say now? She'd never been able to keep anything from Zachary; he knew, the moment he walked into the same room, if she was upset or unhappy. They'd never lied to each other. In fact, lying to anyone was another thing at which she was a complete flop. Maybe she should just tell him what had happened. She knew herself well enough to know it wouldn't be the last time. That compulsion to get an idea on paper would be hard to break, and he'd have to be patient. Anyway, it wasn't as though she'd committed a sin or something.

"Ashley?"

She looked up at him, straightening her back. "Look, Zach, it wasn't really an upset stomach. I got to thinking about the idea Matt came up with for a musical, and all of a sudden the flow began; and I just had to get it down on paper. It's one of those things I'll have to learn to control."

"So you left a party being given in your honor to go lock yourself in the john?" His eyes were still narrowed, but not with concern. "Then told my mother you had a bad stomach?"

"Zachary, why do you sound so angry? I didn't shoot somebody, I just wrote down some lyrics and story ideas. Your mother was very supportive."

"Mother? How did she know?"

Ashley described the scene, including his mother's kindly advice. "I was really touched. She was far more understanding than my own mother's ever been."

Zachary stood up and crossed to the window that faced Marlborough Street, where he pulled back the curtain and looked out, obviously lost in thought. "Are you paying too high a price, Ashley?"

She jumped up and went to him. "Zachary, I didn't say that; it was your mother who did. I'm sorry it happened. But I'm used to working. All this partying, trying to think of things to talk about . . ."

"It seems to me you've never had a shortage of parties in New York."

"Yes, but it's different. They're with my kind of people, who talk about all the things I'm interested in. You know, shows and pictures and who's just sold a screenplay and—" she closed her mouth. Too late, far too late.

He turned to her, his face an unreadable mask. "Your kind of people. As opposed to my kind?"

"I didn't mean it like that. I like your friends and your relatives. It's just, well, I don't know them all that well, and it's harder to keep a conversation going."

"I should think so, when you're holed up in a bathroom!"

"Zachary, damn it all! I'm trying to be what you want me to be, but you can't expect me to change myself overnight! My whole life has been the theater, it's hard to just turn it off like a faucet!" She was getting out of control and didn't know why. The incident earlier in the day had evidently disturbed her more than she'd realized.

"It just seems as though you could keep things in a little better perspective. How do you think my mother must have felt, to find that her future daughter-in-law had abandoned a party being given for her to write lyrics in a bathroom?"

"Your mother said I should never have to apologize for my talent. Yet that's what I seem to keep doing, over and over again. I've been apologizing to my parents most of my life and now to—" Oh, God, her mouth had run wild!

"To me. Might as well finish it." He went back to the couch and sank into it. "Hell, Ashley. I haven't asked you to sacrifice your soul for me! Just to tether a career, put it in a suitable time frame!"

Ashley sat on a straight-backed chair and dropped her head into her hands. "I've been trying. I really have, because I love you so much it's painful to be separated for an hour, let alone for days, and I *want* to spend my life with you. But it isn't just a career, Zachary, something I can *tether*. Oh, Lord, how do I explain it to you?" She looked up at him, her eyes pleading. "It's more like trying to turn off the flow of my blood, or stop the beat of my heart. It's instinct, it's biological reaction, it's an automatic response that takes over." She stood up and paced back and forth, looking for words to describe what to her seemed a natural phenomenon. "I can be sitting in a room, not even thinking of anything theatrical—like yesterday—with all your aunts and your cousins and an occasional uncle who would walk through to see if we were through and he could take his wife home. All of a sudden, I *see* it, onstage. I start pinpointing gestures and mannerisms to define character. Then, I focus on the bride, me, and I think, 'She's got to be as beautiful as possible; we'd use all pink gels.'" She stopped, her hands held palm upward, begging understanding. "I look across a room at you and love lyrics start writing themselves in my mind." She threw up her hands in helplessness. "How do I put that in a 'suitable' time frame?"

Zachary lay his head on the back of the couch and closed his eyes. The silence, cacophonous in its intensity, seemed to go on forever. Ashley could hear her heart cracking, could feel her blood chilling. Her instincts were acute. This was going very, very badly.

Finally, Zachary lifted his head, his face strained, his eyes reflections of pain. "This isn't going to work, is it?"

Ashley's world was disintegrating around her, leaving her no firm ground on which to stand. She wanted to throw herself at his feet, beg him to forget the dumb incident, swear to him she'd never again get distracted by a lyric. But she couldn't do any of those things. Because he was right. It wasn't going to work.

Chapter Fourteen

Ashley lay on the lavender cut-velvet sofa in her living room, staring blankly at the ceiling, trying in vain to thwart the intrusion of dirgelike rhythms into her sorrow-sated brain. Seven long days had dragged by since she'd left Boston. Since she'd left the remnants of her smashed heart in Zachary's home.

She should start returning gifts. She should help her mother cancel the invitations. She should at least get out of her bathrobe and put on some clothes. But all of those things—or even the smallest chore—was beyond her ability to execute.

Her parents had been incredulous, unable to disguise their disappointment, for her and in her. She had no idea how Zachary's family had taken it. She'd talked to none of them since her sudden return to New York. She stood up and went to look out of the window. What in heaven's name was there in this city that was worth losing Zachary for? Surely there was something significant, but it had slipped her memory.

There was a knock on the door followed by two short rings. Matt was here. Either he or Amy had come every day, bringing some small gift to show their love: a bouquet of spring flowers, a package of sachet, a new best-seller, even a crock of homemade chicken soup. Wearily, she trudged to the door and opened it. "Hi, Matt."

He strode into the room, pausing only to give her a quick kiss on the cheek. "I'll play the piano while you go in and get dressed."

"Matt..."

"Ashley, quit hanging around in your bathrobe. You look like a scene from Camille. I've got a song to play for you. It would be for Dr. Jekyll when it really hits him that he doesn't know how to send Hyde back to wherever he came from. It will reflect his utter hopelessness. It's the perfect lyric for you to work on right now."

"Matt..."

"I'm not listening, Ashley, until you're properly attired for late afternoon in Manhattan. Go put on your blue jeans."

Ashley opened her mouth, closed it, shrugged and went to her bedroom to put on her blue jeans. She didn't know what she'd have done, these last dreadful days, without Matt and Amy—probably stayed in bed all the time. Matt, particularly, pestered her doggedly, demanding that she at least attempt to function. When she'd attired herself in her jeans and a shirt, even shoes and socks, she ran a brush through her hair and put on some lipstick. No use trying to skip any of those steps; Matt would just send her back.

When she returned to the living room, she growled, "Okay, Simon Legree, what else? Want me to jump through a hoop or two?"

"As a matter of fact, that's a good idea. Give you a little exercise. Now, sit there—" he pointed an imperious finger at the pink chair "—and listen."

She tried to concentrate on the melody, tried to remember what Matt had told her this was all about, but her mind had posted an Out to Lunch notice. "Matt, my dear and faithful friend, why not give up? You know I can't even remember the gist of the show."

"Yeah, but it'll start perking in that mind of yours sooner or later. I know you."

"Yes, you do. Speaking of which, I must thank you for not saying 'I told you so.'"

"Listen, babe, I'm getting no kicks out of seeing you down for the count again. But people like us, Ash, we're incurable addicts. Trying to cut yourself off from show biz is like cutting the umbilical cord before you can function on your own."

"Wouldn't you think, at my age, that I could?"

"No. Age means nothing. We go from work to death—or senility, whichever comes first. I was frankly astonished that a smart guy like Zachary could make that mistake twice."

"Matt..."

"Okay, okay, we don't mention the forbidden name. Why won't you take his calls?"

"There's nothing more to say. And the sound of his voice would send me right off the edge. I'm clinging precariously, at that."

"All right, my sweet, I'm leaving this music here, so when you wake up in the middle of the night with this immortal tune pounding away in your head, you can come out and play it to yourself. And don't forget you're coming to our place for dinner."

"Matt—"

"No excuses. I'm coming over to pick you up. Be ready to go at seven-thirty."

She sighed. "Do I have to dress up?"

"Yes. Keep your blue jeans on. No bathrobe."

"Yes, sir."

He kissed her lightly, then pulled her into his arms to give her a long, tender hug. "I'm sorry, babe."

"I know you are." She buried her face in his soft cashmere sweater, suddenly aware that a terrible flood tide was erupting within her. When the crying started, it was all-out. Sobs, hiccups, gasping for breath, as though all the fluid in her body was determined to flow from her eyes.

Matt held her, patting her back as if she were a sick child. "Atta girl, Ash, let it out. Get rid of it. Nobody can keep that much hurt bottled up inside and live through it." He held her and comforted her until the storm ran its course.

When she finally stepped back, sniffing into the handkerchief he'd given her, she mumbled, "You're the best friend I've ever had, next to Johnny. Thank you, Matt."

"Friendships work both ways, babe. You've always been there for me, too. Now don't forget. Seven-thirty tonight."

At seven-thirty exactly, the doorbell rang. She went to answer listlessly, not registering the fact that it hadn't been a knock and two rings. When she opened the door, she very nearly fainted. It wasn't Matthew who stood there, it was Zachary. She'd been conned.

"Hello, Ashley." He stepped past her into the foyer, his eyes never leaving hers.

"But, what, how..."

"Matt was busy cooking dinner, so I offered to come pick you up."

"Matt never cooked a dinner in his whole life."

Zachary took hold of her shoulders, his strong fingers digging into her flesh as though he was afraid if he didn't hold on tightly enough, she'd bolt. "You wouldn't answer my calls. I had to figure some other way to get to you."

"And Matt set this up?"

"Yes. He knows we need to talk."

"What's the use, Zachary? What do you want from me, my hide?" The storm was rumbling again, somewhere near the pit of her stomach. If this one got started, the remains of her would probably run off under the door. Which was all right with her. "What are you trying to do to me?"

"Marry you."

She threw back her head and yelled. "Stop it! I can't take any more!"

Zachary, in one swift motion, bent down, scooped her up and carried her to the big, overstuffed chair in the living room, where he sat down cradling her in his lap, running his hand over her hair. "Ashley, please don't cry. Honey, just listen to me for a few minutes. Then if you still want me to go, I will, with no more arguments."

She couldn't answer, she just moved her head up and down, too drained to fight anymore.

"One thing we've always agreed on is that we'd like to be married to each other, right?"

"Uh-huh. But—"

"Shhh. Just listen. Like most men, I figured it was your place to accommodate to my job, to my way of life. The pattern started a long time ago. Remember that the cavemen just bonked their women over the head and carried them off." She looked up at him, frowning, unable to figure out what that had to do with anything. "I'm just trying to excuse myself to a certain extent for being so damned male."

"If you weren't male, we wouldn't have this problem in the first place."

"True." He tipped up her chin, so he could look at her. "I went over to my folks' house to get a little comfort."

"Did you?"

"No, instead, I got what my grandmother called my 'comeuppance.' Mom told me that by pulling you away from your career, I would be doing a great injustice not only to you but to thousands and thousands of people who got pleasure from your great talent." Ashley's eyes stayed fixed on him now; she was all but holding her breath so she wouldn't miss the next words. "So I told her that was what made the whole thing so hopeless." He kissed her lightly on the lips. She didn't mind. "And my mother, who, as you noticed, is a very wise woman, said, 'Son, there are two sides to every issue. And, in this particular case, *two* careers.'"

"That's all?" Disappointment flowed through her.

"That's what I thought, till I got home. Then my mind started grinding it over. And over."

So far she couldn't see any new reason for hope.

"I sat on my big leather chair in my study, staring at the mahogany paneling, and just thought about us. I thought about how much I loved you practically from the first time I saw you. I thought about the fact that I've never found anyone so stimulating or interesting or unique—on top of sexy, of course. I thought about how much fun we had just sitting and talking, sharing our ideas and our successes and our disappointments. I thought about what a good time I had when I came to rehearsals, once I'd let my guard down, how much I enjoyed getting to know Matt and Craig and Jerry and Lyle and so many of the others. You know something, honey, you've opened up a whole new sort of life to me and made my life more interesting and exciting by doing so. I knew what you did for a living when I fell in love with you. And once I quit convincing myself that a proper Bostonian like me couldn't possibly enjoy theater folk and theater activities, I was free to admit I do. I get a real kick out of them."

He stopped for air, and Ashley stared up at him, not daring yet to quite believe what he seemed to be saying.

"So, after I'd sifted through all this, I began to understand what my mother was trying to tell me. And it really belted me right between the eyes. My career is far more movable than yours." She gasped, unable to contain her excitement. Could he really be considering... "Hell, I've already got five New York clients, and eight or nine others who've approached me. And a lot of the kind of law I practice could be headquartered here, as well as in Boston. So, what I'm saying is, why don't we live in New York City, and spend time, when we can, in Boston?''

She was dumbstruck. She just stared at him with her mouth open.

''Does that vast silence mean 'no' or 'yes' or 'maybe?' ''

She opened her mouth a little more and yelled, ''Yes! Yes, yes, yes and yes!'' She threw her arms around him and kissed him with all the ardor and the relief and the joy that had flooded her heart. When she drew back, simply to breathe, she said, ''Oh, gosh. My folks are going to pull out their hair. They probably just about finished canceling the wedding.''

''No, as a matter of fact, I called them and asked them not to. At least until we could sort out our thoughts. So it's still on.''

Her whole face was lighting up, one big glare of happiness. ''Could this really be happening? Are you sure it's not a dream?''

''Well, I don't know. Why don't we go to bed? Then when we get up, we can decide if we've been asleep all this time.''

''What a good idea. Wait a minute, are Matt and Amy holding dinner for us?''

''No. As a matter of fact, they said it would be more convenient tomorrow night.''

She ran her fingers over his cheek, just to check how solid it felt. He certainly didn't seem to be a figment of her imagination. ''Are we really going there for dinner tomorrow night?''

''Sure. We have to celebrate with our friends.'' With that, he stood up, with her still in his arms and, kissing her hungrily, headed for the bedroom.

* * * * *

Take 4 Silhouette Intimate Moments novels
and a surprise gift
FREE

Then preview 4 brand-new Silhouette Intimate Moments novels—delivered to your door as soon as they come off the presses! If you decide to keep them, you pay just $2.49 each*—a 9% saving off the retail price, *with no additional charges for postage and handling!*

Silhouette Intimate Moments novels are not for everyone. They were created to give you a more detailed, more exciting reading experience, filled with romantic fantasy, intense sensuality and stirring passion.

Start with 4 Silhouette Intimate Moments novels and a surprise gift absolutely FREE. They're yours to keep without obligation. You can always return a shipment and cancel at any time.

Simply fill out and return the coupon today!

* Plus 49¢ postage and handling per shipment in Canada.

Clip and mail to: Silhouette Books

In U.S.:
901 Fuhrmann Blvd.
P.O. Box 9013
Buffalo, NY 14240-9013

In Canada:
P.O. Box 609
Fort Erie, Ontario
L2A 5X3

YES!   Please rush me 4 free Silhouette Intimate Moments novels and my free surprise gift. Then send me 4 Silhouette Intimate Moments novels to preview each month as soon as they come off the presses. Bill me at the low price of $2.49 each*—a 9% saving off the retail price. There is no minimum number of books I must purchase. I can always return a shipment and cancel at any time. Even if I never buy another book from Silhouette Intimate Moments, the 4 free novels and surprise gift are mine to keep forever.

* Plus 49¢ postage and handling per shipment in Canada.

240 BPO BP7F

Name	(please print)	
Address		Apt.
City	State/Prov.	Zip/Postal Code

This offer is limited to one order per household and not valid to present subscribers. Price is subject to change.

IM-SUB-1D

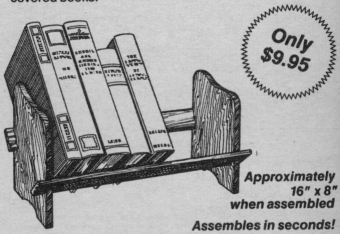

COMING NEXT MONTH

#427 LOCAL HERO—Nora Roberts
Divorcée Hester Wallace was wary of men, but her overly friendly neighbor wasn't taking the hint. Though cartoonist Mitch Dempsey enthralled her young son, convincing Hester to believe in heroes again was another story entirely.

#428 SAY IT WITH FLOWERS—Andrea Edwards
Nurse Cristin O'Leary's clowning kept sick children happy, but her response to hospital hunk Dr. Sam Rossi was no joke. Would the handsome heart specialist have a remedy for a lovesick nurse?

#429 ARMY DAUGHTER—Maggi Charles
Architect Kerry Gundersen was no longer a lowly sergeant, but to him, interior designer Jennifer Smith would always be the general's daughter. As she decorated his mansion, resentment simmered . . . and desire flared out of control.

#430 CROSS MY HEART—Phyllis Halldorson
Senator Sterling couldn't let a family scandal jeopardize his reelection; he'd have to investigate his rascally brother's latest heartthrob. To his chagrin, he felt his *own* heart throbbing at his very first glimpse of her. . . .

#431 NEPTUNE SUMMER—Jeanne Stephens
Single parent Andrea Darnell knew Joe Underwood could breathe new life into Neptune, Nebraska, but she hadn't expected mouth-to-mouth resuscitation! Besides, did Joe really want *her*, or just her ready-made family?

#432 GREEK TO ME—Jennifer West
Kate Reynolds's divorce had shattered her heart, and no island romance could mend it. Still, dashing Greek Andreas Pateras was a powerful charmer, and he'd summoned the gods to help topple Kate's resistance!

AVAILABLE NOW: